Soul of a Human

By

H. D. West

Copyright © 2024 by - H. D. West - All Rights Reserved.

It is not legal to reproduce, duplicate, or transmit any part of this document in either electronic means or printed format. Recording of this publication is strictly prohibited.

Dedication

For my wife, who believed in me from the first word.

Acknowledgement

To every one of r/HFY and Royal road supporting me part for part.

About the Author

Stories and books have always been a big part of my life, but I have never had the courage to try writing by myself until now. All I want to accomplish is to make a single person smile and bring some brightness back into our world of social media and grim news. Always remember, there is a reason to go on, no matter how small or dumb it might seem to others.

Table of Contents

Part 1 1
Part 2 4
Part 3 9
Part 4 14
Part 5 19
Part 6 25
Part 7 31
Part 8 37
Part 9 43
Part 10 50
Part 11 57
Part 12 63
Part 13 70
Part 14 77
Part 15 84
Part 16 91
Part 17 99
Part 18 104
Part 19 110
Part 20 115
Part 21 121
Part 22 127
Part 23 133
Part 24 139
Part 25 145

Part 26	151
Part 27	157
Part 28	164
Part 29	171
Part 30	177
Part 31	185
Part 32	193
Part 33	200
Part 34	206
Part 35	211
Part 36	220
Part 37	225
Part 38	232
Part 39	237
Part 40	242
Part 41	248
Part 42	258
Part 43	268
Part 44	277

Part 1

Welcome to this fantastical, magical world, home of the "Kin." This world is home to the physical strong Stone-kin and their deep mine homes, the dexterous Wood-kin with their aptitude for nature magic, the Sea-kin living deep in the oceans, the Soul-kin in their floating cities of magic wonder and gemstone, and many more. While the kin lives in their cities protected by magic and bastions, the wilds are home to the "monstrosities," strong beasts with magic resistance and thick hides.

Many legends and stories are told about the kin and their exploits, but none more so than the story of the Soul-kin hero, soul bound to a being called the sun god kuh. So gather round and listen up as I tell you the truth of this mythical warrior and his humbling beginnings.

The Hero's Journey by Grand Historian Nalomel Amazonik 122a.C.

***

"Congratulations! Dear students, as headmaster of the Amethyst Academy of Magics, I applaud you for passing the theoretical entry exam. Now, a life of growth and mastery is lying before you, but now, as tradition demands, the word is given to the top scorer of the exam. Student Mor Agaton, please join me on the stage!"

As the headmaster, in his splendid purple robes, takes a step aside, he is joined by an uncomfortable-looking, scrawny boy. Mor is trying to take deep, slow breaths to avoid fainting or, worse, puking with all the attention of the new students, teachers, and the headmaster resting on him.

As Mor nervously stutters at the beginning of his speech, he instantly flinches in surprise as subtle magic circles amplify his voice.

"T...t..tt... thanks... h..headmaster." Trying to get rid of his stutter, Mor takes a deep breath. "I'mreallygratefullforthisopportunityandhopeallstudentswillenjoytheirtime"

A cough from the grandmaster luckily stops the word flood, and an encouraging nod lets Mor compose himself and start over.

"To all students, I'm honored to stay on this stage as your representative. My dream has always been to join this academy like my parents did before me, and while this is a place of learning and growth, I hope to find comrades and friends among all of you. Because my status as the son of an officer is below that of many of you who are nobles, I wanted to refuse this honor. Still, the headmaster insisted on this tradition and the following aptitude test. So, while I wanted to give the honor of first student to someone of a more prestigious family, it was denied."

At this point, the headmaster takes a step forward and takes over the speech.

"As this has gone on long enough, I will test all your aptitudes, starting with Mr. Agaton here."

While this statement resulted in a lot of excited murmuring, someone with keen hearing might have heard a few dissident voices in the crowd.

"Mr. Agaton, please place your hands on this cristal ball and let your magic flow." The headmaster produced a crystal sphere about 30 cm in diameter and held it out for Mor, who slowly put his hands on it and, while taking deep breaths, concentrated on making his innate magic flow.

The crystal sphere slowly gained a subtle purple-blue hue, and lazy energy impulses flowed within. This development lets the headmaster frown and look at Mor with a bit of pity. Finally, he clears his throat and speaks as Mor opens his eyes in expectation. In a voice devoid of reproach or approval, he simply states.

"Mr. Agaton, your aptitude for specialized magic is none. You have no affinity other than basic magic energy. But don't let this discourage you. You can still become a great spellcaster."

The second sentence was nothing more than a platitude. It is common knowledge that without specialized affinity, the magic of the higher circles is outside of reach. While everyone else was taking the aptitude test, Mor silently walked back off the stage to the end of the gathered students, lamenting his lot every step of the way.

Finally, after all tests were concluded, he was the only one without any specialized affinity. His first place on the theoretical tests, low status, and weak magic now instantly made him an outcast among his peers.

Part 2

While the first few weeks were pretty eventless, Mor had this bad feeling that the peace would not last. He excels at magic theory and can hold his own on applied beginner magic. Still, he has a dower outlook as he cannot make a single friend.

But after the lessons, he found a little letter slipped discreetly below his dorm room door, which instantly changed his outlook. So, as he opened the envelope, it smelled slightly of flowers. Mor read the elegantly written letter inside, and a dopey smile grew on his face.

"I really don't know how to start this letter, but I really admire your smarts and think you are really cute. I would like to meet you tomorrow after the lessons at the training center where we can talk and get to know each other better. Zaletha Angelith"

As he went to class the next day, his head in the clouds, he finally felt like everything would be alright. It was finally his popular phase. While he dreamily sat through the lessons, his imagination ran wild. Sometimes, Mor even glanced shyly at the girl who wrote him the letter. His heart fluttered a little as she noticed him and gave him a bright smile.

Mor could not wait for the end of lessons and was finally released from his torment. He was almost rushing to the meeting spot, not wanting to let this opportunity go, and he would not be made to wait long.

A few minutes after he arrived at the meeting spot, the sparkling form of Zaletha walked up to him, smiling brightly and instantly going for a hug, which set Mor's brain in a state of shock and exhilaration.

He was instantly thrown into a dreamy, dopey state and did not notice the other visitors who intruded on the intimacy of the two to be lovebirds.

"Look at that, the princess and the peasant!" One of them exclaimed, and the other two snickered.

"Maybe you should rather get yourself, someone of your status, like a little beggar girl. You magicless loser." The intruder continued on.

While those words were hurtful to Mor, he just ignored those idiots. But then his view fell onto the face of Zaletha.

He saw her fear of those bullies, and instantly, a cold furry began to burn in his chest. Turning around, furious, Mor began to channel his magic, glowering at the three other boys.

"Fuck off, Ruby, and take your flunkies with you, or I will beat you up!" He shouted, and all three laughed at his outburst. The leader, called Ruby, raised an eyebrow at Mor.

"You would attack someone from royalty? Know your place, trash. I, Ranbor Ruby, am this school's most talented flame caster and can burn you to cinders if I wish!" The one called Ranbor said haughtily.

A slight bout of fear manifested inside Mor's conscience, but as his view flickered to Zaletha clinging fearfully at his back, it was quickly squashed. His rage reached new heights, and he unleashed a bolt of pure arcane power, which instantly was stopped by a magic barrier cast by one of the flunkies.

Mor was then caught in a whirling wall of fire, burning away his flesh, hurting like nothing ever hurt before. He would die. Right here, right now, but at least he could protect Zaletha. Smiling like an idiot, he embraced death, just as with the snip of fingers, the flames disappeared, along with something, and a feminine giggle started behind him.

There he was, standing, looking like an idiot, his actions finally catching up with his brain and draining all color from his face. He mechanically turned to look at Zaletha, but his admiration for her was gone entirely. While she just laughed at his stupidity.

"He really fell for it. That lowly peasant thought he could have a chance with me!" She laughed.

And now he understood, with his longing for friends, for someone to have social connections, and his hope for that letter to be real, Mor was caught in illusion magic.

Forming his thoughts, giving him fake feelings, and making him make a stupid mistake, as it was against school rules to use magic against another student.

Now, there he stood, four people laughing at his idiocy and with no witness of his own to change the narrative. He was caught and would now be expelled.

"Well, well, well, peasant. You are really in a sticky situation here, aren't you?" Ranbor gloated.

"But don't fear, we won't tattle on you, but let's say for our understanding and silence, you need to grant us a few small favors, nothing too bad, so don't fear. How about you do our homework for today? That seems fair for the scare you caused." The boy added.

With that, Mor knew his bad feelings had been right. He would now be at the mercy of those bullies. Because who would believe a low-born over the statement of a group of nobles? His school life of dread would really kick off now.

Through the coming torment, his grades stayed good, at least, as he would always do the homework of five people from this point on and seclude himself as often as possible in his room while they had free time to evade his tormentors.

Still, every time they crossed paths, they would torment him with illusions if no teacher was nearby and be all buddies while a teacher was watching. This drained him and let his magic control waver, meaning his applied magic training got worse and worse.

Mor would often think of writing a letter to his parents about his dismay, but he could not bring himself to disappoint them, so he would lie about how he made many friends and how great everything was.

Sometimes, he would try to unveil the lies of his bullies in front of a teacher. Still, his attempts were always seen as a "friendly" rivalry between the generous nobles and the peasant recluse, with who they tried to socialize against his will.

As soon as the teacher was out of sight, he would pay for his insolence with illusory pain and anything to hurt him that would not leave any marks. It was plain hell, and as his thoughts went to quitting everything more and more, another desperate plan formed in his brain.

If he were strong enough, if he had specialized magic, Mor could fight back, show those bullies he could not be taken lightly, and finally break this abusive cycle.

Mor would do something forbidden. A once-in-a-lifetime ritual designed to join the souls of two Soul-kin together. A ritual intended for bonding with your soulmate and lifelong partner, joining your magic pool and affinities together, and enhancing both.

In some children's stories, a lone hero would use this ritual to fuse his soul, not with kin, but with a mighty elemental force. Therefore, becoming far more powerful than any kin, with the cost of staying alone forever, never having a "true" soul bond.

In the deep night, Mor began to draw the required magic circles. He used his own blood and earth from the gardens as a medium to call upon an earth elemental force. Then, with a last bit of exertion, he funneled all his magic into the ritual, falling unconscious simultaneously.

At the same time, fate called, or perhaps it was just chance, when a pick struck something that should never been rediscovered, and something was awakened that should have died in eternal slumber.

Part 3

Rosana Amethyne was worried. Mor Agaton, who she knew only as her slightly reclusive muster student, didn't appear in class this morning, and after questioning his friends, she only got the answer that "they didn't know."

So, while she was on her break, Rosana went to the dorm room of the missing student to find it locked from the inside. After knocking a few times without getting an answer, she used her magic and authority as a teacher to unseal the magic door lock.

Rosana entered to the sight of something awful. Her student, Mr. Agaton, lay unconscious next to something that looked like a hastily drawn and obviously failed runic circle, which she instantly recognized as a faulty soul-merging ritual.

She rushed to Mor's side and tried to get him awake, but nothing she did would rouse him. He might have overestimated his magic reserves for this ritual. She quickly used a teleport spell to get him to the academy's infirmary and instantly called the headmaster and the healing adept on the station for help.

As the three mages converged in the infirmary, Rosana told the Adept and her grandfather what she had found. This erupted into a heated discussion between them all. After they let the adept do her work, Rosana and the headmaster went to Mor's room.

Headmaster Amethyne walked around the chaotic room, looking at the carnage while mumbling to himself until he finally reached a conclusion.

"He really tried to do a soul binding, but it failed. Look here in the runic circle. Wrong symbols are used, and I can't even begin to describe the foolish idea of using plain earth as a medium." The headmaster explained and then, looking at his granddaughter, asked. "Rosana, do you know why he would do something like this?"

Rosana just shook her head at the question.

"No idea. I thought he would finally fit in after he made some friends. The first weeks of loneliness must have been very depressing, but after he started hanging out with the heir of the Ruby family and his group, his grades improved a little. Well, at least the ones for the theoretical classes." She offered an explanation to a nodding headmaster.

"Yes, but maybe this is exactly the reason. You say Mister Agaton became friends with the Ruby boy? Maybe he then felt inadequate, and it is known that a soul-binding ritual if done correctly, will enhance your shared magic energy. I can only imagine he wanted to gain an attribute with this mess and a bigger magic energy reservoir. Probably trying not to be left behind by his very talented friends." The headmaster shrugging

"And maybe for all his school smarts, he is just a young dumb boy. We probably will find out after he awakens and tells us. But first, let's get rid of this mess before someone else gets hurt." With this, they both start incantations to remove every sign of the failed ritual.

Meanwhile, in the infirmary, the Adept did her very best to get Mor to reawaken, using magic that primarily restores the magic energy.

After a while, she noticed the boy's eyelids flutter, and he let out a pained groan.

The Adept instantly called the headmaster and Miss Rosana, and they waited a little bit as Mor came to.

Mor slowly opened his eyes, looking at the unfamiliar space and noticing the grave expression of the three adults in the room.

"What happened? Where am I?" Mor asked, which led Rosana to sigh and answer him.

"You are in the infirmary. Because what you did knocked you out for almost a full day."

This plastered a confused look on Mor's face as he tried to remember and fell short. He silently shook his head as if wanting to shake off some kind of pain. Which in turn let the headmaster speak up.

"You were either an idiot or desperate. We found signs of a soul-binding ritual in your room, and it seems you tried to do something that only works in fairytales. How did you even know how the ritual circle had to look? It was too close to being right to just be coincidence from the well-known children's book scribbles and some half knowledge of a first-year student," he chided the boy.

Mor strained his memory. Yes, there were flashes of desperation. Slowly, the pieces fell back together and let him remember. But he knew he could not tell the truth or why he had attempted it.

"I saw it in some pictures of my parents' ceremony and adapted it as best as I could. I just wanted to get stronger," Mor mumbled and earned a stern look from the headmaster for this.

"So you did not want to be left out of your friend circle, and the best idea for you was to try something that could have killed you or removed any chance of living a fulfilling life with a partner. You, boy, are lucky it failed and did not kill you in the process. That was incredibly stupid and will have ramifications! And before you ask how I know it failed, I can sense your magic! It is still the same. Now for your punishment, I will inform your parents of this, and you will deliver a report to my office in three days on "why using magic above your capabilities is a bad idea." Do you understand?" The last question was voiced without allowing any objection. Mor could only nod in acceptance.

"Good then, sleep for today. You need to recover your magic energy." The face of the headmaster softened. "And eat something, boy. You look like you need it."

After everyone left, the Adept promised to bring him some food later. Mor wanted to cry. "Why did it fail? It's not fair! I don't want to be weak anymore. Why am I always unlucky?" he sobbed as he heard someone ask.

°*What failed?*°

Shocked, Mor looked up and could not detect anyone else in the room.

Slightly scared, he called out, "Hello? Who is there?"

And probably because his luck was indeed bad, the door opened, and four familiar students sauntered into the infirmary.

"Hey, peasant! You did not fulfill your obligations today. Where is the homework you promised us? We almost got into trouble with the teacher! Well, at least you had the sense to pull her away, so no harm was done here. What happened? Did the big baby have an itty bitty nervous breakdown? Want me to bring you some sweets." Ranbor scoffed.

"If you let us hang again, we will really hurt you, but for today, you are lucky and have the whole attention of sweet Zaletha just for yourself. Aren't we nice?" He continued mocking Mor.

Mor tried to suppress his rising fear because it would only give the illusion hold on his mind, but he failed utterly. And because of that, he braced himself for the agony of whatever this witch would put him through this time. So his surprise was great, as nothing happened. Instead, there was this unfamiliar voice again.

This time, it was screaming in rage, °*FUCK OFF!*°

But his bullies seemed not to hear it. Could it be his imagination? Did he finally snap under the abuse and go crazy? At least, it appeared as if the illusion could find no purchase on his mind. Therefore, he was spared whatever torment would have been in stock for him.

Zaletha was confused. Her illusion magic just bounced off the mental fortitude of that peasant, which should have been impossible.

So instead, she huffed, "Not today. It is no fun when he's sitting around all sick. We're leaving so he can dwell in his loneliness."

And with an almost unnoticeable nervous glance, she turned around and stomped out of the infirmary, the three boys on her heels, berating her for ruining their fun.

°*That was something else! But now that this is over, might you want to explain to me what's going on?*° The voice said, and Mor sighed. Yes, he was definitely crazy because the voice was back.

Part 4

°*Hey, hey! Listen!*° The voice had an extremely annoying tone right now.

°*Stop ignoring me!*° The voice shouted, and Mor sighed.

Why won't it shut up? He already has enough problems, and schizophrenia should not be added.

°*Great, if you don't want my fucking help, I will leave. Stupid crybaby holding me up from doing my stuff.*° It huffed, and Mor wondered why it sounded so pissed.

°*So how do I get back... Hey Depresso! How do I get back to Earth?*° It suddenly asked.

Mor instantly sat up, surprising the healing Adept, bringing his food and almost dropping it.

"You shouldn't move so suddenly. You are still hurt," she chided him.

Mor sheepishly apologized, taking the food. His mind was already working overdrive.

The mind said something about going back to Earth, so it worked! But why could the headmaster not detect it?

°*Hmmm, seems not that way. Oh no! Don't tell me I'm stuck here! Hey, intelligence allergic, answer me!*° It shouted, and Mor felt a splitting headache as if something in his mind wanted to break out with force, so he finally focused on answering it.

°*Ouch! What did you do?*° He moaned.

°*Finally... What took you so long? I want to leave. Because someone is just ignoring me instead of explaining what is going on.*° It answered him, annoyed.

°*I'm sorry,*° Mor apologized and was countered.

°*Shut it with your sorry and get on with explaining, or I really will leave!*° The voice huffed.

°*Yes! I'm sor... You said you were from a place called Earth?*° Mor asked.

°*Yeah, as I already told you, but what does that have to do with anything?*° It countered, leading Mor finally into his explanation.

°*I wanted to get stronger, and because my magic affinity is none, I won't be able to cast the highlevel spells. Therefore, I did a ritual to bind myself to the soul of an earth elemental to get an earth affinity and a boost in magic energy. I thought it failed, but now you are here! Please share your magic power and earth affinity with me, and I will be eternally grateful.*° He explained pleadingly.

°*Magic? Like in fantasy? How would I do that?*° It asked, and Mor got thoughtful.

°*Huh? How do you not know that? You are an earth elemental! According to the stories, it should be obvious to you!*° He grumbled.

°*Me? An earth elemental? How did you come up with that stupidity?*° It told Mor, who was slowly getting furious.

°*You spoke about a place called Earth!*° and somehow felt it nodding.

°*Yes, Earth, as in the planet Earth. You know where all humans live? Are you retarded or something, spouting something about magic, elementals, and souls. Get back to reality!*° it chided him.

°*But our world is not called Earth. We call it Kinscradle.*° Mor answered.

°*Huh?*° Came back from the voice.

°*Huh?*° Mor answered.

°*Oh no!*° Both exclaimed.

°*Ok, ok. Let's slow down. We need to get our facts straight. First, please explain to me what you are if you aren't an elemental.*° Mor asked.

°*I told you I'm a human... and my name is....? I can't remember. Why can't I remember? What is this shit? The last thing I can remember... I was on my way somewhere, and then there was a light and then nothing.*° The voice pondered.

°*And you did not think it was strange that you just somehow ended up here and could talk to me?*° Mor drilled further.

°*Everything felt like a dream, you know? Wandering somewhere, forgetting some things, there was no fear, pain, or anything. I was like, "Huh, neat, lucid dreaming. Get to have some fun." then I heard a voice cry out in despair. After I stopped to look, something pulled me, and just like that, the dream got this whiney human with strange eyes in it. But dreams are dreams and don't always need to make sense, so I just ran with it.*° It explained.

°*I fear I might have died, and while my soul? Mind? Whatever, did the things it does, when you die, you pulled me away and towards you. It's strange how calm I am with all of this, but maybe it's another safety feature from leaving your body and moving on or the weirdest dream ever.*° The voice continued.

°*Well for now, I think we just roll with it. Humans will do for a name for the moment, which leads me to the most crucial question. Do you need assistance? Why did you cry out for help? What did *those four clowns have to do with all of this? And what exactly did I get myself into? In detail, please.°* The human asked.

Mor took a deep breath and a sip of his drink before collecting himself and answering.

°Starting at the beginning would be prudent, I think. I'm Mor Agaton, a member of the Soul-kin, and I enrolled only a short while ago in the Grand Academy for magics. But it seems nothing will go my way. First, it was revealed that I had no aptitude for specialized magic, which is terrible.° Mor explained.

°Why?° The human interjected.

°Because, even if you can use every spell, as no affinity will allow, every spell costs an amount of magic energy. The amount depends on the grade and effect of it. But if your "soul" has an affinity, the cost for a spell of the same affinity type is significantly reduced. I wanted earth affinity like my father, so I tried to bind myself to an earth elemental. But, well, as you can guess, I somehow pulled you into my mess. Sorry for that.° Mor explained.

°So, if I get this right, you wanted this specialization because you don't have any. This, in turn, means you are stuck with the basic spells, which will probably put you at a disadvantage in pure power. After all, the high-level spells are too expensive for the magic energy you might have. Am I right? Then why try something like this stupid soul thingy and not just, you know, train yourself to have more magic energy, level up, or something?° The human asked.

°That is not how this works! You can not just get more magic energy with "training." Your magic reservoir will grow when you grow older, and that's it. Because of that, the elders are always the strongest. The only other way is to do this "stupid" ritual and bind your soul to someone who also has a magic reservoir, and those will

°*then be combined into one. But ours did not grow as we soulbonded, which should be impossible.*° Mor told the human.

°*Well, it does make sense because there is no magic in my world, so I probably did not have that "reservoir."*° The human pondered.

°*What do you mean, NO magic?*° Mor was shocked.

"How could anything exist without the magic powers that make up the world?" He asked himself and then added a depressed sigh.

°*I should have tried for my mother's wind affinity.*° He sighed.

°*Your mother has wind affinity? And your dad, earth? Cool, then they have polar opposite powers and probably complete each other pretty well.*° The human exclaimed, and Mor cursed his luck at that moment.

°*I hate my life. Yes, my father has earth, but my mother is exceptionally gifted, with water and wind affinity. Therefore, this gives her a double affinity called ice affinity. She could have easily married into high nobility but chose my father for some reason and gave up her previous title to be with him. I got into this school because of my potential as her son. And even if it is just a guess now, I had a good chance to get the affinity from both parents. This means I probably was lucky enough to also get a double affinity like my mother but unlucky enough to get her wind affinity and my father's earth affinity, which in turn canceled each other out.*° Mor now really wanted to cry.

His life would have been much better if he had a double affinity.

°*Shit, that's some serious unluck. But no point crying over something you can't change. Now, while we are stuck with each other, let's turn this around. Maybe you just need a little bit of human audacity.*° The human told Mor to cheer him up, which almost worked a little.

Part 5

°*So, what now?*° The human asked.

°*Now I'm going to sleep. Today was a lot.*° Mor yawned. °*Good night*°

°*Good night, sleep well.*° The human answered and began slowly wandering the compounds of Mor's mind just looking.

For Mor, this was somehow soothing and let him quickly drift off into sleep. But as sleep took him, so did the nightmares, and while he tossed and turned in subconscious movement, the human watched.

Watched the nightmares, watched the boy, who would be their other self from now on, watched what the four bullies did to him, and felt a protective rage.

°*Those asshats will pay. This ends right now,*° the human promised the sleeping Mor.

On the following morning, Mor acquired some writing implements and got to write his punishment essay while the Human was backseat writing or more backseat questioning.

°*Ah, so if you use a spell where your magic is insufficient, you could die because the missing magic energy will be subsidized with a thing you call "live energy." But both energies are more or less the same, just that the "live energy" is the magic energy being held back for your essential functions. Wouldn't that mean your magic energy would also get stronger if you trained your fundamental strength and endurance? But then, why do the elderly have more energy than someone in their prime?*° The human mused.

°*Could you please shut up? I need to concentrate. I don't want to write it again. And I told you that is not how it works! Also, why would training your strength do anything? You have your body, and that's it. What would you even do to "train" a body? It's stupid.°* Mor complained.

°*Wait! Is that why everyone I saw is so scrawny? You have no concept of training your body? Is it just "I have to be born right, or I can't use the fancy pants spells I read in a book" for all of you?! How did your kin survive until now? What about hunting for food or gathering? What about natural predators?°* The human exclaimed.

°*What stupid question is this now? We grow our crops and everything here on our floating islands. Why should we hunt or whatever? You cast a spell, and all the fruits get neatly gathered where you want them. This has always been that way.°* Mor explained while continuing to write.

°*That's idiotic.°* The human interrupted.

°*Shut it!°* Mor shushed the human.

The rest of the evening was spent in silence, but the human spoke up again just before lights out.

°*Got an idea how we will deal with those bullies of yours?°* They asked.

°*No... I don't even want to think about that.°* Mor confessed. °*But it probably can't be avoided. Best get to it, then. The biggest problem is Zaletha, with her illusion magic, but the last time, it somehow failed. Maybe it has something to do with you? Because you have no fear of her, I was also protected? Illusion magic is strange like that. You need some kind of emotional power over your target, or it has a big chance of failing. But If that's the case, then it will not take long for Ranbor to escalate their abuse. He somehow really hates me.°* He sighed.

°*Yeah, seemed like it. Any idea why? Well, forget it, it doesn't really matter for our problem anyway.*

We still need a good plan to deal with them. It is four against two, and I can't talk to anyone but you. So more like four against one and a half? But if this girl needs to have some kind of hold against me, she will be shit out of luck. Humans are notoriously headstrong. The problem, then, is they may do something else to keep you in line. Maybe trying to intimidate you with more physical means.° The human mused.

°Then they would get into a problem with the school because attacking another student with magic is against the rules.° Mor interjected.

°But what would stop them from claiming it was an accident while helping you train? The best thing we could do would probably ignore them, and if they don't get the hint, we just loudly declare that we don't want anything to do with them.° The human explained, and this made Mor think.

°That might work. The problem is that most might not understand why we would not want to have anything to do with them because it would be helpful for my social standing to liaise with the nobility.° Mor explained, and the human agreed.

°But, let's try this anyway. What could go wrong?° They said.

Agreeing on this plan of action, their talk turned to other subjects until Mor decided it was time to sleep and rest. They would resume talking the next day, and it would again be human who asked the first question.

°Could we use the time, while we are stuck here, for you to explain to me how exactly this magic is working?° The human asked.

°*Yes, of course.*° Mor answered. °*First, as you already know, you need magic energy to cast a spell. Then, you must concentrate on guiding those energies, or the spell will fail. Secondly, while there are some continuous spells, they are hard to keep up because you must concentrate on the energy flow the whole time. That means spells like body enhancement or elemental puppet spells are almost impossible for single mages.*

Body enhancement is more so because a flesh and blood body is more complicated to move with the limits of how the energy can flow. Therefore, most mage teams would fall back on an elemental puppet if they needed someone to keep their enemy at a distance. But those are the last options. At best, you deal with anything at range with your instantaneous spells.° He explained.

°*It would be really cool if we could pull something like that off. It would be like a secret trump card,*° The human joked.

°*Yes, it would, but how could we even start to pull something like that off? First, the energy cost would be far too much for me, and you would need to somehow be able to control the body or guide the magic energy. And that's impossible. In the stories, the bound elemental only gave the mage more energy and affinities.*° Mor retorted.

°*That's why I meant it as a joke. But still, the surprise on the faces of the other mages probably would be hilarious. If it is true, it is impossible for a single mage. Still, I think I got it. Using those instantaneous spells is best because you can just fire and forget them or start casting the next one. The other question is now, how much concentration is required to keep a spell up?*° The human asked.

°*It depends on the spell, but it ranges from almost nothing to wholly occupying your attention. For example, letting a fire spell go on would be on the lowest distraction level, while guiding an elemental puppet would be the highest.*° Mor explained.

°*Ok got it.*° But still, the explanations got the human thinking because something felt off.

Mor used the quiet time to finish his punishment report and catch up on the stuff from the missed lessons. So, while the human brooded over the pieces of information, Mor got himself back on track with his studies with sporadic help from Miss Amethyne. Like this two more days passed, and Mor was finally released from the infirmary. As good as new, according to the healing adept.

However, only Mor and his new partner knew how close "new" was to the truth. Still, Mor had this bad feeling about the almost inevitable confrontation with his tormenters he would definitely end up in. He hoped with all his heart that the strategy of himself and the human would work as they planned.

On the way to class the next morning, it happened, and he heard the call from behind him.

"Hey, peasant, are you finally up again? You have to make up for your laziness now," it said.

"Ranbor..." Mor sighed.

"Hey! You worthless pawn! What kind of reaction is this? Is this how your parents raised you? Seems someone has to teach you respect of your betters again," Ranbor exclaimed, and Mor turned around slowly.

"Excuse me, your lordship. I believe the presence of someone of so lowly standing is no fitting company for someone as illustrious as yourself. But where, sire, is your noble retinue? It does not do for someone as royally important as yourself to be without them. Should I go and tell someone to summon them for you?" Mor replied, trying to keep the sarcasm out of his voice, as the human in his mind giggled.

°*Good one!*° They unhelpfully added.

"You're going too far this time!" Ranbor furiously stated, his ruby eyes glowing balefully with magic energy.

But Mor just shrugged, turned around, and left. °*Are your eyes also this creepy? It looks like you only have a black pupil, and the rest are in whatever color.*° The human questioned Mor.

°*Is that different where you are from? In most cases, the color fits the family, so Ranbor, of course, has ruby red, and mine would be of more an agate green-blue disposition.*° Mor answered the inquiry.

°*It's different for humans. We have white, then a colored ring around the pupil.*° The answer came back.

As they ignored Ranbor, the noble raised his voice in protest. "Don't turn your back on me, you worthless peasant!" He shouted.

Which in turn led the human to giggle again

°*He is really creative with his curses. I diagnose a lack of intelligence.*° They joked.

Which was too much for Mor, and he couldn't suppress an amused snort.

"You're not laughing at me!" Ranbor raged, and as Mor turned around to address that pompous ass, he only saw the red and yellow of a fireball that was flying right toward him.

Mor felt the heat lick his skin, and the shock of the force and the fury of the attack blacked out his mind. While the enclosing darkness would protect him from the pain of burning, he knew that this would be too much and his end. Mor would be just a burnt heap of dust on the floor. With this, the last thing he heard before losing conscience was the voice of his partner.

°*Holy shit! That's interes....*°

Part 6

°*Hey! Come on, buddy, wake up... Please? We are in trouble!*° Slowly, Mor came back to conscience, surprised he was still alive and even more surprised that he was unhurt.

Then suddenly, a cold shiver raked down his back as he noticed Miss Amethyne's expectant look, clearly having asked him something and being furious about it.

°*What happened? Why is she so furious?*° He asked his partner.

°*Well, you see... How do I explain? I just reacted because you blacked out when this fire thing came too close. Without really thinking, mind you, and well dodged.*° The human explained.

°*YOU DID WHAT?!*° Mor interrupted

°*Dodged, listen to me! Then the asshat threw a second one, and I dodged again, closing the distance, and you know, somehow your fist ended up connecting purely by accident, mind you, with his nose? Not my fault at all! He would not stop! Then the lady teach came over and started getting all pissy with us. But, well, I didn't know if it would be possible or intelligent for me to try talking, so I wanted to get you back to reality instead. Now that you are filled in, please deal with it.*° human continued.

°*YOU DID WHAT?! Are you stupid?! Don't answer that!*° Mor exclaimed.

"Mister Agaton, I asked you a question! Why are there signs of magic use in this hallway, and why is Mister Ruby bleeding from the nose?" Rosana brought Mor's internal discussion with his other mind to a crashing stop.

"It was an accident?" Mor started but instantly got shut up.

"Don't lie to me. Mister Ruby already told me you attacked him, and he just defended himself!" Rosana huffed.

"I thought better of you. First, you almost killed yourself with stupidity, and now you attack another student?!" She continued the tirade.

"Huh? That's not how this went! I just wanted to go to class as this asshat came over to bully me because of whatever fucking reason. Maybe he didn't get enough attention as a child, or too much, I don't know! He attacked me with his stupid fire, and I just reacted!" Mor countered angrily.

°*Yeah, tell her!*° The human added.

That outburst caught Rosana on the back foot. There was more going on than she could see at first glance.

"How did you come up with asshat? That is not how to address a fellow student! Besides, if your story was true, why would you retaliate with physical violence? That's barbaric!" She asked strictly.

°*Oh, shit. Think fast! You got this!*° The human said.

"Because attacking another student with magic is against school rules!" Mor blurted out, which gave Rosana pause.

"Well, you are technically correct, but still!" She said.

"You can't let that peasant get away with that! He refused me. I had to remind him of the correct hierarchy of things!" Ranbor raged, but his watering eye and nasally voice almost plastered a self-righteous smile on Mor's face, well nearly.

"I see, that's how it is." Rosana's voice took on a whole other level of coldness.

"We will forget this, but if one of you ever antagonizes the other again," she threw a hard look at Ranbor, "then I will personally kick you both out of this academy! And if your families even dare to try something to overrule this decision, I will ban everyone in that family. Do both of you understand?"

°*That's not fair!*° The human exclaimed but was instantly shushed by Mor.

"Yes, Miss Amethyne, I understand. Will that include using a third party?" Mor asked, and Roasana thought for a second.

"Yes, it would. If a third party is involved, they will be questioned, and if they had any ties to either of you, you will be expelled." She decided.

"What! That's unfair!" Ranbor shouted, catching another cold look from Rosana.

"I did not ask about your opinion. I asked if you understand Mister Ruby." Rosana chided the boy.

"Yes, I understand." Ranbor agreed through clenched teeth.

"Good, now get to class. And remember, I have my eyes on both of you now. You can't misbehave without my knowledge." Rosana told them as she walked away.

Mor was the first to leave for the next lesson. °*You know this will not be over, right?*° The human proclaimed.

°*Yes, he will search for the next opportunity, but for now, we are safe.*° Mor answered.

°*So what is the next lesson about anyway?*° The human asked.

°*History... Most boring class.*° Mor said with a slight groan.

With that, they sat through an exhausting lesson on the history of kin.

***

Initially, there were only kin, no distinction between them. They lived in concert with nature and the beasts roaming their world. Now, while they were peaceful, there were disputes, and the discovery of magic powers only fueled those. Finally, someone used his power to try and propel himself to the top of the world. The resulting war devastated vast stretches of land, killing thousands and starting what we now call the first cataclysm.

As the fighting continued, the formerly free-flowing magic concentrated on the battlefields, the unleashed spells drawing it towards those. In an especially fearsome battle, it reached a breaking point. The resulting gathering of power sucked every drop of energy into itself, killing every living being on the battlefield and creating the first monstrosity.

This sparked a new conflict as more and more monstrosities were found, most of them being the mutated beasts of nature corrupted by overflowing power. This was a different kind of fight, as the monstrosities were almost impervious to magic. Still, with combat prowess and supporting magic, the monstrosities were beaten back repeatedly. Securing a new peace until the second cataclysm and breaking of the kin.

In the great cleansing, the First was not seen again. It just vanished, strengthening itself by hunting other monstrosities and absorbing their volatile magic powers until it was ready. Then, with a deafening roar, it shook the world. Toppling mountains with its lumbering gate destroying newly built fortress cities in days. As the kin rilled under the assault, they used their power to create the ultimate weapon. Sadly, it got lost to history what kind of weapon it was, but the grand magos who made it called it "reyl carnon," and it could immobilize the First, fixing it in place.

But while they were occupied, the monstrous beasts returned, driving the kin into the corner and dividing the world. Now, while the most capable warriors engaged the First, the other kin fought with everything they had. The fighting lasted years, costing untold lives and changing the kin forever. The constant use of magic and the kin's will to survive changed them.

The isolated kin changed according to their environment, splitting into all the different kin we know today. And while the First could not be slayed, even with the grand weapon, it would finally be sealed, and at the cost of every surviving kin of that battle buried deep in the ground to never be freed again.

***

°You know, I feel that something in the lesson sounded familiar.° The human told Mor afterward.

°But I guess I understand now how your people became like that. Your ancestors probably fought lots of those beasts on the ground and needed a safe place to retreat. Then discovered that blasting those things from high above is pretty effective.° They mused.

°Never mind that! Don't we have more important things to discuss? I mean, you told me you dodged those fire spells. How did you do something like this?° Mor replied.

°Don't know, just did.° The human answered.

°Do you not understand what that means? Maybe our impossible endeavor is not impossible at all! ° Mor exclaimed.

°Your right! I entirely wrote that off. Even if you only have enough juice for a single strike, the surprise factor would probably be worth *it. Maybe we can just try it right now...*° As the human talked, Mor's hand slowly went to his face and formed a thumbs-up.

°*This is too hard! It feels like I have to fight you every step of the way and drag you along. I guess knocking you out is not an option?*° The human asked.

°*Of course not!*° Mor protested.

°*Then we either find another way, or it's back to the basics.*° The human stated.

°*And the basics would be?*° Mor asked.

°*Well, practice, practice, and for some variety, practice.*° came the answer.

°*I thought as much.*° Mor's lack of excitement was palpable.

Part 7

On the way to the next lesson, Mor was asked, °*Think, I could use your magic?*° by the human.

°*I don't know. Maybe it's something to try later today.*° Mor answered.

°*Yeah, let's do that.*° The human agreed.

The next lesson was interesting, at least for the visitor from beyond. It was a lesson on the rules of magic. Even if Mor and quite a few of his peers were lulled into sleep by the teacher's soothing voice. The human was surprised that someone could teach something so interesting in such a boring way.

***

As you all know, magic is divided into types known to us as attributes.

Attributes have a positive effect on magic of the same type and a negative effect on the type opposing it.

To give you an example, a mage with fire affinity will not be able to use higher forms of water magic. We know of the following attributes, but sometimes new ones are discovered, so this list is ever-expanding. Please pay attention now, as this will be test-relevant.

We know of the elemental attributes: Fire, Earth, Water, and Wind. The manipulation attributes Healing and Illusion. And finally, the royal attribute, only seen in the royal Diamond family, is called Gravity.

Here, I have to note that there are spells that are not included in any of those attributes and can be used by anyone. These are called

Basic-attributed spells. For example, Those spells include body enhancement, magic bolt, or the widely used message spell.

Now, please note that the attribute distinctions are only one part. The second part is the distinction of potency of the spells. First, there are the single-class spells, moving and manipulating existing materials. You can pick fruits or use a small amount of water to water a plant. They can only do what anyone can with their hands and basic tools.

Next up would be group-class spells where the material to manipulate will be supplied by the magic power. Here, your attributes will matter. The basic martial and convenience spells are located in this class, with a strength that a small group estimated at around five people could produce with their tools.

Then we get into the village-class spells, and as you can guess, those include things that would need the manual labor of a small village. Here, most of you will find yourself comfortable spellcasting.

But after that, we get into the higher forms. Here, you either need a soul-bound partner with the same affinity as yourself to supply the energy demands or have an exceptionally strong affinity yourself. Those spells are called demographic-class spells.

Finally, there would be world-class spells, but the energy requirement of those could only be supplied by a whole convent of perfect attributed mages. At least, that's the theory. Nobody could use a spell like that. It is purely hypothetical.

***

°*Ok, that was really interesting. I would like to see what those high-class spells are capable of.*° The human stated, and Mor answered

°*Yes, but with my magic reserves, we will probably be stuck at group-class magic.*°

°*Laaaame!*° human exclaimed. °*We really need to find a way to get you more magic... This is just stupid.*°

°*Well, it would help if you could cast spells as well. Then we could use magic much faster.*° Mor said, and added °*Well, only a few more hours, and we can test that.*°

°*You're right.*° The human agreed.

With this, both of them either suffered or excitedly listened through the following lessons. Mor was enjoying a peaceful lunch break. At least, it was as peaceful as possible, with a human trying to move random body parts and cursing about how hard it was.

Mor finally made the human stop after he was forced to open his hand involuntarily and drop his juice.

But without the acute danger of the bullies, it was very nice for a change, if a bit lonely. But still much better than before. The only bad thing about the bonding with the human was that his body ached after the human moved it so violently, but it would pass. He was sure of that. Finally, after lessons ended, Mor acquired something for supper and retreated to his room, carefully locking the door.

After they finally "guarded" their room right, Mor refused to add some "surprises" for anyone opening the door. They sat down on the bed and began with what they discussed.

°*I want to try using magic first.*° The human opened. °*Moving your body is hella exhausting.*°

°*Yes, let's try it. First, concentrate on the magic inside our body and make it flow.*° Mor guided the human.

°*How do I concentrate on the magic?*° The human questioned, and Mor explained it further.

°*You have to feel the potential within and then concentrate on it.*°

After a short while, the human stated, °*Is it bad that I can't feel any potential or whatever? Maybe just go like this, and yes, I think I feel something flow!*° The human finally said.

Mor felt elated. Now, they could cast two spells even with his meager energy reserves.

°*Great! Now concentrate on the pillow and imagine it fluffing itself up.*° He said, and once again, the human tried, but nothing would happen.

°*Huh? Why is nothing happening? I feel something flowing and all.*° The human asked.

°*I don't know, I'm telling you what I was told when I started with magic. What my parents taught me.*° Mor answered.

°*Speaking of your parents, don't you have magic communication? Why is that message taking so long to reach them? Shouldn't that be instantaneous?*° The human asked.

Mor sighed °*Your understanding is screwed up. How would you even think that? Message magic is simple, so you need to have view contact with your recipient, or it won't work.*°

°*Well, we have some stories in our world, with magic settings and shit, and there it is always super handy and can do just about anything. While here, it is tedious and full of "that's not how it works."*° The human sounded disappointed.

°*Well, let's get back on track. Let me try some more. Maybe you could watch the flow of your energy, then tell me if I do something right.*° The human offered, and Mor nodded.

Like this, they tried, but Mor could not detect any movement in the energies within him. °*This is not working.*° Mor stated, and the human had to agree.

°*So we are left with trying to let me do the body movement... It's not ideal, but well, let's try something from my world. Take deep breaths and relax. Only concentrate on your breathing.*° The human instructed.

Following the directions, Mor did so, and slowly, he felt his body moving. He was doing everything in his power to not intervene and only concentrate on his breathing until, finally, the human let out a satisfied grunt.

°*Yes, that's better. It is still hard, but now I'm just moving something I'm not accustomed to instead of fighting you.*° The human sounded pretty happy, as was Mor.

But a quick glance at the clock in his room made both of them decide to get some sleep. Being late for class would not be good. Mor awoke the next morning to a world of pain. His whole body just hurt.

°*What is this? It hurts!*° Mor whined.

°*I don't know! I did nothing while you were asleep!*° The human said.

°*You must have! Why else would it be like this?*° Mor scolded the human.

°*Don't get snippy with me! I will slap you! And with your own hand, no less!*° The human countered.

°*And why am I the only one in pain? That is unfair!*° Mor complained.

°*Why would you think that? I feel the pain, too. It's just not as bad as you say. You are just a little wuss.*° The human said.

°*I'm no wuss! I just never had this kind of pain before!*° Mor grumbled.

°*Really? If I had to describe it, it feels like a little muscle soreness... Ah! Maybe me moving your body is more stressful than you moving your own. Even if you are distracted, you subconsciously try to fight my control. That would make sense, but we can't know for sure.*° The human theorized.

°*Really? And now? If this is what happens, this is not acceptable!*° Mor was still whining.

°*Well easy, we will test your theory that you can't train your bodies because, with this new development, I smell bullshit and laziness. Time to train and limber up!*° The human decided, and Mor whinced at that exclamation.

°*We will do nothing like that!*° He exclaimed.

°*We will, and I will force you if I need to.*° The human stated matter of factly.

°*I hate you.*° Mor grumbled.

°*Yes. Yes! Let the hate flow through you!*° The human snickered. °*Still, I won't let you just opt out without trying!*°

Part 8

The following day was hell for Mor. Everything ached, and it seemed that Ranbor not only noticed Mor's discomfort but reveled in every wince and pained groan.

At lunch break, Mor dragged himself to the infirmary to visit the adept for help, earning a bewildered look from her at his appearance.

"Mister Agaton, what brings you back here so soon? Already got yourself hurt again?" She chuckled. "To be young again."

Mor gave her an apologetic smile. "Thank you for taking care of me, Miss Amber." He told the Adept.

Which made her laugh. "Miss, he says, you are one sweet talker, but I'm too old for you." She told him.

Mor turned red at that while the human let out a whistling tune in his mind. °*Shut it!*° Mor shushed the human.

"Please stop teasing me. I could use some help and tips with some healing magic. I have this ache in my muscles, and it hurts. Is there something you can do?" Mor asked.

°*Good thinking, but still a wuss.*° The human teased and adept Amber thought for a second.

"Yes, there is such magic. I could teach you without too many problems. But tell me, how did you manage that? Aching muscles is not a usual problem the Soul-kin must contend with." She questioned him.

"You know, the recklessness of youth. I experimented with something, and well, now it hurts." Mor half lied, and the Adept gave him a strict talking-to.

"Did you not learn from your last "experiment"? This goes beyond reckless to get yourself hurt so soon again." She chided him.

"That's why I want to learn some healing magic, to be safer." Mor interrupted the lecture.

"Yes, then, at least you can administer first aid and keep from dying. But are those experiments that important to endanger yourself?" Amber asked.

"No, I won't do anything that dangerous again. Promise! I just want to try some things because my magic is weak. I want to get stronger and be able to stand next to the others." Mor revealed his feelings to her, and adept Amber nodded.

"I get it, come back after class, and I will teach you. But promise me not to endanger yourself again. I believe nobody told you how close a call your first "experiment" was, and it wouldn't do for my first admirer to die off like that. This would ruin my reputation as Adept." She teased again.

°*Nicely done, Romeo, you did well. Healing magic always comes in clutch. We will be invincible, always healing.*° The human congratulated Mor, who in turn rolled his eyes.

°*Again with your over-the-top beliefs. I told you that is not how all of this works!*° He sighed.

"I saw those eyes. Only because I'm old doesn't mean I don't notice something like that. But a cutie like you is excused." The Adept smiled warmly, misinterpreting Mors reaction to the human.

"Now, get back to class. You don't want to be tardy," she told him, and Mor gave her an excusing smile as he took his leave.

°*I like her, we should probably get her something for teaching us. Are there any snacks we could get?*° The human suggested, and Mor agreed.

That's why, after classes, Mor got some sweets for the adept and made his way to the infirmary for his additional lesson.

After a few hours of teasing and bewildering explanations, he knew that he would have to come more often to learn the required spells. Ultimately, it took Mor the whole week to learn the basic healing spells.

The positive thing was that while Mor attended those lessons, the human did not enforce his threat and didn't drag him through physical training.

Instead, the human encouraged him to get as many healing spells as possible. After his week of practicing and learning, he got a good grasp on the spells "close wounds," "recover stamina," and "reduce pain." All of them were at single-class level, but they would be enough.

°*Great now that we have this in the bag, back on track. Cue the training montage and play Eye of the Tiger!*° The human exclaimed, and Mor dreaded what would come.

°*What even is a tiger...*° Mor grumbled.

And just like that, the human training camp from hell started. Mor was forced to wake up early and go through a strange sequence of movements, which the human supposedly "knew" would be suitable for more flexibility.

After that, he would cast reduce-pain on himself to lessen the pain from the day before and the actual day. Mor would go through his lessons, and after classes, the human would practice taking control and doing simple movements like turning a book page while Mor did his homework.

The days flowed into each other as Mor was kept busy with his learning and human training. He only recognized an increase in hunger and food consumption, but the human said this was expected and normal.

Mor started to believe, more and more, that there was something about training your body, and those movements were somehow starting to feel relaxing and calming his mind for the day. Just like the human said.

All this lasted until about three weeks later when he received a letter from Diamond Isle. A letter he completely forgot would be coming. His parents, they had sent their answer, now he was in deep shit. With dread, he opened the envelope and was surprised as two letters fell out.

Picking up the first, he noticed the penmanship of his mother, and after the first sentences, he dreaded the rest of it.

*My dear baby boy,

Mommy is really, really angry with you. Why didn't you tell me that you are unhappy at your new school? You even lied to me. ***Sob sob*** Mommy is really sad. You are always welcome to come home to me. You don't need to stay at that stupid place if it makes you unhappy. Just come back to me. It doesn't matter if you are bad at magic; Mommy will take care of you regardless. I'm sure Daddy will see it just like me. We can all be a super happy family again.* The letter was going on and on and on, filling both sides of the piece of paper.

°*That is... painful to read. My condolences.*° The human said, and Mor nodded.

°*Yes... She is a great mage, but her motherly love is smothering. I wanted to go to this school to get out from under her bosom. I guarantee you. Father told her to keep it on one sheet of paper...*

Well, on to the second letter... fathers.° Mor opened up the second piece of paper and read.

*Mor.

Don't dare lie to me again. We will talk when you visit at the big break. Morokahn Agaton*

°*That is short!*° The human exclaimed °*How did your parents get together with this difference?!*°

Mor shrugged °*I don't know. Mother told me she was "super duper lovey-dovey" in love with Father, and he just went along with it, I guess. But if they are happy, who am I to disagree?*° He answered.

°*True, but still!*° The human said and began to chuckle. °*The difference is too funny.*°

Mor started laughing at this exclamation as well.

°*The letters are not as bad as we feared. It seems this will have to wait until that ominous break. Meaning back to business for us.*° The human stated, and Mor sighed.

°*Yes, but I should at least answer them.*° He said.

°*Yes, later. Now, back to training!*° The human urged, and they got back to training.

Later that evening, Mor hit the mattress of his bed completely exhausted, and any thoughts of letters and answers were forgotten.

The next morning, while going through their exercises, Mor spoke up.

°*We never talked about why you are so helpful to me. Isn't that kind of weird? I would be furious if I just got stuck in some other place.*° He asked.

°*Yeah, but somehow, right from the start, I had this instinct to protect you and this body. Don't know why, but whatever! Right now, I'm having too much fun just living and doing stupid shit. This magic stuff is also really interesting. Also, we humans are known for our great adaptability. So no harm done, don't think about it.*° The human replied.

°*Still can't remember your name?*° Mor asked.

°*Nope, I don't know my name or anything personal, like my age. I don't even remember my family. But somehow, it doesn't concern me, probably because I died or something. You just leave everything behind and move on.*° The human guessed.

°*But sometimes you make strange jokes or talk about things like a "Tiger," whatever that is.*° Mor replied.

°*You got no tigers? Well, they are big cats and very dangerous animals. Also, while I can't remember my personal stuff, other things from human culture I knew are still there. No matter. I already came to terms with the strangeness of this situation.*° The human answered.

°*What are cats? Or those animals? Are they some monstrosities?*° Mor was confused.

°*Why would you even think that? Are there really no animals here?!*° The human asked.

°*No. Only monstrosities, but in History, they talked about beasts. Maybe those things were animals once a long time ago.*° Mor put forward.

°*Your world is stupid!*° The human replied, ending the discussion.

Part 9

Mor grew comfortable with his morning exercises and even enjoyed them as more time passed. Part of this was that he could now see changes in his body. What was scrawny became lean and limber. In addition, his scholar robes weren't fluttering around him anymore. Instead, they were starting to sit somewhat comfortably while still hiding all his progress. The human told him if they keep this up and go on to the next stage, he might need new ones soon.

The lessons also went well because the human was paying as much attention as Mor himself, or still tried to use his magic when they got bored, without any kind of advance, mind you. It would not work, no matter what the human tried.

The headmaster revealed this year's half-year aptitude test about a quarter into the year. It would be a duel, as the rise in the appearance of monstrosities raised the need for more combat-oriented mages, or at least mages able to protect themselves.

It would be done tournament style, with each school year having its own bracket. The pairings would depend on your grades, both in magic theory and applied magic.

Mor glanced at Ranbor briefly at this announcement, and they met eyes. Ranbor's chance had finally come, and he would crush Mor for every perceived insolence. The look they shared made clear that neither would back off now.

°*Seems like the fun part will start now. Are you ready for a war meeting? We need a strategy to press that looser into the dirt.*° The human edged Mor on, who in turn replied.

°*We know he specializes in fire magic, and as a high noble, his magic reserves are probably much higher than ours. In addition to that, I'm sure he knows at least one village-grade firespell.*°

°*But we can't just concentrate on a hard counter for the big idiot. This is tournament style, and we don't want to be forced to drop out before meeting him. Additionally, we are at a*

disadvantage. We have neither friends nor allies. While he has his flunkies. If we meet them, they

will fight with everything they have to tire us out, but if they meet Ranbor, they will probably just forfeit so he can save his energy.° The human theorized, and Mor had to agree.

°*Yes, too bad we can't raise our reserves or at least replenish them fast. So we need to win as efficiently as possible.°* Mor said.

°*Well, we have the most efficient spell possible.°* The human snickered.

°*That would be?°* Mor asked.

°*We. Can. Cast. FIST and the higher level spell Break Nose!°* The human unveiled, which led both to chuckle, and Mor was promptly reprimanded for interrupting the lesson.

After class, the human invited Mor to walk outside while they talked, just moving the body to move the mind.

°*Now, to get to the matter, we need to specialize in something while not giving up our most significant advantage. We are generalists and can fall back to any attribute. So, any Ideas?°* The human asked.

°*Well, we have the following additional advantages. Firstly, we can use any attribute spell.*

Secondly, we don't have to stand still while casting continuous spells because you can move us. Our disadvantages are our comparatively small energy reservoir and lack of affinity. Therefore, we are limited to performing group-class spells.° Mor offered.

°*Yes, that sounds about right. Do you think we could use body enhancement magic? We could then enhance our mobility advantage, which is never a bad tactic.*° But Mor shook his head.

°*We would run out of energy too quickly. It is just a too complicated spell.*° He explained.

°*Too bad, but if you think so. We should probably at least try it. Maybe it is still an option to get a surprise attack in. Depending on mobility advantage would still be a good tactic, and if we couple that with some ranged attacks, we would be hard to deal with, more so if your peers have to stay stationary for the truly problematic stuff. The rest we can dodge or defend against.*° The human put forward, and Mor agreed.

°*We should go with ranged magic but probably ignore fire because Ranbor will just shut that down with his more powerful fire control. Wind is also out because it is terrible against fire in its base form. We would need to get deeper into wind affinity magics to have a chance, and then we would be back to the efficiency problem because of the raised energy demands.*° Mor explained.

°*Why not try earth? You are fond of that affinity, right? And we could bring some stones to where the duel is taking place. Meaning we could use single-class magic to "throw" stones. In addition, as a trump card, we could get some more potent earth spells and some spells of the other attributes.*° The human suggested, and Mor got thoughtful.

°*But this spell is incredibly weak. Look.*° Mor picked up a Stone and let his energy flow.

It did cost almost no energy, but it was also disappointing. The stone flew for about 3 meters and then flopped to the ground.

°*What the heck? Ok... look, humans are stone-throwing experts, and we learned in class that magic has much to do with imagination, right?*° The human asked, and Mor nodded.

°*So this spell is probably based on your view of your usual throwing strength, which, for your kin, is probably none. I'm sure you could throw it further than that right now with your own strength, but let's get some string and a little bag or something, and I will show you how you really "throw" a stone.*° At the humans' urging, Mor procured the requested material.

°*Just like that... Fixing this to here.... and done!*° The human seemed happy with their construction.

°*What would that be?*° Mor asked.

°*A sling, of course!*° Came the proud reply.

°Now just watch, I will show you.° The human took over Mors' movements and showed what was possible even with the sling. Even if the flung stones did not have any semblance of accuracy. But then it also was just a made sling.

The primary purpose was fulfilled, and after Mor tried the stone-throwing spell again, he noticed that the speed of the stone was definitely enhanced, even if it was a little bit more energy expensive now. Still, the energy demand was much less than any group-class spell but with comparable power.

°*That is nice! Let's go with that one!*° Mor excitedly told the human, who agreed.

°*Then, we will add enhanced magic training to our daily regime and gather up some useful stones.*° The human decided.

°*Wait, add? We will do more training?! But what about learning? We can't let our grades drop.*° Mor whined.

°*Easy, you will learn while I do the physical training. Your grades won't drop, and I will get a better feeling of moving, which will help with our duells. But now that we are done with this, it's time to head back. The homework will not do itself.*° The human told Mor, who in turn looked up surprised.

He hadn't paid attention to his surroundings. He just kept walking while they talked. Shocked, he recognized how far they had come and without him being tired.

°*Told you those exercises would help.*° The human proudly declared, as a bright smile grew on Mor's face.

°*Don't you think, if we can train our body, there must be a way to train our magic reserve?*° He asked, and the human had to agree.

°*If we find that, we will be unstoppable, but where to look, or who to ask?*° The human questioned, and Mor shrugged.

°*I don't know. We will probably have to experiment on our own. There's perhaps no one who can tell us anything about that because...*° Leading both to exclaim at the same time,

°*That's not how this works!*° and laugh.

°*Then, my friend, we have a plan. Let's do this!*° The human excitedly exclaimed as Mor returned to his room.

While Mor finished his homework, the human did some leg raises below the desk, using a footrest as additional weight.

With their strategy firmly in place, the training took off, and the other students often saw Mor wandering the school grounds, a book in hand, reading while expertly evading any obstacle.

While the boys tried to trip Mor, when he was occupied it was met with no success. Mor seemed to effortlessly move around their pranks without really noticing them, and some girls took second glances because something about that boy was different.

At times, Mor would even be seen running, which led to even more bewilderment because what would he run from? Most just accredited this to some strange commoner thing and ignored it.

Ranbor snickered every time he saw Mor because, to him, it was clear that the peasant wanted to run away, and that's why he was running around like a coward.

°*This gets really boring! Why are those idiots even trying anymore? Don't they learn they can't trip me? I mean, I can see them sticking out their foot and all.*° The human complained.

°*How would they know? All they see is a distracted outcast wandering about, not caring for his surroundings. And with them constantly failing, we only make a more worthwhile target. We're a challenge now.*° Mor answered while they dodged the next poor attempt.

°*Still annoying.*° Poutet the human.

°*Other topic! Any progress in our "Raise the energy reservoir" project?*° The human asked, changing the subject.

Mor shook his head. °*Nothing until now. All books I can get ahold of say that it is impossible. Just as impossible as training your body. Slowly, I believe you are right, and they are all stupid.*° Mor sighed.

°*I have an idea, but it could be dangerous. That means we shouldn't do that without someone to observe it, meaning we need someone we can trust with this.*° The human stated, and Mor's interest was clear.

°*What idea? We just about tried anything, using magic every day. Just like we would move our body to train muscles, but it did not work at all.*° Mor said.

°*Well, if we empty our reservoir completely and dip just a bit into our "life energy," then maybe if we do this often enough, we can get our reservoir to "think" it must grow to supply the new demand.*° The human explained, and Mor nodded.

°*Sounds risky. Too risky to experiment on our own with it. But the only one I might trust with this would be the old Adept. She seemed inclined to listen to arguments if we explained what we wanted to do right.*° He said.

°*Good thinking, Mor! Let's put that on the list for after the turnier. For now, we have to work with what we got. We don't want to drop out because we did some experiments that might fail.*° The human told Mor.

°*Yes! We only have two more weeks. At least our training is going well.*° Mor agreed.

°*That's why we will do intensive training for next week and rest up the week after to be in top form.*° The human said.

°*I don't like the sound of intensive training.*° Mor carefully offered.

°*Nothing bad, we will just do 100 sit-ups, 100 push-ups, 100 squads, and 10 km of running each day, every day. Doesn't sound too bad, right?*° The human asked.

°*I only understood some numbers and running in this sentence, I don't like this.*° Mor complained.

°*Don't worry, I will do those exercises for us.*° The human calmed Mor, but Mor's bad feelings were not so easily quelled.

Still, he had no choice if he fought the human in those exercises. It would just be more exhausting.

Part 10

Mor thought he knew now what pain was after the last brutal muscle aches before the human got him to do morning exercises and stretches, but this "not so bad" intensive training was hell.

He almost felt like he was losing hair. But at least it was over now, and the human stayed true to their word. The last week before the tournament was just resting up.

Still, Mor couldn't calm down because he didn't know what to do with his time now. At least the human would let him keep doing his morning exercises.

Because of that, he was incredibly excited as they had just three days before the tournament revealed the pairings.

°*Ok, where are we?*° Mor searched for his name and found it completely to the right.

°*There, meaning we're on the first fight. Now, where is Ranbor?*° Mor asked, and after a quick search, he found the name of his ex-tormenter entirely on the left.

Meaning they would not meet before the finals.

°*I recognize tampering when I see it.*° The human states and Mor had to agree.

°*Miss Amethyne probably doesn't want this duel to happen at all, but rules are rules.*° He said.

°*Still, that means we have to get to the finals first. Good, we already planned for it.*° The human said, and Mor smiled.

°*Then let's look at who we are up against first.*° The human added °*E. Emeror, you know him?*° they asked further.

Mor shook his head at the question and answered in turn. °*No, I don't remember anyone with that name, but Emeror is probably a branch family from the Emeralds, so he's probably windattributed.*°

°*Well, there is no sense in wrecking our heads about that now! Time to get some food, stretch to take the nervous edge off, and sleep. Then we are in the best shape possible.*° The human told Mor, and both went to end the day early.

Sometime later, Ranbor looked at the same list and smiled. "Amethyne has made sure we don't meet up, shame. But she made a mistake. Don't disappoint me now, Emtsor. The peasant is yours. Just stomp him completely into the ground and make him pay to disrespect the nobility." Emtsor Emeror nodded at his order.

"As you wish, Lord Ruby. I will drown the commoner in my storms." He said, and Ranbor let out an evil chuckle.

The next morning, after a restful night, Mor went through his morning routine, getting some stretching and then breakfast. Followed by readying his bag of stones and making his way to the gathering hall for the headmaster's announcement of the exact tournament rules.

As he went to his spot, he noticed Ranbor smiling at him, and Mor shuddered at that.

°*I don't like that look.*° He told the human, who had to agree.

°*Something is up. We have to be careful.*° The human said, but further musings were cut short as the headmaster took the stage.

"Dear students, please pay attention, as I will now announce the rules for this midterm. First, you are allowed to go all out while you are in the arena with your opponent. The arena is fitted with protective magic, keeping you from being seriously wounded. Secondly, you will be graded according to your performance, and finally, keep your rivalries and fights in the arena! It will have the harshest consequences if someone is caught trying to "even the score" outside the arena. But now, without further ado, let the midterm test begin!"

The headmaster left the stage with hoots and applause from the students, and the other teachers herded everyone toward the arena. Mor was just walking along when a feminine hand touched his shoulders. He turned around at the touch, looking at Miss Amethyne.

"Mister Agaton, you are in the first round. Please follow me," she told him, and Mor followed.

He was led to a side room and made to sit down.

"Now, Mister Agaton, I need to ask what you have in this bag of yours because weapons or something like that are not allowed. This is, after all, a contest of magic." Rosana asked.

Mor just shrugged and showed his collection of stones to her.

"Just stones." He told her truthfully and got a confused look as a reward.

"Why would you bring stones for your magic test?" She asked him, and he explained.

"I want to use single-grade magic and therefore need some materials. I didn't know if the arena had what I wanted, so I brought some."

Miss Amethyne nodded. "I understand this will be allowed, but remember, this is about magic. You're already on my watchlist, and if I see you hitting someone with that bag of stones, like some sort of barbaric berserker. I will disqualify you. We are of the Soul-kin and not the berserkers of the Ice-kin after all," she said sternly.

Mor nodded and answered. "I didn't plan on using it as a weapon, just for the throw-stone spell," which satisfied Miss Amethynes' questioning.

"Good, then you are ready to go. Here's the door to the arena, and after your duel, just leave through it again. I or another teacher will then bring you to the stands to watch the following duels." She finally closed.

Mor smiled at her and left through the door, stepping outside the darkened room and instantly getting blinded by the burning sun.

As Mor entered the sandy arena, which had some metal pillars designed as cover or obstacles, he heard a lot of booing.

°*Seems, we are not so popular.*° The human stated the obvious. °*But let's raise hell!*°

Mor had an evil smile plastered on his face because of the humans' enthusiasm.

°*This will be fun. Let's keep surprising them until we win the whole thing!*° *The human* told his partner.

Emtsor entered the arena, squinting his eyes. Why did they have to keep this room so dark? If he is only blinded by the sunshine afterward? As his eyes got used to the brightness, he saw his opponent, the commoner Ranbor, wanted to be crushed. He shrugged, sometimes you just have to do what the higher nobles want, and it wouldn't be tragic for the commoner.

The commoner would just get put back in his place and could be happy knowing his betters cared so much for him. The only thing giving him some thought was the warning Zaletha gave him.

She told Emtsor that after the commoner's accident, he was somehow different. Now, after he took a better look, he saw the smug smile on the commoner's face. Oh, he would put him back in his place. This uppity behavior is not acceptable for commoners. They should bow to him and the other nobles and be grateful for everything.

With a loud gong, the first fight was on.

Emtsor watched the commoner run towards some of the metal pillars and smiled to himself.

That was more like it. At least the commoner hat that much sense to hide from Emtsors magic.

Now, the rumor that he was "running" in his free time even made sense, but Emtsor did not care. He was ordered to go all out and crush the commoner, so all out he would go. Emtsor gathered the air around him, and with a spike of power, he let all his power flow....

Mor watched in horror as his opponent entered the arena, and he finally got a face to the name. °*Oh no!*° Mor exclaimed.

°*Isn't that one of Royal-butthole's flunkies?*° The human asked.

°*Why did you not know his name?*° They chided Mor, who got defensive in turn.

°*He never introduced himself! And I didn't think Ranbor would tolerate a lesser noble in his entourage! I thought his "friends" would at least be upper nobles!*° Mor exclaimed.

°*Well, too late to cry over spilled milk!*° The human said, and Mor asked

°*What's this milk now?*° His nerves were getting the better of him.

°*Not important right now! Get ready!*° The human admonished and got ready to move.

As the gong sounded through the arena, the human exploded Mors's body into movement, getting into cover.

°Come on, we can do this! We trained, just keep going, we are stronger than this pompous ass!° The human tried to motivate Mor, but then it happened.

The air grew eerily still, and even the human could feel the powers unleashed by their opponent.

°Oh, shit!° The human exclaimed, and Mor's face went pale.

°That is not good!° He fearfully exclaimed.

°Quick! I have an idea, just ...° The human started.

The unleashed storm hit the arena like a hammer strike, the iron obstacles giving off stressed metal sounds but holding. Sand and dust became a torrent of razor-sharp projectiles, and both contestants vanished from view. Ranbor smiled excitedly. Yes, now the peasant would know true power, and Emtsor would quickly run out of energy, but nothing the peasant could do would keep him from losing and, of course, getting a bad grade. Ranbor bribed one of the applied magic teachers with favors from his family and, therefore, knew that this tournament was just a ruse. It was just to motivate everyone to do their best casting offensive spells. The only advantage winning had was that you get to show off more often, but going all out in the first round would at least get a passing grade. With Emtsor's dominating power, the peasant would not get to show off at all and would fail. Ranbor laughed. His plan was perfect!

Rosana watched in horror as the storm toppled one of the metal pillars. The tournament was not meant to be fought at this power level! The spell unleashed was a continuous spell of village-class, probably scratching on demographic-class power levels. Even she was unsure she could escape a spell like that without using all her power. However, this kind of spell would come at a cost, as Mister Emeror would not fight his second round. He would be entirely out of energy in just a few seconds, but that would be all he needed for this win. She did not understand what pressed the young mage to such an extreme reaction.

Slowly, the storm wained, and the dust settled. A single figure could be seen bent over through the haze, panting but still standing. Emtsor looked around, breathing hard. That spell took everything out of him, but no trace was left of the commoner, and he smiled at a job well done.

"This is what you get for messing with nobles without being strong yourself." Emtsor thought.

Ranbor laughed as the crowd gasped in shock. The peasant had just vanished, probably getting ground up by the flying micro debris. He would need to give Emtsor something for that performance. He really got rid of the pest.

Headmaster Amethyne watched carefully, keeping his calm. The spell was impressive and worth passing marks, but it could not have obliterated the other contestant. The protective magic was too strong for that.

"What is going on?" He whispered to himself.

Part 11

It was cold, dark, and deafeningly loud. The boy huddled down, hoping the quickly made stone plate would hold, and finally, after a moment seeming to last forever, the noise quieted down, leaving an eery silence.

°*Do you think it's over?*° He asked.

°*Don't know, let's take a look!*° Someone answered.

Headmaster Amethyne watched, as did everyone else, when a part of the arena ground opened up, and the disheveled hair and head of the second contestant came out, looking around carefully. Headmaster Amethyne was surprised.

How did the boy withstand such a powerful spell without using equivalent magic? He should have been able to survive that attack, but it should have decided the duel and not in his favor.

Headmaster Amethyne smiled. Something interesting was going on, and he would question that boy in just a moment about it.

Emtsor was still panting and getting slowly nervous. Why was he not declared victor? He eliminated the nuisance, after all. He even completely removed that bastard. It was just a commoner, so no harm was done. A sudden murmur went through the stands, and he could almost hear Ranbor shouting something at him, but he just wanted to lay down, the exertion taking his toll, making him unfocused.

Mor heaved himself out from his impromptu foxhole and looked around.

°*So what now? The flunky seems to be ready to forfeit. Probably spent all his energy.*° He asked.

°Well, why not ask him if he wants to tap out? We used a little bit. This "Dig-well" and "stone foundation" were great for what they cost. Even if you initially told me practicing "convenience" magics would be pointless. But I won't be like that and spare you the "Told you so!" ° The human answered.

°Yes, I guess you are right, never thought we use it as protection against storms.° Mor conceded the point.

"Hey! Want to forfeit? You seem pretty done, and I'm still fine!" He called out to Emtsor.

Emtsors gaze focused on Mor in surprise. "*How was that commoner still okay? That is not possible! Rage built within him. He was almost out of energy, and this peasant was still fine? Preposterous, it was a lie. Commoners always lie. The commoner must be even more tired than him!*" He thought his pride not allowing him to forfeit on such a ruse.

"Shut it, commoner! It is not over yet!" He called back, breathing heavily.

°*You heard the man.*° The human said.

Mor shrugged, put his hand in his bag, and retrieved a stone. Emtsor took a deep breath, channeling the very last of his power in a finishing attack, but before he could unleash it, he felt a sharp pain hitting his stomach, and everything went black.

°*Well, that's that.*° The human said, and Mor agreed.

Headmaster Amethyne watched in amazement as Mor did something using almost no power.

Emtsor just folded up, knocked out cold. It was just too fast for him to see, and he glanced curiously at his granddaughter as she blew a surprised whistle.

"Rosana, might you explain to me what happened? I could not see the spell that ended the fight." He asked a blushing Rosana, who answered.

"Mister Agaton there wanted to bring some stones for a "Throw-Rock" spell, and even though it looked like exactly what was used, it was far too powerful. But nothing else fits what we could see from here."

"Intriguing," Her grandfather said. "I'm going down to get Mister Agaton to the stands; I want to know what he did."

Headmaster Amethyne stood up and called out Mor as the victor, then left quickly for the little preparation room. Another teacher would collect Mister Emeror, and the next contestants would wait in two other rooms. He rushed to Mister Agaton's preparation room and was greeted by a shocked expression of the boy.

"Headmaster!" He called. "Why are you here?"

"Because you did something impossible, Mister Agaton. How did you protect yourself against that spell?" The headmaster asked, and Mor blushed.

"I used some convenience magic at the group level. Made a hole, hid in it, closed it with a stone foundation, and waited until everything blew over?" Mor put forward, the human snorting at the pun.

"And how would you come up with such ideas?!" The headmaster looked like an excited kid who had found an exciting toy.

This excitement scared Mor more than anything right now.

°*Time to lie!*° The human advised.

Mor almost wanted to make an incredulous remark about how he would not be that dumb to tell the whole truth, but he kept his quiet and answered the headmaster instead.

"Well, sir. As you know, I don't have an affinity, and my magic energy reserves are also not great. So I must think hard about what I want to spend this energy on to get the most efficient result." He explained.

"You say that, but I noticed your "Throw-Rock" spell. It was more powerful than this spell had any right to be. At most, the stone should have flown a few meters and then fallen to the ground." The headmaster drilled Mor further.

He is good. I didn't think many could identify the spell we used because it looks so different now.° The human said, and Mor had to agree.

"Well..." Mor put forward. "The magic teacher always told us that imagination has a lot to do with how your spells would work, but it could not be something impossible. A single-class spell will never be able to do anything you couldn't do with basic tools and on your own. This got me thoughtful. I asked our teacher in the class reserved for the study of kin history how other kin, who are not as blessed with magic as we are, would throw rocks very far and get a short explanation of a tool.

I built this tool and tried it, and it changed my view on "Throw-Rock" because the tool made the rock travel much further and faster. Then, my imagination aligned with what was possible with that simple tool, and the spell represented that ", he explained.

Mor just hoped the headmaster would not ask the teacher because that last part was entirely made up. But he could not tell the headmaster that the human devised this idea.

"Fascinating!" The headmaster said, "I look forward to what you come up with next!"

With that, Mor was led to the stands by the headmaster and watched the next duel. It was pretty lackluster because both contestants were evenly matched and seemed to try to save as much energy as possible until, finally, one won.

°*This must have cost more energy than just trying to finish in a decisive blow.*° The human stated, and Mor agreed.

°*Good for us, then we have the advantage.*° He said.

Ranbor was furious. Not only was Emtsor still out cold from magic exhaustion and probably would be for at least a day, but the peasant was sitting there seemingly unfazed by the ordeal he had just gone through. He should be lying on the arena floor!

Something was up. He knew it. The peasant was somehow cheating! But let him get to the finale now. He would burn that peasant to a crisp. Ranbor's rage was fueled by a little fire burning in his soul. Yes, he would kill the peasant.

As the rounds went on, almost always a slugfest of who had more energy and could unleash more power, and only sometimes someone who used some strategy or tactic, Mor nodded off. The human had told him to relax. They would wake him if something interesting was happening.

That moment came as Ranbor entered the Arena °*Hey wake up! Asshat's on. We need to pay attention to what he can do.*° The human called out to Mor.

Mor woke up startled. °*Allready? I just dozed off for a few minutes!*° Mor said and got a slight chuckle in return

°*Try an hour.*° The human said.

Both aimed their attention to the duel below, where Ranbors opponent was a girl with bright sapphire eyes.

°*Isn't this the daughter of the Sapphire family?*° Mor asked.

°*How would I know? But if we go with that logic, wouldn't she be a water specialist?*° The human retorted.

Yes, and a potent one. It seems like Ranbor will lose this round. Water is a bad matchup for him, and I can't see him letting go of his pride using anything other than fire.° Mor answered, and they watched, curious how this would go.

But nothing prepared them for what happened. It started pretty normal, with Ranbor bowing and the Sapphire girl giving a curtsy.

"You should give up now, Saphine!" He called to her. "You are no match for me, and I don't want to hurt you."

She gave him a beautiful smile in turn as she answered. "I don't think so. I have the advantage with my water. My family was always called upon if yours went out of line, and this will be no different."

And with the bantering out of the way, the duel was on; it started like any other before.

They both were just trying to find some weakness and flinging spells left and right, but the energy level was much higher. As expected, though, it seemed Saphine would win if this continued. Then suddenly Ranbor laughed, and it happened...

Part 12

Saphine hid behind a metal pillar after firing a lance of water at Ranbor. While hiding from the retaliatory fireball, she could feel the metal pillar slightly heating up, so she changed her cover while attacking again. As she moved, Ranbor fired again, but this time, she just used a spell of her own to cancel the fire spell and give herself some cover from the emitting steam cloud.

"Only brawn, no brain," she thought to herself.

Ranbor hasn't moved once this whole fight, just using fire spell after fire spell. If he wants to tire himself out, she would be okay with it.

Ducking behind another pillar, she readied her next spell, hurling another lance of water at the still-standing Ranbor. He tried to block it with a wall of fire but just wasn't fast enough.

She smiled to herself at the hit and changed position again as Ranbor shouted, enraged. "You bitch! How dare you!"

Saphine, stunned for just a moment, shouted back, "This is not how you should address a lady, you boor! It is your fault if you just stand there!" as she evaded another fire spell.

"I'm a high noble. I will not hide like some scared commoner!" He answered her, and she shrugged.

If he wants to be that way, then she would let him. She thought, *"Losing will bring him down a peg or two,"* while hurling another water stream at Ranbor, who now put more energy in his fiery shield and blocked.

Like this, their duel went on and got increasingly heated, as somehow Ranbor kept up that high energy output. Saphine, meanwhile, got slowly close to her limit. She knew she had to do something about that, and gathering most of her remaining energy, she unleashed a tidal wave that flooded the whole arena. With shock, she witnessed Ranbor withstanding this spell with his fire.

That's when she heard him chuckle and raise himself into mad laughter. Ranbor unleashed a grand spell himself, instantly evaporating every trace of Saphines' water, breaking through her quickly raised water sphere shield, almost burning her to a crisp. Luckily, the protective magic of the arena saved her life.

°*Holy shit, how much power does that ass have?! But at least he should be low on energy now.*° The human said, but Mor was unconvinced.

°*Are you sure? I don't see any sign of exhaustion in him.*°

With dread, both concluded they probably bit off more than they could chew. Still, they had no time to panic, as they would be up next, and a teacher came to get him.

As Mor entered the arena once again, he noticed that the sand in the arena was glittering. A closer look revealed to him that almost all the sand had turned to glass, and some of the metal obstacles had a kind of runny look. Mor's gaze fell on his next opponent, a girl whose name he also didn't know. When the gong sounded again, the duel was on, and again Mor exploded into movement, getting into cover and tried taking a look at his opponent, who was nowhere to be seen.

°*Where is she?*° Mor asked.

°*How would I know?*° The human said.

°*Let's keep moving. Standing still is just an invitation to get hit.*° Mor decided.

They began to move again, holding a stone in preparation for an opportunity to attack. Suddenly, a spear of stone shot up from below, almost hitting Mor as he jumped to dodge. Still, he could not locate the girl.

°*Could it be that she's using our first trick?*° The human asked, and Mor agreed.

°*But why can she see us?*° He asked back.

As soon as his feet hit the ground, another thorn of stone shot up to skewer him, ripping through his robes from the almost hit.

°*The ground! She can somehow see us if we touch the ground!*° The human said, and Mor sighed.

°*What can we do about that? Flying is not something we can do with our energy reservoir. Also, attacking while flying is not possible.*° Mor asked as they had to dodge another attack.

°*Well, either we keep moving and hope her energy runs out before our stamina does, or we need to do something more proactive.*° The human put forward.

°*Great, what proactive thing do you have in mind?*° Mor asked.

°*I don't know. I didn't think that far ahead,*° came the answer.

°*Great, how to be more useless...*° Mor chided as they again dodged an attack.

°*Shut it if you don't have a better idea! Rather than bitching, get the dust of the stamina recovery magic we trained. We need that shit going.*° The human complained.

Mor began concentrating on the spell, at the humans' urging while the human kept moving and dodging. The headmaster watched in amazement as the boy Agaton moved and used some kind of healing magic.

"This should be incredibly hard, but dodging attacks while doing so should be impossible," he thought.

"Was this evasive action maybe trained as some kind of reflex, but even then, how would you go about something like this? And all that while seemingly channeling some sort of body enhancement magic to move like that." His thoughts continued.

"This boy is too interesting," he whispered as a broad smile grew on his bearded face.

Then another close hit ripped Mor's robe around his chest, revealing Mor's toned body. This was followed by a gasp from the stands, mainly, the headmaster noted, from the female students for some reason.

°*How are we holding on to our energy reserve?*° The human asked, moving their sweating body out of another attack.

°*We're still good, but we should do something soon. We don't know how much energy she has. So much for "tired herself out in the last round,"* ° Mor said.

°*I have an idea. Maybe she forgot to use the stone slab to close her hidey-hole. So let's get water into this arena, and where it seeps away faster than somewhere else, she is probably hiding.*° Mor nodded and stopped concentrating on the healing magic while the human dodged another attack. °*This may cost more than we would like, but I also have no better idea.*° Mor said.

He channeled more power to water the soil of the arena. They then watched for suspicious places. The human jumped after Mor channeled another spell to give them more jumping power. As they looked around while up in the air, they saw a hole open up, their opponent surfacing from the ground, looking surprised for a second.

°*Found you.*° The human said, and Mor grinned.

They touched down on the ground and sped towards the hole, coming up from her blind spot and stopping just behind her. Mor let out a slight cough. Their opponent turned around, shocked, and Mor smiled.

"If you don't want to get hurt, could you please give up?" He asked her sweetly, and the human added in Mors' mind °*Yeah, it's over! We have the high ground!*°

She sheepishly looked at Mor, blushed, and looked away. In a tiny voice, she said, "I give up."

Mor then reached down, offering his hand, which she took, pulled her out from her hidey-hole, and gave her a smile, to which she shyly replied.

"Why did you come out from your hiding spot?" Mor asked, and she looked to the ground.

"I thought it would get flooded, and I didn't want to drown." She told him dejectedly, and Mor laughed.

"I understand you very well. This hiding spell is great for dodging many things. But it's dark and cramped, and letting water flow inside is not something I want to experience." He told her.

°*Hey lover boy, back it off!*° The human interjected, which confused Mor.

He was just happy to have won, and she was a graceful loser, so he wanted to be nice to her.

"What's your name?" She asked quietly and got another smile from Mor as a reward.

"Me? I'm Mor Agaton." He said.

"The commoner?!" She said, shocked. Quickly putting her hand on her mouth.

"I'm sorry. I'm Clare Celestyne. Nice to meet you, Mor, but we probably should leave the arena. The next contestants are probably already waiting. Maybe see you sometimes at school?" She asked, and Mor happily agreed.

Finally, he had the chance to make his first friend.

°*I thought I was your first friend.*° The human interrupted again.

°*Yes, but this is something different. We are not only friends. We are partners.*° Mor said, and they left the arena.

Exchanging a last wave with Clare. Mor was brought back to the stands, and the tournament went on as expected. Halfway through the second round, the headmaster called a stop and closed the tournament for the day. It had gotten pretty late.

The next duels would be continued on the next day. For today, all students would be recommended to get some food, look to the infirmary if they got hurt, and get to sleep. Homework and reports would be extended with the duration of the tournament.

This made the first-round losers somewhat happy, as they could enjoy the show the next day until the tournament was concluded.

Mor took the recommendation to heart. He quickly got a new robe from the school store and food from the mess hall and retreated to his room. After doing some evening stretches and cleaning up before falling into bed and instantly drifting off into dreamless sleep of the exhausted.

The next morning, Mor felt rested and ready for the next duels. But as he went to get breakfast, he felt someone watching him. No matter how suddenly he turned to catch his stalker, no one was to be seen.

°*What's up with you?*° The human asked as Mor spun around again.

°*I feel like we are followed.*° He answered, and the human snickered.

°*Stop being an idiot and get breakfast. I'm hungry.*° The human instructed Mor, and they got on with their day.

A familiar figure waved to Mor as he ate his breakfast and approached him.

"Can I eat with you?" Clare asked, and of course, Mor agreed while the human let out a whistling tune.

°*Shut it, parasite*° Mor chided the human, happy to maybe have found a friend.

Part 13

The next duels went as expected, but you could see the exhaustion from the previous day on almost all the contestants, as their magic regeneration hadn't replenished the spent energy. Except, it seems, for Ranbor, who destroyed his opponent with overwhelming firepower. He was still showing no sign of exhaustion. He didn't even reduce his energy output, and Mor slowly got scared of that much power.

°*Something is up!*° The human said.

°*Yes. I think so, too, but no technique or potion could replenish that kind of power in such a short duration.*° Mor explained.

°*I have a bad feeling about this.*° The human said.

Mor's next fight was against another higher noble, but at least none of Ranbor's flunkies. He stood there in true, noble fashion, relying purely on his magic power.

°*Well, if he wants to be like that, I will not complain.*° The human stated, and Mor agreed with a chuckle.

Mor dodged the first attack and retaliated with a "Rock-throw" of himself, which got blocked by an earth thorn of the noble. Mor was momentarily surprised as the noble smiled, making a multi-thorn attack on Mor.

The dodge was close, and again, his robe was damaged, this time luckily without completely shredding it.

°*He doesn't take this seriously at all!*° The human complained.

°*Time to step up our game and show him why this is a bad idea. Time for spray and pray!*° The human added, and Mor grinned.

The noble looked briefly confused at the commoner's behavior, and then a hail of twenty rocks flew from Mor, who had started a quick barrage. The noble tried to block this onslaught but had to throw himself to the ground, cursing. The noble was trying not to get hit, and Mor laughed at this.

°*Five rocks left.*° The human informed Mor. °*Time to end this quickly.*°

Mor channeled enhancement magic for his legs again and closed the distance in a mad sprint. He almost ran full force into a quickly set up stone lance. Mor reacted quickly enough and could reduce his speed somewhat, but still took a hit to his stomach and fell to the ground gasping.

The noble smiled, assured of his victory. "That's what you get for underestimating someone of noble descent. Be proud that you lost to someone as great as me. No matter how hard you train, you will never reach someone of noble descent!" The noble said.

°*Is he really holding a monologue now?*° The human exclaimed, surprised.

°*Seems like it, still that blow hurt!*° Mor agreed, still groaning from the hit.

°*Is he stupid? We only get more time to recover!*° The human complained.

°*Be thankful for this, or we would have lost right now. Any other Soul-kin would be knocked out cold from this. Once again, our physical training proves very handy.*° Mor answered and took hold of another rock.

°*Why are nobles all this prideful and stupid... Takes out all the fun of this.*° The human complained further, and Mor slowly got on his knees.

"I see. You still don't have enough commoner. Then let me teach you another lesson." The noble said haughty and then fell over like a sack of potatoes as Mors magically accelerated stone and hit directly on the chin.

°Ow, that must have really hurt.° The human said, and if they still had a body, they would have winced.

°I couldn't aim better with the time I had.° Mor complained.

°Yeah, I know. It's a good thing there is healing magic. If not, he would only get liquid food for a long time.° The human answered.

°Well, one more win in the bag. How many are left?° The human asked, and Mor answered.

°We are now under the top 50, so probably four to five rounds?°

With a bit of pain in the now bruising spot, Mor limped back to his waiting room and was led by a teacher back to the stands. He crumpled, exhausted, into his seat, trying to take a quick nap.

"Excuse me? Could we switch seats?" A voice asked, but Mor was too exhausted to open his eyes.

"Yes, of course!" came the reply, and Mor was relieved that the question was not directed at him.

Suddenly, a warmth flowed into his body, reducing the pain and getting rid of the nausea that had plagued him. He slowly opened his eyes and looked into Clare's face, concentrating on a healing spell.

"What are you doing?" Mor sat up from his "lounging" position.

"Healing you, that hit must have really hurt, but you did very well." She answered him with a bright smile.

"Thank you," Mor said, wondering why the human stayed still during this interaction.

"No problem, just rest. I'm rooting for your win." She answered, and Mor drifted back to a resting nap.

She wouldn't be able to replenish his energy, but he didn't use that much, and if he didn't need to get rid of the wounds before the next round, it would save him energy in the long run.

°*Good thing we didn't use healing magic ourselves but tried to power through the pain in case the hurt was not incapacitating for the next round.*° The human's comment was the last Mor heard before blackness took him.

Ranbor was in good spirits, his second duel was an overwhelming victory, and the blow the peasant caught with his stomach was just plain funny to him. Still, his next round was coming up, and he strode to the waiting room without waiting for a teacher to get him. This got him into some trouble, but he gracefully ignored it.

As his next round started, Ranbor reached deep into his reservoir and ended it again with overwhelming fire. He loved the power he could channel, and he was unbeatable. Even the Sapphire girl had been no match for him, and his fiery soul burned with pride. Now, he only had to wait until the peasant dropped out or, better, get to the finale and then be burned to a crisp by him. Yes, today was a good day.

After the third round, more students dropped out because they were too exhausted, even when they won, leaving only about twenty more contestants in the tournament. As Mor got ready for his next fight, feeling much better thanks to Clare's healing, the human informed him of Ranbor's fight.

°*He seems to have a limitless supply of energy when using his fire spells, which is scary.*° The human described what had happened.

Nevertheless, they had no more time to ponder all that as they were ushered into the arena.

°*Remember, we could not replenish our stones, so only four left.*° The human reminded Mor.

°*That means we have to take our throws carefully.*° Mor said.

But when they entered the sandy ground, their opponent was already waiting.

°*Who's that? He looks so self-assured.*° The human asked, and Mor shrugged.

°*I don't know? Someone from a different class?*° He guessed.

°*I always forget you are a friendless recluse. Why do I even bother asking anymore?*° The human complained.

°*I don't know why you are unable to learn. Maybe you are an idiot?*° Mor offered in jest and got a sigh from the human in return

°*Seems like it...*° The human said.

Strangely, their opponent approached them, offering his hand, and Mor shook it, surprised.

"I looked forward to meeting you, Mor Agaton." He said, "I'm Orth of the Obsidian family."

Mor just looked shocked. Another high noble? "It is a pleasure, your lordship." He offered, and Orth laughed heartily.

"Don't worry about the formality. I'm a big fan of the black knight, so it would be great if we could be friends after this." He said.

Mor looked even more confused. He began to ask who the black knight would be, but the starting gong interrupted him.

"Well, let's do our best!" Orth told Mor and walked back to his side of the arena.

°*What was that about?*° The human asked, and Mor shrugged.

°*Do you know anyone with the title black knight?*° The human questioned further, and Mor shrugged again.

°*Really, why do I even ask you...*° The human sighed.

After Orth retook his position, he gave Mor a nod, and then the fight was on. Mor instantly opened up with a "Throw-Rock" to get an early hit. He did get that hit. It just had no effect, as Orth was instantly protected by an armor of stone.

°*Holy shit that is cool!*° The human exclaimed.

°*Yes, but what do we do about it? Our stones will do nothing against that!*° Mor complained.

°*Yeah, we have an error in our strategy. We didn't plan to get paired up with someone who could do shit like that.*° The human agreed.

°*Well, let's keep moving, looking for an opening! Nothing else to do.*° The human said, and they again exploded into movement.

As they circled the armored mage, who turned with them and suddenly moved on his own. Orth cut off their path and let his giant, stony fist slam toward them. Skidding on his knees, Mor evaded that hit barely. Even getting in a quick water spell to damage the armor, which did jack shit. Jumping on his feet and starting to run again, Mor gained some distance using a wind-cut spell, which at least nicked the stone armor but did not penetrate it.

°*Yes, that's the way to go! Keep our distance and fire this wind magic.*° The human said. But then the Armor of Orth just repaired the damage.

°*Shit.*°, both Mor and the human said simultaneously.

That way, the fight went on. Mor tried to keep his distance and used the Air spell as fast as possible. Orth, in turn, just shrugged off the damage and tried to smash Mor into the ground with his armored fists.

°*How is he so fast? That armor should make him a standing target!*° The human asked.

°*He is moving it with his magic, of course! Don't look at it like it is some sort of clothing!*° Mor said.

°*So it is some kind of Mecha? That's so cool!*° The human said and got confused °*Mecha?*° as an answer.

°*Not important right now. We need to somehow break through it!*° The human told Mor.

°*And how? We can't cast any strong enough spell!*° Mor asked, and the human came up short.

°*Desperate attack? Just pump as much juice as possible into body enhancement, and we try it with a fist?*° The human put forth, and Mor whinced.

°*We have no alternative left. But still, I hate it.*° Mor complained.

Mor then skidded to a halt, turning around and dashing towards Orth, who also stopped in surprise for a second.

Mor shouted as his fist connected with the stone armor of Orth, using as much power as he could, slowly cracks forming on the stone around his fist and finally breaking, Orth letting out a gasp.

°*Serious punch!*° The human shouted.

Part 14

Mor smiled. It had worked! He got through the armor with their enhanced blow! Now, he just needed to finish it up with some other magic while he had the armor penetrated.

Mor gathered energy for a fire spell. It might not be as powerful as most other spells in his repertoire, but with Orth stuck in the armor, it would be much more effective. Just as he unleashed his magic, everything went black, and pain flooded his body. It flowed from his fist, which had hit the stone, and simultaneously radiated from his guts. With a silent curse, Mor fell unconscious. It seems that Clare's healing had been not enough, and the strain on his body may have undone what she did, bringing back the pain stronger than before. Even the human let out a gasp.

Orth pulled his fist back after punching into Mors' gut with a lot of power. He let the unconscious boy carefully glide down to the arena floor while his armor slowly peeled off his body. He looked down at where Mor's fist had struck his armored form and could see a bit of a charred spot on his robe.

"You almost got me, just as expected from you. Too bad your energy reservoir is not nearly big enough to beat me while I'm serious." Orth said to the prone Mor.

"That was fun. I want to repeat that sometime," Orth said and left the arena with a big smile. Waiting only long enough for the teachers to recover Mor's prone form and bring him to the healing adept.

°*You alright?*° A voice brought Mor back from the darkness.

°*Yes, we lost, haven't we?*° He stated, °*So much for our arrogance. We thought that only because we could use some new tricks, we could surprise everyone until we won. We're pathetic.*° Mor was close to tears.

°*Don't! We did our best!*° The human interrupted Mors' dark thoughts and went on.

°*This only means we need to work harder, get stronger, and make a comeback!*° The human went on.

°*Yes, I understand, but still, it is infuriating!*° Mor answered.

°*Yes, yes, it is. But you saw the power of Ranbor. We struggled through each round while he just blasted through. I'm sure we will get another chance at this, and then we will be ready. But for now, rest. "We need to recover our strength if we want to resume training as fast as possible.*° The human said, and Mor drifted into a restorative sleep.

For Mor, almost no time has passed as another voice roused him from his dreams, which vanished like fog in the morning sun.

"They got you good, boy." Mor felt his hair getting ruffled.

Then, a powerful warmth flowed into him, restoring his strength and helping his magic energy recover. Mor slowly opened his eyes to the view of the healing adept Miss Amber.

"Hello, Miss Amber," He said weakly and got shushed from her.

"Keep still and rest. I will take care of you. I'm already used to it anyway," she joked.

°*Yeah, listen to her; we at least broke something. This Orth did not hold back at all. The headmaster's protective magics probably saved our lives. Now, go back to sleep!*° The human ordered, and once again, Mor surrendered to the Adept and his partner and closed his eyes.

While he slept, he was moved back to the infirmary. Later, after he woke again, Amber told him about the results of the tournament. The finale was between Ranbor and Orth. She was told that even the headmaster was impressed by the power of both of them. Still, the victory was a close one in favor of Ranbor.

°*Great now, he will be even more insufferable. Good that we are saved from him...*° The human said, and Mor agreed.

°*I'm more worried that he might amass more flunkies from all of that. At least we also got some friends from this tournament.*° Mor said, and this time, the human had to agree.

He stayed in the infirmary for a much shorter time than last time, and this time with company. The other students hurt in the tournament would tell him what happened in his last fight. Then, after being given a clean bill of health, Mor left while waving Amber goodbye.

Feeling hungry from the whole ordeal, Mor decided to get some food. As he entered the mess hall, he was met with a surprising number of people, who soon detected the reason for it. Ranbor was sitting there like a king at a feast, surrounded by lots of students who wanted to congratulate him on his victory or gather some favor by kissing up to him.

Mor just ignored all that silliness in favor of food and decided to take his lunch back to his room.

"Look at that buffoon, like he saved the whole world." A suddenly appearing Orth said, surprising Mor.

"Yes. Just let him. I don't want to have any part in that." Mor said, and Orth chuckled.

"I wanted to congratulate you on a good fight. It was entertaining. If you ever want to have another go, tell me," he offered.

"Thank you. But I heard of your fight with Ranbor. Did you have that much energy left?" Mor asked, and Orth looked a bit bashful before answering.

"Yes, sorry. Still, you can be proud of yourself. You made me use more energy than I wanted to. If you want, I would like to offer you a position as a Military adviser and trainer after we graduate. Your adaptability and creative thinking are very inspiring. But don't decide just yet. We still have a few more years at school. Still, my father always said, "Get good talent early before someone else notices it." The only thing I'm sad about is that you were blessed with a strong body but not overly strong magic. If all of your physical power had been magical, I might even have had the chance to convince my father that you would be my right-hand man, even without being a noble." He said truthfully.

Mor nodded at that and smiled. "Yeah, thanks for the offer. I will think about it."

Now it was Orth's turn to smile. "Great! Then see you around! And if some other noble ever wants

to pull Rank on you, just tell me. I will drop them a peg or two. We're all students at this academy." he then left without waiting for a reply.

°*Shit! Missed our chance to ask about the black knight again.*° The human said.

°*Yes, but right now, food is more important.*° Mor said, and they went to get something, leaving Ranbor to celebrate his victory.

Ranbor saw the peasant from the corner of his eyes, but right now, he was in too good a mood to let himself be disturbed by Mor. Even as he watched Orth talk to the peasant, it was not enough to get him in a bad mood. The weak flock together. That's how it always went, and if Orth wanted to get the peasant into his entourage, he was welcome to. He would pick the best of his new admirers to bolster his influence. That's the difference between the first son of a noble house and the later born. As the firstborn, he will be the next family head, while Orth, only the third son of the Obsidians, will probably end up in some dead-end administrative position.

After every hurt student was finally released from the clutches of Miss Amber and the lessons could resume, all students were told that an oral exam would be done. They would start with the tournament winner and work their way down to the first dropouts, questioning their perceived performance and knowledge.

Mor was called to the reserved classroom, and he noticed that not only the headmaster himself but a somehow pissy Rosana was in the room, and he suddenly got nervous.

"Greetings, Headmaster, Miss Amethyne." He greeted them.

"I thought this examination was done by the normal teachers?" Mor asked further, and Rosanas's face grew sour.

The headmaster pointed to a chair before speaking.

"Yes, but my granddaughter insisted that she would like to do yours, and I took this opportunity to tag along." He said.

"You're in trouble, Mor." Rosana began, but the headmaster interrupted her.

"Rosana! Be quiet, don't throw accusations around."

Mor flinched at this outburst and asked. "Did I do something?"

The headmaster gave him a warm smile. "Well, Mister Agaton, might you want to explain what you did in your fight with Mister Obsidian? Your final gambit got my granddaughter to throw a little tantrum."

"Grandfather!" Rosana complained and instantly got silenced again.

Mor looked between them, unsure what to say.

°Seems like they argued about you. Just do what the headmaster tells you for now.° The human unhelpfully added.

Mor cleared his throat and started to talk. "With my remaining magic power, I couldn't get through Orth's armor, so I had to improvise, and the best thing I could come up with was to use body enhancement and break it that way, then..."

"I told you! We are no barbarians!" Rosana interrupted him and got a stern look from her grandfather.

"Quiet girl! Let him finish." He chided her.

Mor was even more cowed but continued, this time with a slightly shaky voice.

"...then I wanted to use the last of my energy for a fire spell, which should have been more effective, as the enclosed armor would have contained the heat."

The headmaster nodded and opened his mouth to speak, but Rosana was faster again.

"Why would you even punch him? Why didn't you just cut off the Airflow in his vicinity!" She asked.

This was seemingly the extent of the headmaster's patience as he sternly talked to Rosana.

"So you know he could use that spell? Did you teach him?" He asked.

This time, Rosana shrunk back, whispering a quiet "No." but the headmaster thundered on.

"Then you know that someone else thought Mister Agaton that spell?" and she again answered with a quiet "No," then he took on a somewhat softer tone.

"Mister Agaton, do you know a spell like that?" He asked, and Mor shook his head. The headmaster focused his look back on his granddaughter.

"See, girl, it was a desperate gamble because he knew no better. In addition, not everyone is as blessed with as much magic energy as you are. In this case, body enhancement was a good choice because his body is unusually strong. Now, Mister Agaton, please continue."

°*Headmaster one, teach zero!*° The human said, and Mor continued his tale.

"In retrospect, that gambit was stupid because I could feel the armor getting a hold of my wrist, fixing me in place, and stopping my strike. Then, as I fell unconscious, I thought the injury from the round before knocked me out by overexertion of my body. But if I can trust the tales from the other students, Orth did hit me with a strike of his own and knocked me out that way."

The headmaster nodded, "Yes, he did, but you were already pretty low on energy, so no wonder you lost. Still, I'm proud of you. You showed ingenuity and even got some of the other students to think and not just stand there, trading blows. Miss Celestyne is one of them, and she showed great promise with your "hiding" tactic. I'm glad this whole tournament turned out so well." He said warmly, and Mor was excused from the questioning.

°*Seems, like the lady teach wanted to rip you a new one for punching someone, but luckily, the headmaster intervened.*° The human said, and Mor could only agree.

Part 15

°*You know. Isn't it strange that no one thinks twice about our body? I mean, we are far from muscular, but at least we no longer count as "scrawny."*° The human asks suddenly.

°*Not really. The big school robes hide a lot, and you know "training your body is impossible." The only ones who might recognize the change would be my parents and Miss Amber. The question would, therefore, be, why didn't she tell the headmaster or someone else?*° Mor asked in turn.

°*That means we should ask her about it, which is not that problematic, as we want to talk to her nonetheless.*° The human said, and Mor directed their steps to the infirmary.

Entering the infirmary, they were instantly welcomed by the Adept. "Mor! Did you hurt yourself again?!"

"No, Miss Amber, I just wanted to talk to you about some things," Mor answered her inquiry.

"Then I guess you want to go on a date with me?" She teased him, and Mor blushed. °*Be smooth now.*° The human joked.

"Well, any man would be honored to take you out, Miss," Mor said with a bright smile, and she chuckled.

"Smooth talker. Now, if you are finished, tell me what you are here for," she said.

"I wondered about something. You are aware of my physical changes, right?" Mor asked, getting straight to the point.

"Yes?" Amber answered.

"Why didn't you tell the headmaster about it?" Mor asked, and Amber looked a bit surprised.

"How would you know if I told anyone? Are you stalking me?" She asked, half jesting.

"Well, if you had told the headmaster, he would have reacted differently while questioning me today," Mor explained, and Amber nodded.

"I understand. Yes, you are correct. I told nobody because nobody would believe it and just think of it as the rambling of an old woman. In the worst case, they could even think I'm unfit to continue working as a healing adept." She ruefully explained.

"Thank you for explaining to me. I think I understand your reasoning." Mor answered.

"But you have to tell me, how did you do it?" she asked him, and he smiled.

"Oh, it's not that hard. Well, at the beginning, it is. But it gets easier every day. You just have to move your body a lot, without using magic, and then get used to the muscle pain." Mor explained.

"Interesting, but that explains why nobody tried it for longer than a few days. The pain would discourage many people, and depending on how bad it is, it would lead to everyone just using magic for strenuous activities. Therefore, neglecting to move your body. It does make sense." Amber said.

"Yes." Mor agreed, "Just like that. And it's painful enough that if I didn't use pain-reducing healing magic, I wouldn't have been able to move at all." He explained, and Amber winced at that.

"Then, no, thank you. It sends shivers down my spine even listening to it. I will keep on using magic. But I'm interested in where this is going, so why don't you come by regularly and let me document your progress?" She asked. "Only if you can do me a favor." Mor began

°*Good thinking!*° The human added.

"I want to do something a bit dangerous and need someone with medical expertise watching so I don't get hurt badly," Mor said, and Amber threw him a questioning look.

"That would be what?" She carefully asked

"I want to see if I can "enlarge" my magic reservoir like I trained my body. I would like to empty it fully and go a step further. Not enough to kill me. Just a little, to test if it will expand due to the higher demand." Mor explained.

"Are you stupid, boy?!" Amber scolded him, but Mor stood his ground.

°*Make it or break it. The contest is on!*° The human cheered.

"If you don't want to help, I will do it on my own. Or ask Clare to help me." Mor huffed, and Amber deflated a bit.

"Why do you, young ones, always think you are smarter than your elders? Can you only learn from the mistakes you make yourself? Every year, I have at least one of you idiots," she sighed.

"Well, the "elders" thought it was impossible to get stronger by training your body, and as you have recognized yourself, that's wrong," Mor stated calmly.

"Be that way then. Alright, I will help you. But only once! But only because I like you. You are not as pompous as those other kids." She gave in.

"Thank you!" Mor said and gave Amber a quick hug, which she took with surprise.

"Ah, sorry." He said shyly.

"I get it, boy. It is a possibility to get stronger and catch up with the others. Still, it won't work." She told him.

"Well, if you want to drain your magic energy, you might as well be useful with it. Let me teach you a spell to transfer your power to someone else. Then you will use your magic to heal others and keep my magic topped up." She said, and Mor agreed.

°*Seems easy enough.*° The human added, and with that, they got to work.

They assisted Miss Amber in curing and healing the unexpected number of injuries a magic school produces on a daily basis. After a few hours, Mor was exhausted, slowly feeling the headache as a leading sign of magic deficiency.

As the day neared its end, the headache was more splitting than unpleasant, but Mor still powered on.

°*Ow, ow, ow! I begin to think that this really was a stupid idea.*° The human complained, and Mor winced.

°*Be quiet. This hurts me just as badly, but we need to know,*° Mor said.

"Good, that's it for today. Do you still want to go through it?" Amber asked.

"Yes, please," Mor said, wincing again.

"If you are so sure, then let your energy flow to me," she said, and Mor did as he was told, blacking out in the process.

A short while later, he opened his eyes again, completely exhausted and unable to move.

"How long was I out?" Mor asked, groaning.

"Just a few minutes. Did it work?" Amber asked him.

"I don't know. I probably need to regenerate my energy before I can answer that." Mor said.

°*Yeah, it's a good thing we tried to get close to our limits a few times and have a good feeling on how many spells we can do. The most accurate reading would be by using "Throw-Rock."*° The human said.

°*Yes. Until now, we were at a constant 300 casts until the headaches became bad enough to stop.*° Mor answered.

°*Then let's rest up and try it after completely replenishing our energy.*° The human said, and Mor agreed.

"Are you still with me, Mor?" The adept asked.

"Yes, sorry. I'm just exhausted. I will just take my leave and go to bed." Mor said, slowly standing up and taking his leave.

He slowly walked to his room and instantly fell asleep on his bed without even removing his clothes. Then, on the next morning, he woke up to a world of pure pain.

°*Outch! What is this? Why does everything hurt so much?!*° The human complained.

°*I don't know.*° Mor answered and tried to cast a pain-reducing spell, which just gave him an instant headache.

°*Owww! Fuck this!*° The human cried out.

°*We can't even use magic right now!*° Mor complained, and they both regretted their curiosity and came to the same conclusion... The rules for magic are bullshit!

Mor dragged himself back to the infirmary, each step a new flood of pain and exhaustion. "Mor! Good morning. How are you feeling?" an unusual chipper Amber said, welcoming him.

"Bad..." Mor groaned.

Amber then looked at him and said. "Told you so! Get yourself a bed. You are excused from the lessons today."

Mor took her up on that offer, falling into a restless sleep and awakening often because of the pain.

He just wished this day of pain and despair would finally end. And the human did as well.

°*No choice but to rest up. At least we know why no one would try this more than once and why it is considered dangerous.*° The human said, and Mor agreed, or at least groaned in an agreeing way.

It took two more days before Mor could move around without having constant pain.

°*Why wasn't it like that after your stupid ritual? I can't remember it being that painful.*° The human said.

°*I don't know? Maybe something is different if you use the ritual and don't have enough magic? But we would have to find out more about soul-binding before we can have a definitive answer to that.*° Mor said.

°*Means we have no choice but to shelf it for now.*° The human said. °*All this magic shit is stupid...*°

Finally, after a few more days, Mors' magic energy was refilled, and they could finally test if that ordeal merited some kind of success. They walked to the training room, and somehow, Mor felt like many eyes were resting on him.

°*Seems like someone is now popular with the ladies.*° The human joked, and Mor groaned, "As if they didn't have enough problems already."

°*Nothing will come of that because of the difference in status. It is probably just some sort of morbid curiosity.*° Mor said, and the human laughed at that.

On the way to their goal, Mor gathered a bunch of stones for his magic energy reserve test. After a few moments, a rhythmic plock was heard from the training room. While Mor used his "Rockthrow" repeatedly, and the human counted every cast of the spell. They went on until the headache set in.

°*And 300! Shit! No change at all, not even one more...*° The human finally revealed.

°*Maybe we have to do this regularly?*° Mor asked, and the human thought.

°*Maybe, but this would either destroy us or your grades. And we can't let those slip.*° The human answered, and Mor agreed.

°*Meaning we are still at square one and have no clues on how to get more magic. Now what?*° Mor asked.

°*I don't know. For now, we can only strengthen our bodies and try to get more used to our current spells. Maybe another opportunity will arise that will help us. Still very frustrating.*° The human said.

°*Yes, feels a bit like all our work is for naught if we can't get to the level of Orth or Ranbor.*° Mor said, and both quieted in grim silence.

Part 16

The next morning, Mor woke up and started the day with his usual morning exercises, but somehow, his heart was not in it anymore.

°*What's up? You seem out of it.*° The human asked, and Mor interrupted the exercise and sat down on the floor.

°*I was thinking...*° Mor started.

°*Allways a dangerous thing.*° The human jokingly interrupted.

°*What's even the point with the body training anymore? We can't get more magic, so why should I even try to get stronger?*° Mor complained with a depressive sigh.

°*Don't make me hit you!*° The human growled. °*Remember you did your stupid ritual to get stronger. True, you might not wanted to end up with me, but me is who you got. Trust me, for now, we can get stronger by training our body. You don't need to use magic for every little thing.*°

°*I wanted to get stronger in what matters, and that's magic! Without magic, you are nothing! But by summoning you, it isn't possible because you didn't help me with my magic deficits! Because you don't have any magic! You are useless! I only went with what you said because you told me I would get more magic!*° Mor shouted.

°*Yeah, asshat?! Wanna see how far you can go without my help? Mister "I wAnteD To GeT StrOngEr In WHaT MatTerS"! Have it fucking your way, then.*° The human shouted back and then went silent.

°*I'm frustrated because everything we did trying to get me more magic didn't help!*° Mor said and was greeted with silence.

°*You want to stay silent, great, and to use some of your fancy human words. Fuck you!*° He cursed further, again getting no answer.

Mor left his room, smashing his door closed angrily and stomping to the mess hall for breakfast.

"Mor! Good morning!" An energetic voice greeted him, and he turned around to see Clare running after him. Her bright smile turned into a frown as she recognized the sour look on his face. "What is going on? Are you angry?" she asked, concerned.

"No. It's nothing." Mor answered, and Clare's frown deepened at his tone.

"How about we get breakfast, and you tell me what's wrong? I'm a great listener." She gave him another warm smile and grabbed his hand, pulling him along.

Mor followed, grumbling, but he noticed how weak Clare's pull was. He could easily resist if he wanted to. Are all Soul-kin that physically weak? After both of them got something to eat, they sat down at a table and, at first, ate in silence. Clare did not want to pressure Mor, and Mor did not know if and how he wanted to describe his grievances. Finally, he let out a deep sigh.

"I want to get more magic, and a friend told me he could help me with that, but he lied to me." Mor started, and Clare nodded, encouraging him to go on.

"I just don't want to be that weak anymore... after what Ranbor did to me, I want to be able to stand up to him and show him that he can never shove me around again. At first, I thought I could just win the half-term tournament and show him that way, but then Orth beat me without really trying, while I had to go all out just to scratch him." Mor complained, and Clare gripped both of his hands, feeling how cold they were.

"I think you are strong. You got far in that tournament, and nobody who matters thinks you are a pushover anymore. Yes, you might not have as much energy as those high nobles, but you have something more important. You can inspire people to try new things and have new ideas on using spells that no one has given a second glance for hundreds of years. So you are smart, creative, and have a strong body. It now should just be a matter of how to use all this. Also, you will get more magic as you grow, and if you find someone who wants to share your future, you can share your power." She told him, slightly blushing.

Mor thought a bit about her words, then slowly nodded.

"I think you are right. Maybe everything is not as hopeless as I made it out to be. I was just frustrated because there are so many stronger than me who can do anything without trying half as hard as I." He said.

"Life is not always fair, but I think your hard-working self is very charming. Your "friend" probably thought so too and just wanted to support you." Clare said, and Mor nodded after taking a deep breath.

"You know, it is very hard to stay depressed if you smile at me like that and come up with all those reasons," Mor said, and Clare's smile grew even wider.

"I'll take that as a compliment and am happy to help," she told him.

"Really, thank you. I was going to a dark place, but hearing it from someone else was very helpful." Mor said.

"No problem. We should still get going, or we will be late for class," Clare said as she stood up and left with Mor for their classes.

°*I'm over it. Can we go on with our training?*° Mor asked his partner, still getting no answer.

This went on all day. No matter how often Mor tried to talk to the human or apologize, the human stayed stubbornly silent. After the lessons, Mor went on a walk to get some fresh air.

Then suddenly, a feminine voice called out to him. "Hey, Mor!"

When he turned around and saw Zaletha waving to him, Mor instantly became cautious about her familiar behavior.

"Angelith, what do you want?" He asked her.

"Why so cold? I just wanted to say hello she told him, pouting.

Mor raised an eyebrow at that exclamation, not believing her at all.

"You don't need to be so guarded. I don't want to do anything to you. I'm not with Ranbor anymore. He is truly an idiot." Zaletha said to him.

"Good for you, but I need to go," Mor said, turning around.

"Don't just let me stand here." She shouted after him, and Mor sighed as he turned back around.

"What?! I'm busy and don't have any nerve to deal with you." Mor told her, getting annoyed with her.

Zaletha instantly recognized his annoyance and channeled all her illusive magic power to get a foothold on his mind with that feeling. After trying and trying again, constantly failing for some reason, Mor never even seemed to notice her trying. Never, until right now. She felt her magic grasping around Mor's mind true. Annoyance is not the best entry for illusion magic, but it is something. She just needed to put in more power to get a complete grasp on his mind.

Mor's body froze up as she sauntered closer to his. His body no longer obeyed his commands. His mind fought against the intrusive magic and failed. Zaletha gave him the most evil smile such a beautiful face was capable of.

"Finally, I got you." She purred. "Because of you, I lost my place next to my Lord. Because you somehow resisted any of my attempts to give you nightmares. But now I got you."

Mor tried to speak, but his mouth would not obey him, and Zaletha chuckled at his resistance.

"Too late! I only allow you to keep your senses to tell you all of this for now, but soon, you will fall into a never-ending nightmare. If you think I would get into trouble because of that, because you are Miss Amethyne's little pet, don't bother. She left the school yesterday to go somewhere far off." Zaletha said, gently caressing his cheeks and raising on her toes to give him a smooch on his forehead.

"Now, my little stupid commoner, have a good time in the terror of your own imagination." She said, sauntering away, leaving him with dwindling senses and forcing his mind to live through a magically created nightmare.

***

Mor woke up, gasping a thick forest around him.

"Fuck she got me!" He called out.

"Why didn't you help me!" Mor shouted into the darkness, getting no answer.

Instead, he heard something growl at the limit of his hearing. He broke out in a cold sweat, turning around to try to locate the source of the sound. Suddenly, a pair of yellow glowing eyes pierced the darkness of the never-ending forest, the growling getting stronger, followed by earth-shaking steps. Mor felt his fear numbing his thoughts and a dampness filling his pants. On the edge of his vision, he could have made out a bipedal shape, shaking its head in disappointment, but the monstrosity coming closer completely demanded Mor's attention.

Mor turned around, stumbling deeper into the forest, his legs somehow weaker than he could remember. He couldn't run as fast as his body should be able to, constantly stumbling, always hearing the breath of the monster close behind him. He ran further and further into the forest, soon losing every sense of direction, as everything was just an ever-repeating darkness and trees. His instinctive fear of what was hunting him was the only thing on his mind. To face a monstrosity alone always means death. Every child knows that. His fear paralyzed his mind, and he no longer recognized the illusion. The bipedal shape slowly walked along, covering the same distance as Mor while he was running with all the speed his fear gave him, staying silent and watching.

After another big stumble, Mor fell to the ground, getting a face full of something awful smelling. He scrambled to get up and run away again, something heavy pressed on his back, claws digging into his skin, a deep growl and stinking breath coating his neck. It had him, he thought with complete panic, tears flowing freely in terror.

°*I'm sorry! Please help me! I was an Idiot.*° Mor called out to his friend, still getting the silent treatment.

A grave calm flowed through his body as he heard his bones breaking, the claws drawing blood. He was finished.

°*Thank you for sticking with an Idiot like me all this time. I now get it. You only wanted to help me fulfill my dreams the best way you could,* ° he said in an ever-weakening voice.

The bipedal shape appeared right before him. Still, he couldn't make out specifics. It crouched down before him, giving him a flick on his forehead.

°*Finally, I didn't want any apology. I'm your friend, but you should be at least a bit thankful for my help. So how about we get out of this illusion and kick that bitches ass?*° The human finally answered.

Mor broke out in tears again, this time though they were tears of relief.

His strength began returning as the human stood up, grasping the giant nightmare monstrosity on the snout.

°*You are not welcome here, fuck off.*° The human said, and the nightmare was erased with a whimper of the monstrosity.

°*No, one fucks with my mind.*° the human said, and Mor slowly returned from this dream world back to reality.

***

He woke up lying on the ground with soiled pants, breathing hard, his heart almost exploding in his chest, and completely exhausted.

°*You almost died of shock.*° The human explained.

°*Yes, you could have helped earlier! But I guess I hurt you.*° Mor said, half complaining.

°*Yeah, I needed to teach you a lesson, to teach you not to take me for granted. I'm not your servant. I'm your friend. I wouldn't have let you die, but this was your punishment,*° the human said sternly.

°*I understand. Thank you for sticking with me. I'm sorry for taking you for granted. Are we good again?*° Mor asked.

°*Of course, and now let's get revenge. How about taking Orth on his offer? Zaletha DID try to kill us.*° The human said, and Mor nodded, a new kind of confidence filling his soul, letting him smile.

°*Maybe just get new pants beforehand. You stink!*° The human added in a nasely voice.

Part 17

After getting new pants, Mor went to find Orth. He asked around and was then directed to the library, where he found Orth reading a history book.

"Hello, Orth. Do you have a minute?" Mor greeted the noble, who in turn looked up from his book.

"Hey, Mor!" He said, and then he gave Mor a strange look. "Everything alright? You look like someone rolled a boulder over you."

"Not a too far off guess. I had a run-in with Ranbors ex-flunky Zaletha, who was pissed at me for being too resistant to her illusions and therefore losing her place next to "her Lord." Mor explained, and Orth took a thoughtful look.

"What did she do?" Orth asked, concerned.

"Well, she got through a crack in my mind's defenses and dragged me through a nasty illusion." Mor shrugged. "Probably wanted to kill me, but I got out before dying."

"How can you be so calm about it?!" Orth asked incredulously.

"Well, it helped me to get my head straight, but I can't just let it go. So I wanted to ask about your offer to help me if some other noble tried something with me." Mor explained.

"This goes far beyond "trying something." We need to get you to the headmaster and let him deal with that," Orth said, standing up and putting the book back. "Come with me."

Mor followed Orth as they walked through the halls towards the headmaster's office. Orth knocked on the door and opened it without waiting for an answer.

"Mister Obsidian, you are a noble, but that does not excuse this kind of behavior." The headmaster chided Orth instead of a greeting.

"Excuse me, headmaster. I didn't want to show a lack of respect, but it is important. My friend Mor Agaton told me he got attacked by another student, which is clearly against school rules." Orth explained, and the headmaster let out a sigh.

"As if I didn't already have enough problems..." the headmaster whispered to himself, not quite loud enough for Mor and Orth to hear.

Then he looked at them both. "Well, Mister Agaton, please tell me what happened."

Mor told the story of Zaletha's attack, leaving out how exactly the illusion was broken. The headmaster frowned at this tale.

"Let me examine you. If it was such a powerful spell, you should have residue on you," the headmaster said, concentrating on Mor.

"You can do something like that?" Mor asked, interested.

"Yes, please be quiet. This is very demanding." The headmaster replied.

As Mor stood there in silence, the headmaster examined him from head to toe and finally nodded.

"I see. You are telling the truth. You were definitely influenced by powerful illusion magic. I will take care of this, so don't worry anymore. Mister Obsidian, would you be so kind as to escort Mister Agaton back to his room? He looks somewhat pale." The headmaster asked.

"Thank you, headmaster," Mor said, but he did not leave immediately.

"Headmaster, could you please teach me this spell to detect magic?" He asked instead, and the headmaster looked at him.

"You will learn it in class when your lessons have progressed enough. I don't have time to give you a private lesson on this. Now leave," the headmaster answered, evicting Mor and Orth from his office.

"You heard the headmaster. Let's get you back to your room. Let the people in charge deal with this." Orth said.

"Yes, that's probably for the best. Can I ask you something, Orth?" Mor said, and Orth looked at him, questioning.

"Do you know why Miss Amethyne left the school? Zaletha told me, and that's why she was so sure she could get away with it." Mor asked, and Orth shrugged.

"I only know there was some kind of emergency, and she was chosen to deal with it. Something about ancient traditions, but I also don't know more." Orth said.

°*Something is up. He isn't telling the whole truth.*° The human said.

"Orth, please don't keep something important secret from me." Mor tried to get more information.

"Sorry, Mor, but I can't tell you more right now. Get some rest. Everything else will be explained tomorrow." Orth said, leaving a confused Mor in front of his room.

°*It is very strange, but it won't do to pressure him further. I hope he's right, though, and everything will be explained tomorrow,*° the human said, and Mor nodded.

°*Let's get some rest. We had enough trouble for one day. At least you are talking to me again, which is nice.*° Mor said, and the human chuckled.

°*It was your fault.*° They said.

°*Yes, you made sure I understand that.*° Mor answered.

After they had completed their evening exercises and some stretches and cleaned themselves, Mor went to bed. However, this night's sleep was not restful, as every time he closed his eyes, he was back in this dark forest. He spent the night tossing and turning and awoke the next morning dead tired.

°*Bad night?*° The human asked.

°*Yes, seems Zaletha's illusion hit a bit too close to home.*° Mor answered.

°*I just don't get why. Yes, this thing was scary, but it was still only a beast in a dream, so why are you reacting so extremely at this?*° The human asked, and Mor shrugged.

°*I don't know. It's an illusion of a monstrosity, so maybe some ancient instinct kicked in? I mean, many children's stories have tales of monstrosities, and they are almost unstoppable forces of nature every time. In those stories, lots of heroes are needed to defeat one.*° Mor said, and the human got thoughtful.

°*Then maybe this was the natural enemy of your ancestors, and this instinct helped your kin survive.*° The human mused, and Mor agreed.

While Mor sat through his classes, he noticed that something was up. There was a sudden extra history lesson and an after-school assembly scheduled. The lesson was about the origins of the monstrosities, but the assembly was a mystery.

***

Monstrosities were once the beasts, living along the ancient kin, but while the great kin war raged, the habitat of the beasts was drained of magic. Every scrap of power was pulled towards the battlefields, and the beasts were starved of the energy. Many of those beasts needed that energy to stay alive, though. Now, with their survival on the line, they used the last bit of magic they could get ahold of and transformed themself. They did so in desperation to get the much-needed energy in some other way, by hunting other beasts or killing the kin, as they were now the best source of magic. In addition, the emergence of the "First" also seemed to influence the beasts. They quickly became more resistant to magic and physical attacks, seemingly as a defensive measure to protect themselves against the hunting of other beasts, the kin, and the "First."

***

After the lessons, all the students gathered again in the gathering hall, and the headmaster once again climbed the stage and took a deep breath.

°*Doesn't he somehow look nervous?*° The human asked, and Mor nodded.

°*Whatever is going on, it seems bad.*° Mor said, and the human agreed.

Part 18

"Please, quiet. I have an important announcement!" The headmaster started.

°*Doesn't he sound kind of shaky?*° The human asked.

°*Be quiet! He will tell us what's up. So pay attention.*° Mor answered.

"We got confirmation that the Andesite city of the Stone-kin was destroyed. We don't know what caused such a thing, but there is increased activity from the monstrosities. Therefore, an attack of those would be the most likely reason.

Please stay calm. The Soul-kin cities are all safe, and the royal Diamond family is acting to keep them that way. Still, the higher rate of monstrosity-related incidents and the destruction of Andesite city have invoked ancient law," the headmaster explained, a nervous murmuring starting among the students.

°*Could this really have been monstrosities?*° The human asked.

°*I don't know for sure, but if there were enough and all the stories were not overly overblown, then it is at least possible.*° Mor answered.

°*And what's this ancient law the headmaster is spouting about?*° The human continued asking.

°*I don't know, but he will probably tell us now.*° Mor answered.

"Quiet, please! There is no reason for any chatter. I'm not done. As I said, the ancient law of kinship was invoked, meaning an observer of the Ice-kin will join us to see how we have changed according to their traditions!" The headmaster continued.

°*Cool, someone else. Weren't the Ice people, not the barbarians?*° The human asked excitedly.

°*Yes, but why here to this school?*° Mor answered far less excited.

"Now, many of you will be confused about why we would get this observer, and the reason is simple. Our island is the closest to the main Ice-settlement. Miss Amethyne is already gone, so we need to get our guest and bring him here. Please be advised that they have different traditions and laws than ours. They are very honor-bound, so please do not provoke them. If you still refuse to heed my warning, I won't be able to intervene at all." The headmaster explained further.

°*I can think of someone who will do precisely that.*° The human snickered, and Mor had to suppress a burst of laughter.

°*Maybe he will get his nose broken this time.*° Mor added, and if on cue, they heard the voice of Ranbor huffing close by.

As the students filed out of the gathering, chattering amongst themselves, Mor was stopped by a familiar face.

"Hey, peasant!" Ranbor shouted, some nosy students slyly looking in their direction.

°*What does he want?*° The human sighed.

°*Let's ask him.*° Mor answered.

"What do you want?" He asked the other boy.

"How could you dare, to get Zaletha transferred to another school?! It is beneath her to learn with all those commoners." Ranbor raged.

"That's her own fault. She broke the school rules. All I did was get some advice and report it to a figure of authority if that is her punishment, fine by me. Also, why do you care? Didn't you kick her out of your super special flunky circle?" Mor countered.

"Yeah, because she is weak, but that doesn't mean you are allowed to get her punished!" Ranbor raged, and Mor sighed.

"Go have that talk with the headmaster. Leave me alone," Mor said, and Ranbor got even angrier at his nonchalant defiance.

"You heard that Amethyne is not here right now. So better mind your manners!" Ranbor went on as another voice suddenly cut in.

"Ranbor, what are you doing?!" Orth asked, walking up and standing beside Mor with another student in tow.

"He's being an idiot, Orth, nothing new. Leave him if he wants to get kicked out, too. His loss." Saphine added in a dismissive tone.

"You're right, Saphine. There is no sense in starting a fight with that idiot. Come on, Mor, let's go. I wanted to talk with you and Saphine a bit." Orth said, pushing past Ranbor, who glared at the little group.

As Mor, who was now following Orth, passed the furious boy, Ranbor whispered, "Watch your back. I will get you."

°*How can a single person be so resentful?° What did you do to him?°* The human asked.

°*I don't know. I beat him in the entrance exams, and you punched him on the nose, and now getting Zaletha kicked out of this school. But that's it. I don't understand why my presence is such a big problem for him.°* Mor answered.

°*We might never know.°* The human said as they left Ranbor behind.

As Orth, Saphine, and Mor walked a bit, looking for a good spot to talk, they found a place in the mess hall. They got some light snacks, and Orth finally revealed why he wanted to talk to them.

"My brother sent me a letter. This attack on Andasite City was not done by monstrosities. He also doesn't know what did it, but the monstrosities couldn't have leveled the whole mountain this city was built into and left no survivors. While searching for clues, they excavated parts of the ruined city, with other Stone-kin to help, and what they found was concerning." Orth explained, whispering.

"What was the problem?" Sahpine asked, while Mor just looked concerned.

°*That sounds even worse than what the headmaster told us.*° The human said, and Mor agreed.

"The concerning thing was that there was no sign that anyone was trying to flee. So either they were surprised and instantly eliminated or bound by some kind of magic, so they didn't even notice they were killed. Both pieces of evidence will eliminate monstrosities and other kin as culprits. Because bringing that mountain down is way above anything the kin can do." Orth went on.

"What could it be then?" Mor asked.

"We don't know," Orth said, and Saphine nodded.

"I get the conundrum, and I understand why you would tell me, but why this boy?" She asked.

"Mor has a good head on his shoulders and might get us some different insight into all this. Also, he might be able to cook up a good plan if we get him more information." Orth explained to a doubtful Saphine.

°*Didn't we hear in history about something called a "First"?*° The human asked.

°*Yeah, but this is more of a legend to explain the rapid evolution of the monstrosities.*° Mor answered.

°*But what if not? What if this thing really exists?*° The human went on, and Mor shuddered.

"Are you alright, commoner? You are shivering. Are you scared?" Sahpine asked in a haughty voice.

"Yes, I'm alright. I just had a random thought. What if this was no simple monstrosity attack but instead the return of the "First"? History taught us that it was only sealed and never killed, and it would be the most powerful monstrosity. Maybe it would be able to do something like that?" Mor offered, and Saphine laughed at that.

"Oh, I understand why you like this commoner, Orth. He has a good imagination and is funny." She wheezed. "Let me explain to you. There is no such thing as the First. This is fiction to scare little kids."

She looked at Orth, who, instead of laughing with her, stayed completely serious.

"But what if," Orth said. "I need to tell my brother this. If this is really what is happening, all of kin are in deep shit. Whether it exists or not, something powerful did this might as well believe in the worst case." He pondered.

Saphine threw Orth an incredulous look. "Really? You think the commoner could be right?" she asked him.

°*Tell her this, "When you have eliminated the impossible, whatever remains, however improbable, must be the truth." It's a famous quote from Earth.*° The human told Mor, who nodded and repeated the quote to the two others.

"This is pretty convincing and sounds smart," Orth nodded. "I will include that in my letter to my brother. Sahpine, would you please do the same with your family?"

"If you want to. But I still don't believe that," she shrugged.

Part 19

Mor returned to his room after talking to Orth and Saphine, as it was getting late.

°*So what do you know of the Ice-kin?*° The human asked.

°*Well, what everyone knows. They are barbarians who don't have any talent for magic. Instead, they fight with their bodies. Therefore, they are blessed with strong muscles, though, based on what I know now, I think they may be training hard in addition to just being strong.*° Mor answered.

°*Now I'm really excited to meet one!*° The human said, and Mor grimaced.

°*What?*° The human asked.

°*I'm not sure I want to. They sound scary.*° Mor said.

°*Yeah, but think about it: aren't the different kin all coming from the same race? A race that used magic to rise to the top of the world and subsequently almost destroyed themselves with it? If we can believe what the history class told us.*° The human said, and Mor thought over this statement.

°*True enough. But kin history usually is pretty precise. They probably gave up on their magic ancestry to get physically stronger.*° Mor said, but the human was not convinced.

°*Maybe they just don't show off their magic capabilities, and therefore being seen as mindless brutes?*° The human offered, and Mor shrugged.

°*It's possible, but why would they do something like that?*° He asked.

°*I can't say, but maybe they want to keep this a secret weapon, or whoever talked to them didn't care enough to ask?*° The human said.

°*Well, it doesn't matter right now. He will be coming, and we will see.*° Mor answered, and the human agreed.

°*We also have another problem we need to take care of.*° The human said, and Mor let out a sigh.

°*You're talking about Ranbor...*° Mor said.

°*Yes. As long as the lady teacher is not here, we should not be out and about alone and stick to Orth or maybe Clare, so he doesn't have an opening to do anything to us without someone else as a witness. So, for now, solo training outside of our room should be postponed. No more running and no using the magic training room alone.*° The human said.

°*That sounds good. Finally, I can slack a bit.*° Mor joked but was also a bit relieved.

°*Don't be so relieved! We will substitute running for something else. It's time to dust off the intensive training, minus the running,*° The human said, and Mor shuddered at that.

°*Please, not again! What you describe as intensive training is torture!*° Mor complained, but the human just huffed.

°*Shouldn't have been that relieved about skipping training then.*° The human said.

°*Sometimes, I hate you...*° Mor said, and the human chuckled at that.

°*That's the spirit, son.*° The human said.

°*Shut it...*° Mor answered huffy.

The next morning, Mor went to the mess hall, keeping watch to see if Ranbor would try something. This time, though, it seemed he wouldn't, so Mor made it without incident.

°*Let's wait here for Orth or Clare and ask them to stick with us today.*° The human said.

°*Yeah, at least while we're having a break and after class. While we are in class, I don't think he would try anything. There would be too many witnesses.*° Mor said.

While eating, they spotted Clare first, and Mor waved her over. "Good morning, Clare." Mor greeted her, and she smiled at him.

"Good morning, Mor." She said, sitting down with him.

"Can I ask you a favor, Clare?" Mor started, and she raised an eyebrow at that question.

"Sure, what can I help you with?" She asked.

"Well, Ranbor has it out for me again, and I need someone to stay with me, so he can't get me on my own. At least until Miss Amethyne returns." Mor said, and Clare got thoughtful.

"What's in it for me?" She asked him.

°*Uh, what now? This is unexpected.*° Mor asked the human.

°*Well, just ask her what she wants.*° The human answered snickering.

"What would you like?" Mor asked Clare.

"Let's see. How about you just owe me a favor for now?" She told him, smiling.

"A favor?" Mor asked.

°*Yeah sounds good, just agree. Don't think too hard about it.*° The human said, still snickering.

"Yes, don't worry. I won't ask for anything you can't do," Clare told Mor.

"I don't know, but well sure. I owe you a favor." Mor said, and Clare smiled brightly.

"Then I will stick with you today." She said.

After eating, they went to their lessons, Clare clinging to Mors' arm.

"You don't need to stick that close to me," Mor said, and Clare looked up at him, still clinging on.

"I do have to! What if we get separated? Then I would break my promise," She insisted.

°*Let her.*° The human said, between fits of snickering.

"But look, right now, there is no danger of us getting separated. There are not that many others here?" Mor went on.

°*Dense like a piece of Osmium.*° The human said, disappointed.

°*What's Osmium?*° Mor asked, and the human let out a sigh.

°*The most dense material from my homeworld, Earth.*° They answered.

°*And why am I "dense" like that now? I don't get what you want to say.*° Mor asked, confused.

°*Sorry, my fault. You are even denser than Osmium...*° The human answered, and Mor became even more confused.

"You can never be careful enough if Ranbor is after you," Clare said, clinging a bit closer, and Mor shrugged while the human was laughing at something again.

Like this, they spend the whole day. Clare was almost always clinging to Mor, and somehow, this strange pair got some for Mor unidentifiably looks from nearby other students. Which in turn cracked the human up even more.

Ranbor waited for his chance, but it seemed it would not come as this traitorous bitch was always hanging on that peasant. He must have blackmailed her somehow because no noble would stay that close to any peasant. True, she was not a high noble like himself, but still, she should have some more pride! This, in fact, made him even more furious. Somehow, sometimes, this bastard will pay for everything.

Like this, Mor and Clare spent three more days, sometimes noticing a fuming Rambor in the corner of their eyes, but at least he wasn't trying anything. Once, Orth asked them what they were doing, giving Mor a friendly clap on his shoulder and laughing when they answered him.

Even though Mor asked for only a day, this continued until Miss Amethyne finally returned. At that, another student gathering was held by the headmaster. The thing that confused Mor was then confused, as somehow, Clare was unhappy about that and pouting. He asked the human about it but only got laughter as an answer. Sometimes, the human was less than helpful.

Part 20

As they all gathered again and the headmaster retook the stage, he was accompanied by a

woman with ghostly pale skin and snow-white hair. This person's eyes were icy blue.

°*Huh, she doesn't look like what I expected when they said an Ice-kin would be joining us. She is smaller than the headmaster.*° Mor said.

°*What did you expect? Some kind of big milker muscle, Mommy? Also, she is at least half a head bigger than you.*° The human said, confusing Mor.

°*A what now?*° Mor asked the human, who just sighed.

"Dear students! Here with me is Miss..." the headmaster began, pausing for the woman to offer her name, which she didn't, resulting in a few seconds of awkward silence.

°*What's that stick she has on her back?*° Mor asked.

°*Look better! This is no mere stick. It's a war bow! See how big that thing is.*° The human said.

°*A bow? I thought the Ice-kin was all about physical power.*° Mor asked further.

°*Are you this stupid? If she can draw that without magic, she can probably fold you up easily.*° The human explained.

°*But I got a lot stronger, I think I won't lose.*° Mor said confidently.

°*Yeah, right, idiot, I will drag your sorry ass back to Miss Amber after this one is done with you.*° The human said.

"Well, please be nice to her, and if she asks you any questions, answer truthfully. Please remember she is an honored guest." The headmaster continued while the woman stood there, eying the students.

°*Is this a leather armor she's wearing?*° The human asked.

°*What's leather?*° Mor asked back.

°*You kow, cured animal skin? But there aren't any more animals, and it looks dark and oily.*° The human pondered.

°*Huh, you're right. Maybe she will answer us if we ask her?*° Mor said.

°*I really don't know. She seems like the silent type.*° The human said.

°*But you know, looking at her and comparing her to our women, she seems more defined.*° Mor said.

°*Yeah, most of the Soul-kin are almost malnourished. Because of your "Magic is everything" mindset, a balanced diet is almost a foreign concept for you,* ° *the* human said.

°*Yes, food is only there so you don't die?*° Mor said, questioning.

°*And you're stupid again. Why do you think you need more food now? Food fuels your body and muscle growth. So, contrary to every woman you know, she is eating right and caring for her body. By human standards, she would be labeled as fit.*° The human explains.

While the headmaster kept talking, the women wandered off at some point, leaving a confused headmaster alone on the stage.

"Well then, get back to your classes, please." The headmaster ended his speech.

After everyone returned to their lessons, Mor saw the Ice-kin a few times, sometimes sitting in at a lesson, sometimes just walking by, but never showing any emotion.

"I'm disappointed," the woman thought. It *seems the Soul-kin have lost their sense of honor and their sense of battle. All I can gather from them is complacency for whatever they were gifted with at birth, no need for self-improvement, a very sorry display."*

While she was sure no one was near her, she let out a sigh of frustration. "It seems my time here will be over faster than I expected without good news. I expected something more of a training center than sitting around listening to fireplace tales and a few magic exercises. They won't be completely helpless, but nothing on how to fight for real." Her thoughts went on.

After the lessons, she continued to wander around and observe, but her first impressions were generally reinforced. After their classes, the students lounged around, socialized, or learned from books, which was disappointing. Then, while she walked by a few students, she overheard them saying something.

"Look, there, he's running again." The first said, grinning.

"How can he be so stupid? No matter how much he runs, he will never get stronger," the other said, and both broke out in laughter.

The Ice-kin looked to where the students were pointing, and indeed, other than all of his peers, this one was running. She could instantly recognize that this was not just to get somewhere faster.

There was a rhythm to it, a rhythm she knew very well. Maybe her first impression was false. Perhaps the souls were not as useless as she thought. With that, she began to follow this strange student.

°*Can you guess why the Ice-kin doesn't talk to anyone?*° Mor asked while they were running.

°*I can't, but if I had to, maybe she was shy or annoyed that she needed to be here.*° The human said.

°*Maybe... If it is something like that, our peers may not be helpful with their attitudes. I surely hope she doesn't run into Ranbor. Then, our credibility is done.*° Mor said.

°*I think this might be a bit funny because she could probably beat that asshat senseless.*° The human jocked, and both snickered, Mor just a bit breathless.

"He's laughing!" She thought, "Is he having fun running?"

Even the old tales of the Soul-kin never told of someone fond of running. They were always known to be magical powerhouses, with training in the battlefield- and support magics. So she kept following.

°*I think that's enough running for today. Let's get to the training room. After our three-day pause, it's time to hone our magic again.*° The human said, and Mor nodded before breaking into a sprint for the last distance to the training center.

"Something is off with this one. This one might even be worth speaking to," she thought, hiding around a corner as the strange one sprinted by and took a close look.

"Form is rough but good. Too bad I can't see anything of his body with those robes," she thought regretfully and once again trailed the student.

°*Well, let's get going! It's time to drain your magic.*° The human said.

°*Still didn't give up hope for finding some way to get more spells out of our meager reserves?*° Mor asked.

°*Of course! There has to be something because if not, the older folks wouldn't have more magic than someone in their prime!*° The human grumbled.

°*Yes, I understand. This doesn't make sense to you, so you don't want to accept it.*° Mor sighed.

°*Good, then less talking, more using magic!*° The human ordered.

She watched in amazement as the strange one picked up a stone and said something about "First the classic." He held the stone and made a throwing motion. The Ice-kin was surprised as the stone raced away from the youth's hand, crashing into a target and leaving a sizable dent.

"This is scary." She thought to herself.

She would need a sling to get a stone to such a speed. It's still nowhere close to her bow, but still... If that hit right, it would drop someone without protection. Unbeknownst to her, a small smile crept onto her face.

"This one would have been a good choice for the coming-of-age ritual of the Ice-kin." She mused. She was so distracted by the strange one that she didn't hear someone else walking up behind her.

"Look at that, the barbarian is watching the peasant," Ranbor said, smiling, and was promptly ignored by the woman.

"Hey, you. If you want to see what the Soul-kin can do, you should watch me!" Ranbor boasted further.

The Ice-kin slowly got annoyed. If that idiot was shouting so much, she would be noticed by her target. She slowly turned around and put a finger to her lips to quiet that nuisance.

"Seems she wants you to shut up, Lord Ranbor," Emeror said, and the other two escorts shook their head disapprovingly.

"You're right, Emtsor. That is very disrespectful to someone who can't even use magic. They should show more respect for their betters!" Ranbor said, raising his voice.

The Ice-kin sighed at that. This one is the perfect example of the Soul-kin vanity. Worse, the strange one seemed to have heard the commotion and stopped his exercises. She could hear his steps coming closer to see what the interruption was about.

°*Did you hear that?*° The human asked.

°*No? What?*° Mor asked back.

°*I thought it sounded like Ranbor trying to bully someone again.*° The human said.

°*Let's go look. I don't like the idea that someone has to go through the same thing as me. We can probably help!*° Mor said, and they went to take a look.

Part 21

The Ice-kin began to leave, hoping to get away before being detected by the strange one, but this other Soul-kin would have none of that. As she turned around and began to walk, he shouted at her.

"Don't ignore me!" Ranbor was getting pissed.

"Why is he that resentful?" The new woman in Ranbor's entourage asked Emtsor in a quiet voice.

"He is a high noble. It's his right to get his will. Don't antagonize him. More importantly, don't question his decisions. If you just follow him, you will get far in life." He answered her inquiry.

The Ice-kin continued to ignore Ranbor and kept walking, enraging Ranbor even more.

"I said stop!" Ranbor shouted and followed a few steps after the woman.

"Last, warning bitch. If you don't show me the respect I deserve right now, I will burn you!" He threatened.

The Ice-kin stopped and deflated a bit before turning around, throwing Ranbor an incredulous look, almost as if she wanted to ask if he was this stupid. At this defiant look, Ranbor growled, conjuring a fireball. The Ice-kin changed her stance slightly and got ready for the attack. Mor walked out of the training room just in time to see the impending shitstorm.

"Ranbor! Don't be..." Mor started to shout, but it was already too late.

°*I can't believe this. He is the definition of a brain-dead idiot.*° The human said.

The fireball left Ranbor's hand instead of burning the Ice-kin to a crisp. She did something, and steam exploded from her as the fire hit. After the view had cleared up again, she stood there holding two long knives, which were glittering in a slight blue light. She took a deep breath and fixed Ranbor with her gaze.

°*Look at that! She's like a predator, and Ranbor is now her prey.*° The human said.

°*This is incredible. How did she defend against the fire?*° Mor asked

°*I don't know, but we might find out if this continues.*° The human answered °*No! We need to stop this before it completely goes out of control.*° Mor disagreed.

°*Laaaame!*° The human complained but was ignored.

"Ranbor, stop this madness! Let her be!" Mor shouted, and Ranbor looked at him angrily.

"Silence, peasant, know your place! Emtsor, take care of this nuisance, and Anna, you will help him. Cornel, you are with me. Let's show them that they are lesser than us!" Ranbor growled.

The Ice-kin looked surprised at the strange one, the "peasant" as he was called.

"Why did he get himself in trouble for her? Does he have a sense of honor?" She asked herself.

°*Well now we are in deep shit. Good thing we're not done with our training, and we have a good chunk of energy left.*° The human said.

°*Yes, but we couldn't just let this happen. It's wrong!*° Mor answered.

°*True enough. I'm proud of you. Let's give them hell. The first order of business is to get to the ice woman. If we let the group stay between us, we will be divided and conquered!*° The human said, and Mor nodded, a slight grin forming on his face.

°*Time for a rematch, we beat Emror once and can do so again,*° Mor said.

°*Yeah! Still, be careful. This Anna woman is new. We don't know her capabilities.*° The human said.

°*Yes, but this time, our victory condition is not beating him but getting away!*° Mor said

Anna looked confused and a bit scared to Ranbor and then at the commoner, who started to smile. She didn't think this was a good idea. They would all get into trouble for this. Because of her hesitation, she missed the commoner moving, and Emtsor cried out in pain.

Mor exploded into movement, as he did so often. Standing still is an invitation to get hit, and at the same moment, he tried something new. He kicked a pebble with all the force his enhanced self could offer, and with the guidance of the human, the pebble hit Emtsor in the arm, drawing a cry of pain from the noble.

The strange one had a fantastic sense of combat. The Ice-kin instantly knew what he tried and knew he was right. They needed to link up to avoid getting beaten separately with the enemy's numerical advantage. After that, they might be able to do a holdout or separate one and, therefore, whittle down their numbers.

Ranbor invoked a wall of fire, shouting, "Don't ignore me!" at the Ice-kin. Splitting himself, Cornel, the Ice-kin from Mor, and the other two.

°*Shit!*° The human exclaimed.

°*I have an idea! Take over the running and slide when I give the sign!*° Mor said.

°*I like it! Let's go! Now you finally have some spunk in you!*° The human celebrated

Emtsor tried to hit the running commoner with an air spell but missed because of the pain in his arm, while Anna stood there stunned.

Mor ran directly towards the flaming barrier and tripped, the momentum sliding him right into the firewall. Emtsor smiled at that, but then the commoner just vanished.

°*Now!*° Mor said.

The human threw them in a slide, sliding below the wall of fire, through the earth tunnel Mor had just created, jumping back on his feet on the other side.

°*Boo, YA!*° The human shouted.

°*I thought you could use the "well spell" not to dig straight down but along the ground.*° Mor said proudly.

The Ice-kin was driven into a corner at the onslaught of two fire mages, slowly giving up ground, but still, no spell seemed to connect to her. Suddenly, the strange one slid through the wall of fire without suffering a single burn and stumbling to a halt next to her.

"We need to get away. The loud one is powerful and an idiot!" The strange one shouted at her

But she shook her head. Now, they could fight back. This was now a two-on-two, at least until the fire barrier came down and got them to the back again.

"Why not?!" The strange one shouted, and she smiled at him, pointing to the one called Cornel.

"Yours." She simply stated, and Mor looked incredulously at her.

°*Is she stupid?*° Mor asked

°*No, she has her own pride. This can't be just let go without retaliation.*° The human answered.

°*I'm getting allergic to this whole pride shit.*° Mor complained, and the human laughed.

°*You wanted to help and help we will. Let's get the flunky for her.*° The human said, and Mor sighed.

°*Battlemaniacs, all of them...*° Mor cursed.

The wall of flame slowly died down, as it was no longer sustained with magic energy. Mor knew they only had a little time. Still, luckily, he had gathered a handful of stones while sliding through the earth tunnel. Mor used all of them in a barrage against his opponent, still evading the returning fire, only getting charred a few times. He did hit only a few, but they were enough of a distraction to make the fight between the Ice-kin and Ranbor a one-on-one.

Ranbor raged, unleashing fire spell after fire spell but never getting through the defenses of the barbarian woman as she closed in. When she was close enough, her elbow crashed into Ranbor's stomach, and he was swept off his feet by her follow-up low kick. Her daggers found Ranbors throat in an instant. The Ice-kin drawing a bit of blood and throwing Ranbor an ice-cold look. In the same instance, Cornel dropped to his knees with a pained cry and tears in his eyes. Mor had hit him with a "Rock-thorn" right in the groin. Mor was breathing heavily at the exhausting fight while the wall of fire faded completely.

°*And be thankful it was not a thrown rock! That one would have shattered your bones and ended your bloodline!*° The human shouted.

°*He can't hear you.*° Mor said, looking to the ice-woman.

"We need to get a teacher and explain this." He said.

The woman just looked at him, shrugging her shoulders and knocking Ranbor out with the pummel of her dagger. Then, standing up and leaving without a word.

°*Not even a thank you?!*° The human asked.

Mor stood around confused for a second and realized too late that they were now in much deeper trouble than before. Just after the Ice-kin was gone, a voice behind him asked something and sounded very angry.

"Mister Ruby, Mister Agaton, WHAT DID I TELL YOU?!" Rosana shouted at them, Ranbor blissfully unaware of her fury.

°*Fuck this shit...*° The human sighed.

°*This is unfair!*° Mor complained.

"This is not how it looks..." Mor started but was shushed by Rosana's furious look.

Part 22

Rosana was angry. She was tired from getting the Ice-kin here and annoyed at the Ice-kin for never uttering a word of thanks. To top it all off, her mark on the Ruby and Agaton boys alerted her that those two did get into trouble with each other again.

Now she came to a scene of utter brutality, the Ruby boy lying there unconscious, the one next to him. Carnelis was his name, right? Was lying on the floor groaning and holding a spot between his legs while two other students looked from the sidelines, and the Agaton boy was standing there and spouting some nonsense like "Not how it looks." Does he think she is stupid?!

She had heard that after she was gone, Agaton ran into trouble with the Angelith girl because of some slight he had done against her. Because of this, the headmaster transferred her to somewhere else. Rosana could not understand why. It would have been better to transfer the commoner to a commoner school and restore the cracks in this one.

Then she was informed that Agaton had butted into an argument between the Ruby and Obsidian boys. An argument he shouldn't have any say in, and worse, she had to endure a lecture from her grandfather because of him.

True, as a teacher, she couldn't let those feelings cloud her judgment, but still... The commoner has no place here, and the rumors of his continuous needling against the Ruby boy were confirmed by many different students. But now it seems to have escalated, and he beat both the nobles in a surprise attack.

"Mister Agaton, stay quiet!" She told the boy, who looked defiant at her.

"You and I will go to the headmaster's office, and there you will receive your just punishment." Mor wanted to protest, but she cut him off again.

"I told you to stay quiet!" Rosana shouted, and Mor flinched.

She then focused her gaze on the two bystanders.

"You two, get those two here to the infirmary. I will deal with them after I'm done with Mister Agaton." She ordered in a tone that did not allow any protest.

Emtsor and Anna just nodded, gathered up the unconscious Ranbor and the whimpering Cornel, and left. Rosana grabbed Mor at the scruff of his robe and pulled, getting confused that the boy didn't even move a bit, even though she pulled with quite a bit of force.

°*Let's go along. She is not inclined to listen to us, but maybe the headmaster can salvage this,*° the human said, and Mor reluctantly agreed, finally letting himself be dragged to the headmaster's office.

Mor was dragged through the school, and quite a few of the students laughed at his predicament until an exhausted Orth crossed their path, panting a bit.

"What's going on here?" He demanded, and Mor gave him a slightly dejected smile as a greeting.

"Stay out of this," Rosana said.

"No, I will not. Why are you punishing him while Ranbor was the aggrevator?" Orth asked.

"You don't know that I will punish him. Also, how would you know?" Rosana answered, getting an incredulous huff from Orth.

"Right, that's why you are dragging him like you fear he might run away. And I know because I know Ranbor!" Orth protested.

"Orth, don't..." Mor began.

"I told you to stay quiet!" Rosana chided Mor, who shrugged.

"Mister Obsidian, stay out of this, or you're getting punished for interfering with teacher business," Rosana said coldly, and for a split second, Orth seemed unsure.

"I can't let this go.." Orth began, but Mor shook his head, silencing Orth.

°*Don't worry. We will get out of this.*° The human said thankfully.

°*He can't hear you.*° Mor answered.

°*Yeah, but it was nice for him to come to our aid and see how exhausted he is. He must have run to catch us here, and tomorrow, he will be questioning his decision because of the muscle pain. You Soul-kin are all wimps.*° The human said.

°*Then we should express our thanks by alleviating his pain tomorrow.*° Mor said.

Mor was dragged off again, just as Clare came into view, behind Orth, who, after a nod of Mor, stopped her in her tracks and talked to her, seemingly calming her down.

Rosana burst into the headmaster's office, Mor in tow. And then stood still, surprised, as the headmaster already had a visitor. The Ice-kin looked surprised, too, as Rosana entered the room. She was just in the process of informing the headmaster of what had happened and that she had dealt with it according to Ice-kin law.

"Rosana, please knock next time if you want to enter my office," the headmaster said, disappointed.

Rosana stood there speechless for a second.

"Headmaster, I caught Mister Agaton here, attacking two other students, and therefore he needs to be punished," Rosana said.

"Four." The Ice-kin said, and Rosana looked at her questioning.

The headmaster sighed. "Our honored guest here just informed me of the incident and explained to me how she had handled it. But now you come to me and make it something bigger than necessary," he told his granddaughter.

"I don't understand?" Rosana said.

"Miss Snow here told me what happened. She was doing her observing duty when she was confronted by Mister Ruby, Mister Emeror, Mister Carnelis, and Miss Aragonite. She ignored them, as she had nothing to discuss with them. Mister Ruby seemed to get offended at this and instructed his "friends" to help him put her in place." The headmaster said sternly.

"She further told me that Mister Agaton, who you dragged here through the whole school, was jumping into that evolving conflict to stop it. And after his words were dismissed, he was targeted by the other four. But instead of running away, he helped our guest not get hurt!" The headmaster growled, slowly getting louder.

°*Oh, shit, now he's pissed. Better shut up and let this play out.*° The human commented.

°*Yes, but it's interesting that the ice kin went here to set things right instead of just staying.*° Mor said.

°*Maybe she wanted to tell this to the boss?*° The human offered.

°*Maybe. Probably another Ice-kin thing.*° Mor said.

The Ice-kin whispered something to the headmaster.

"I need to correct myself. Miss Aragonite did not partake in the fight. She was somehow "sidelined"?" The headmaster said, questioning, and the Ice-kin nodded.

"Still, the whole thing was resolved with Miss Snow here, knocking out the leader of the enemy group instead of KILLING him, like the Ice-kin law would normally dictate. And now all that should have to be done was for Mister Ruby to APOLOGIZE to Mister Agaton here. But of course, my stupid granddaughter had to blow this out of proportion." The headmaster morosely said. Rosana looked very uncomfortable right now.

"Mister Agaton, would you have accepted an honest apology from Mister Ruby if such a thing was even possible?" The headmaster asked Mor in a forced calm voice, and Mor nodded.

°*Yeah, right, as if that pompous son of a raging bitch would ever apologize to a "lowly peasant" like you.*° The human said sarcastically.

°*True, but we butted in, and well if this is what the Ice-kin would have wanted.*° Mor said, not wholly truthfully.

"Let me guess." The headmaster went on. "You are still pissed because I undermined your first protest at the tournament, but you are a teacher. Don't let your bias decide who is innocent and who is not!" The headmaster continued, scolding his granddaughter.

Rosana was getting agitated and began to shout back. "What do you know! You are just sitting here in your office, not knowing the feelings of your students and the other teachers! A commoner has nothing to do here at this academy! We are for the nobles only!" Letting her feelings out in a last-ditch to rectify her reasoning.

"Mister Agaton should be transferred to the commoner school, and then there would be nothing of that bad blood here!" Rosana continued and got interrupted by the headmaster

"Excuse me, Miss Snow, Mister Agaton. Could you please leave me and Miss Amethyne alone for a second? This does no longer concern you." He calmly stated, but Mor could feel cold fear running down his spine.

After he and the Ice-kin left, the door was closed, and after that, they could hear the headmaster shouting but couldn't make out his words.

"You are an honorable fighter." The Ice-kin said, and Mor looked up at her, surprised.

°*Well, it's some kind of thanks.*° The human said.

"Thank you, Miss Snow, right?" Mor said, and she nodded.

"For your help, you have earned my trust and caught my attention. So if you have any questions, I'm honor-bound to answer them because if not for you, I couldn't have upheld the law." She said, embracing him in a hug, his face pressing into her chest by the height difference.

°*Let's go, Casanova!*° The human laughed, and Mor grew redfaced at the softness of her chest.

But as he wanted to free himself from the embrace, he realized that her strength was something he couldn't overcome. Still, Mor continued to struggle futilely.

°*Told you, she's much stronger than you right now.*° The human laughed further.

Part 23

After Mor was finally let go of the Ice-kin woman's embrace, he noticed she seemed confused about his resistance. Mor first took a few deep breaths to calm himself before speaking again. °*Yep, this is a real woman. Nothing like the flat boards, who go to this school with you.*° The human teased, but Mor was too flustered to give a witty reply.

"What was that?" He asked the woman instead, and the Ice-kin looked at him confused.

"What do you mean? This is the traditional way my people show that they trust each other," she answered, and Mor coughed.

"Sorry, I was just surprised. This is highly uncommon for Soul-kin," Mor said.

"I understand. Forgive me if I did something inappropriate." She answered him.

°*Idiot. You just had to stay silent and enjoy.*° The human teased again.

"I think we should first introduce ourselves. I'm Mor Agaton, and if I got it right, you are Miss Snow?" Mor said, and the Ice-kin nodded.

"Just call me Snow. It will suffice." She answered.

"Could you please explain why your name is Mor Agaton, but the others call you peasant and commoner? I don't understand," she asked, and Mor got uncomfortable with this question.

"Almost everyone in this School is a noble, and well, I'm not, so most use the terms "peasant" and "commoner" to reinforce their status over me," Mor answered.

"I get that it is some kind of insult against you, but what is a noble? Is that some kind of village elder?" Snow asked further.

"How to explain that... The distinction is how you were born. The nobles have always been stronger than the common folk, with the royal family standing at the top of those nobles. Therefore, the nobles are the ones in the leadership roles." Mor explained.

"If I understand this right, it only depends on how you were born and not your merit. Isn't this stupid?" She went on.

°*That's what I said!*° The human commented.

"Well, it was always like this. You can only become a noble if your magic power is strong enough, and you can marry into a noble family." Mor shrugged

"I don't like this either because I'm weak, but that's what it means to be a Soul-kin. Your magic energy is everything." Mor said dejectedly.

°*Yeah, like I said stupid.*° The human added.

"But how do you know that those "nobles" are fit to be leaders?" Snow asked.

"They just are? That's why they are nobles." Mor answered, slightly confused.

°*I would like to add again, plain stupid!*° The human said.

°*Be quiet if you don't have anything better to add.*° Mor chided.

"Huh, that explains a lot, so this chief here is not in this position because he is the best and therefore voted into his leadership. But somehow, because he is a noble, he is fit to lead?" Snow tried to understand.

°*Chief?*° Mor asked

°*She means the headmaster, as he is responsible for this school.*° The human explained.

"Yes, the nobles are still given positions according to their abilities by the king, but in summary, only nobles are allowed to lead," Mor said.

"This is stupid!" Snow protested but accepted it for now, deciding to concentrate on something else.

"Say, if magic is all for your kin, then why are you training your body?" She asked.

"Well, that's not so easy to explain. I don't have that much magic energy, and I am something like a free thinker. Meaning I like to experiment," Mor explained.

"Meaning?" Snow asked.

"I once thought, like everyone else, that you can never be something you are not born to be, but a few things happened, and now I know that it is not so. Getting over the first barrier of muscle pain was hard, but it really paid out, and now I'm a lot stronger, and now I just need to find a way to raise my magic energy." Mor explained and got a smile in return.

"I like you. If I were younger, I would have asked you to accompany me on my coming-of-age ritual, but I already have done that," she said.

"What is that?" Mor asked.

"Don't you have that, too?" She asked back, and Mor shook his head.

"When an Ice-kin gets of age, he will need to find some comrades among the other adolescents and hunt a monstrosity. However, to fulfill the ancient tradition, the hunting party may only consist of four hunters. So it is both a test of strength and insight." She explained.

"A monstrosity?! But you don't have any magic, and the legends say those things are almost invulnerable to physical attacks!" Mor said, surprised.

°*Now it get's interesting.*° The human said.

"Yes, but we have other means to wound those things," Snow said, pulling out an arrow and handing it to Mor.

"See the tip. This is made of a special crystal we work into all our weapons. This crystal can store magic power and generate a magic field around it, enabling our weapons to penetrate the monstrosity's defenses and hurt it. It's still a hard fight, and you must be careful not to die, but we are not helpless." She explained.

°*Do you think what I think?!*° The human asked.

°*Yes, we can store energy in those crystals and use it later!*° Mor answered.

"So, how do you get the magic into those crystals?" Mor asked.

"You just pull it from your surroundings? How else?" Snow asked back.

°*Wait! That's possible?!*° The human exclaimed.

°*Not that I knew! Magic just sort of replenishes itself after a while.*° Mor said.

"We don't do that. We have an internal magic reservoir, and if it is empty, we need to wait until it fills again on its own," Mor answered Snow.

"Interesting, we don't have this reservoir and can therefore not use those "spell-things" you Soul-kin use, but we can use magic, and filling those crystals is one of them," Snow said.

"Can you teach me?" Mor asked, and Snow nodded.

"Yes, you are interesting, and we kin need to help each other out, but I will teach no one else. Teaching other Soul-kin will be your decision and responsibility," she said.

"Why?" Mor asked.

"Because it's tradition," Snow told him. "Let's meet in your training room, after your lessons. Then I have enough time to fulfill my duty." She added.

"Yes!" Mor said excitedly.

°*Now we are getting somewhere!*° The human celebrated.

As they finished their arrangement, the door to the headmaster's office opened up again.

"You can come in again." The headmaster told them both. "Excuse this interruption," he said.

Mor entered the room and saw a cowed Miss Amethyne. He decided at that moment that he would never get on the wrong side of the headmaster.

"Now, Mister Agaton, your punishment will be simple, and before you protest, let me finish. You will be responsible for accompanying Miss Snow if she wants to go somewhere and answer all her questions. You wanted to help her, so do it until the end. Is this acceptable, Miss Snow?" He said, and the Ice-kin nodded gracefully.

"Good, for the punishment of the others, I will think about something. I know you deem it a closed matter, Miss Snow, but my granddaughter made a mess of it by dragging Mister Agaton through the school. Therefore, punishment must be given to all students breaking the school rules." The headmaster explained.

"I understand," Snow just answered.

°*Best punishment ever!*° The human said, and Mor suppressed a smile.

"I understand, headmaster, I'm sorry," Mor said, and the headmaster gave him a friendly nod.

"Good, at least you seem genuinely sorry for the happenstance," the headmaster said.

"You can leave now, Mister Agaton, Miss Snow, if you would like to stay for a bit. I have some more things I would like to discuss with you," the headmaster added, and Mor excused himself.

But before he could leave, he was caught in another embrace by Snow, the headmaster raising an eyebrow at this display. Luckily for Mor, Snow quickly recognized her error and let the bright red Mor go.

°*Get used to it. I think this is some kind of Ice-kin greeting.*° The human teased.

Part 24

Deep in thought, Mor was on his way back to his room when his path was blocked by two students.

"Mor! Are you alright?" Clare asked concerned

"Yes, I got off lightly, thanks to the headmaster," Mor said calmly.

"But you still got punished?" Orth asked.

"Yes, but it's not that bad. I'm now kind of the assistant of the Ice-kin. All in all, I'm happy with it." Mor answered, and Orth nodded.

"I'm still not satisfied that you got punished, but if you are fine with it." Orth shrugged.

"What! That's awful!" Clare complained.

"Why?" Mor asked her.

"What do you mean, why? She's a barbarian. Who knows what she'd do!" Clare went on.

"Clare, don't talk bad about her. It's true. I got into trouble for helping her, but that's Ranbors fault, and she at least went to the headmaster to explain everything. That's why I got off so lightly." Mor explained calmly.

"But! Your reputation! You're already..." Clare said, and Orth intervened

"Clare! Be quiet!" Orth shushed her.

"I'm what?!" Mor asked, agitated. "Tell me, Orth." °*I can guess what's coming now...*° The human added.

Orth gave Clare an annoyed look but then deflated a bit.

"Most students and teachers don't like that you are here, a commoner at a noble school. I asked the headmaster, but he didn't want to explain and just told me it would be fine." Orth explained.

°*Yeah, thought as much.*° The human said.

"Makes sense. I mean, I had no friends before you and Clare, but this puts me in a unique position. No one will bat an eye at the commoner needing to babysit the barbarian. That's not a task fit for a noble." Mor said, and Orth nodded.

"I still don't like it," Clare mumbled.

"And best of all, Snow wants to teach me some of the Ice-kin magics!" Mor told them excitedly.

"Snow?!" Clare exclaimed, surprised. "You know her name?"

"What Ice-kin magics? Do they even have magic?" Orth asked at the same time.

"Yes, Clare...The headmaster had something to discuss with Miss Amythene, and we had to wait outside, so we talked a bit. She even thanked me for helping her again, Ranbor." Mor said.

°*You did more than talk.*° The human teased.

°*Silence!*° Mor chided.

"Yes, they do Orth, but they seem to have no energy reserve, so there are no big spells for them. They have a technique, though, with which they can pull energy from their surroundings!" Mor told them excitedly.

"So?" Orth said. We will learn that in our last year at the school." Clare added, and Mor looked surprised.

"You know of such a technique?!" He asked.

"Yes, don't you?" Orth asked, and Mor shook his head.

"Guess the commoners are not good enough to learn something like that," Mor said, dejected.

"I didn't know that," Orth said, and Clare looked a bit sad.

"Well, I'm using my chance to learn it now and everything Snow can teach me," Mor said.

°*Everything?*° The human joked.

°*Shut it. I'm not in the mood for your stupid jokes,*° Mor said.

°*Yeah, I get you're pissed, but I just wanted to cheer you up,*° the human said, understanding.

°*Sorry,*° Mor said.

°*Don't worry. We will show everyone what a barbarian can teach a wizard,*° the human said.

°*What's a wizard?*° Mor asked.

°*Magic user,*° came the answer from the human.

Mor left Clare and Orth and walked to this room, but before he could take a few steps, Clare called after him.

"Mor! I'm sorry. I didn't know," she said, but Mor didn't look back.

"Not right now, Clare. I have to think, I'm not mad at you. I just need some time." Mor answered her and left for good.

"This is bad," Orth said. "I never knew there were such barriers put in place between us nobles and the commoners." And Clare nodded.

"Why, though? Wouldn't it be better for all Soul-kin if we would have more talented mages?" Clare asked.

"You would think so. That's probably something I should ask my family about. Maybe I can change it when I'm old enough." Orth said.

"I will help you," Clare promised, and Orth nodded.

The next day started with Mor getting dirty looks from many other students. Finally, the rumors of Ranbor's punishment reached him. It seems the headmaster went fully nuclear. The only one who got off lightly was Miss Aragonite, as she didn't do anything but be part of Ranbor's entourage.

Miss Aragonite just had to copy the whole school rule book, which would be about a day's work.

The two other boys got the added punishment of helping out the cleaning staff with their duties to appreciate the work of the "commoners." Ranbor got the worst punishment. The headmaster severely limited his magic, only giving him enough energy to complete the day-to-day mundane tasks of their school life.

Mor would have liked to get Ranbor kicked out, but as Ranbor attacked the Ice-kin, she said it was settled, but that was seemingly not on the table. The headmaster might also wanted to avoid any significant conflict with the Ruby family.

The most surprising thing about all of this might be Miss Amethynes' transfer to another school island, one for commoners, it seems. The headmaster seemingly told her to respect every student regardless of their status and that she was unfit as a teacher at his school. Mor was a bit conflicted about that one.

As promised, Orth and Clare gave Mor space to think about everything.

°*You know, they probably didn't realize that the commoners were being held down by the nobles.*° The human said.

°*I know, but still. I just want to be alone a bit and learn from Snow.*° Mor answered.

°*I guess. But remember, both of them are your friends. Don't cut them out completely,* ° the human advised.

°*Yes, I won't. I probably just need a few days to get to terms with it. I never thought the nobles would keep secrets from the lowerborn, but it makes sense in a morbid kind of way.*° Mor said.

°*I get it. In human history, we also had a system like that, and the nobles used their power to keep the common folk under control.*° The human said.

°*You say, had? That means it was changed, right? What happened?*° Mor asked.

°*Well, we had a few catastrophes, and well, the nobles wanted to keep their living standard and couldn't understand the needs, pleas, and worries of the common folk. In almost all cases, this led to uprisings amongst the commoners and the death of the nobles.*° The human explained.

°*You killed them?*° Mor asked.

°*Yeah, we did... After that, we changed how we did things and set up voting systems for our leaders. They are also not perfect, but at least a bit better. But don't worry, for now. If everything is at least somewhat fair, nothing terrible will happen. If there are too many rifts between commoner and noble, someone should get to fix them as soon as possible, though.*° The human answered.

°*This sounds scary.*° Mor said.

°*It was, but human history is full of atrocities. We are not peaceful people, no matter what someone else says.*° The human went on.

°*Got it, enough of that... Let's get the lessons over with and concentrate on getting better.*° Mor ended the discussion.

°*Yeah, I also don't like this dark theme. Let's get back to helping you,*° the human said.

"Commoner! What did you do to Orth?" A very agitated Saphine asked Mor as she caught Mor on his way to the classrooms.

"Nothing, I just wanted some space." Mor sighed.

Part 25

Saphine blocked Mors' way, defiantly putting both hands on her hips and giving him a stern look.

"What do you mean nothing? I talked to Orth yesterday, and he was not his usual self. After I asked him, he said it was nothing, but I'm sure it was something YOU did." She spat.

"Because I'm a commoner?" Mor asked with a dangerous tone.

"Yes, exactly. There can never come something good from a high noble like Orth mingling with a commoner like you." She huffed.

"You know nothing," Mor growled. "Get your facts straight, and then come talk to me again, and don't use that snotty tone with me!"

"You dare?!" Saphine began.

"Yes, I fucking dare! First, I had to deal with the oh-so-great Ranbor who trampled all over me, and now that I'm finally free of his torment, you show up and do the same!" Mor shouted over her.

"I just want some time for myself without you condescending nobles. You think you are so much better than the common rabble, but honestly, I am beginning to think you are much worse, and maybe..." Mor continued.

°*STOP! Don't say anything more! You will only get in trouble again.*° The human interrupted Mors's tirade.

Mor took a deep breath.

"You know what, never mind," Mor said, annoyed, and just left.

Saphine stood there stunned for a second at the ferocity of the commoner. What has happened? She thought to herself.

"You shouldn't treat your comrades so poorly." A suddenly appearing Snow told the girl.

"What would you know?" Saphine countered.

"I know this one is done with being held down. He wants to move on his own path, a path none of you would ever understand." Snow continued on.

"I don't understand?" Saphine said.

"I know," Snow replied and followed Mor, leaving Saphine stunned again.

"What is going on?!" Saphine shouted into the corridor.

Snow quickly caught up to Mor and followed him quietly.

"Don't you want to ask me what's going on?" Mor said quietly.

"Not my business," Snow answered.

"Thank you," Mor told her.

"Don't mind it," Snow said.

Mor let out a deep sigh.

"I found out that the nobles kept at least one secret from us, commoners..." Mor said.

"And you think they might keep a bunch more," Snow said, and Mor nodded.

"What if they only think of us as disposable pawns while keeping their influence and power intact," Mor said.

°*Yeah, this is probably it. Orth and Clare are probably rare exceptions from that,*° the human said.

"I understand. You fear that if this gets known among your kin, there might be a conflict brewing." Snow said.

"Yes, and I don't know what I should do about it. Should I keep quiet, or should I talk?" Mor said, and Snow nodded.

"Quite the conundrum." She said.

"Yes, what would you do?" Mor asked.

"I will not answer this. It is for you to decide. But you need the power to follow your convictions anyway." Snow said.

"You're right. I can't do anything if I'm powerless." Mor said.

°*Why is she helping you so much? This goes way beyond being "thankful,"*° The human asked.

"Why are you so helpful to me?" Mor asked, and Snow smiled.

"I'm here as part of the "kin-ship," but you are the only one, except the chief, who doesn't view me as the stupid barbarian. You give me the respect that kin deserve from each other and are humble. Also, I can see the soul of ice in you. It just makes me want to help you." Snow explained.

"The soul of ice?" Mor asked.

"Yes, you struggle to overcome yourself every day anew, trying to become the best you can. We Ice-kin are respecting that," Snow answered.

°*I get it. Your hard work is paying off now,*° the human said.

°*I don't,*° Mor said.

°*In short, out of all the Soul-kin, she can relate to you most and, therefore, is willing to share her techniques with you. She probably also knows that no one at this school would want to learn from someone outside the Soul-kin, no one except you.°* The human explained.

"You are helping me because I listen to you and want to learn from you?" Mor asked Snow.

"Now you understand, if you offer respect, you will get it in return," Snow said again, embracing Mor for a second.

"What's up with all this embracing?!" Mor asked, flustered after he was let go.

"I told you it's how we show that we trust someone," Snow said.

"How did you end up with something like this?!" Mor continued.

"Simple. When you live in ice and Snow, warmth becomes a valuable resource, but it also makes you vulnerable to attacks on your back, so sharing your warmth with someone else is a sign of trust", Snow explained.

°*Makes sense.°* The human said.

"I get it," Mor said, somehow feeling better after this hug.

They walked the last distance to the classroom in pleasant silence. Snow stayed with Mors's class the whole day, and after the final lesson was over, they both walked to the training room.

"Snow? What's that armor of yours? I have never seen anything like that," Mor asked.

"I told you about our coming-of-age tradition, right?" She answered, and Mor nodded.

"After you have slain your monstrosity, you bring the body back to the village. There, it will be processed into food, armor, and ammunition." She pulled out an arrow. "The fins on the back are feathers of a flying monstrosity." Snow explained further.

°*That's cool!*° The human said.

°*"You are eating them?*° Mor asked, surprised.

"Yes, we can't let anything go to waste, and fruits are not growing where we live. Therefore, we need to hunt the monstrosities regularly or starve. Also, we need to keep their numbers low because we don't have as strong a protection as many other kin, unlike your floating cities or the underground cities of the stone-kin. Getting used to your food is not that easy. At least you have some nuts, or your food wouldn't be filling for me." Snow explained.

°*Told ya.*° The human said proudly

°*You didn't, though. You said they were eating right and not they would eat mostrosities.*° Mor countered

°*It is the same thing! Meat is good for your muscles.*° The human said.

"But if you hunt them for food, why make clothes out of them?" Mor asked.

"I told you, nothing can go to waste. Also, the material keeps many of the original properties, so it is resistant against cuts and even protects a bit against magic." She explained.

"Is this why Ranbors fire couldn't hurt you?" Mor went on.

"The loud idiot? No. I blocked this one's attacks with my daggers after imbuing them with power." Snow said.

"Meaning, you can fill those crystals with magic and then block other attacks?!" Mor asked, and Snow nodded.

°*This will be so much more helpful than we thought at first!*° The human celebrated.

°*Yes, we need to learn this technique and get our hands on some of those crystals.*° Mor said.

°*Then we can do a two-in-one, saving energy for later and using it as a shield in the meantime!*° The human said, and Mor agreed.

Part 26

After arriving in the training room, Snow asked Mor to sit down opposite her. As they both got comfortable on the floor, she fixed Mor with her gaze.

"You want to learn how to gather magic energy from your surroundings, right?" she asked him, and Mor nodded.

"Yes, but could you also teach me the full technique?" Mor asked back.

"Sure, I don't know what you could gain from learning to imbue a crystal. I can teach you." Snow answered.

°*Nice, now we are getting somewhere.*° The human commented.

"Then we need to start at the basics and don't expect to succeed immediately. This is a rather difficult technique every step of the way." Snow explained.

"I understand," said Mor.

°*Yeah, could have guessed, so it's business as usual.*° The human added.

"Good, then let's get started," Snow said. "Firstly, just try to feel the magic around you."

Mor took a deep breath and concentrated, trying to even get a feel for any other magic than his own. Of course, on this first try, nothing would happen.

°*Yeah, guessed as much. No choice but to keep trying.*° The human said.

This went on for a whole week. He would go with Snow whenever she wanted to see some part of the school, attend his lessons, or train after class. To Mor's relief, Ranbor was nowhere to be seen for all those days.

Then, finally, after a few pointers from Snow, Mor had his breakthrough. He could feel the energy around him; even Snow radiated magical energy, which Mor accounted for as her life force. He got a big smile.

"I got it." He told Snow.

"Very good, faster than expected." She nodded with a smile. "Then on to the next step, getting the energy from your surroundings into the crystal."

"Wouldn't it be better to learn how to absorb it myself first?" Mor asked, and Snow shrugged,

"I can't help you with that. I can only teach you how to get it into the crystal. After that, you have to find out everything else yourself," she explained to Mor.

"Oh, I get it," Mor answered.

"Good, then take this crystal." She handed him a spare arrowhead. "Get a feeling of how empty it is, and then try to guide the surrounding energy into it."

°*Sounds easy enough.*° The human commented. °*Can I try again? We never got me to guide the energy.*°

°*Can you even feel the magic?*° Mor asked.

°*I can feel something,*° The human said.

°*Well, no harm in trying.*° Mor agreed and let the human try, but no progress was made after trying for a few hours.

°*Fuck, why can't I do it!*° The human complained.

°*I don't know, but maybe it is because you don't have any magic?*° Mor put forward.

°*This is bullshit...*° The human pouted.

The next day, it was Mor's turn. He concentrated on the crystal, felt the energy flow, and instantly, it filled with energy and shattered. Mor looked surprised for a second and then cursed.

"Shit! What happened?" He asked.

"You concentrated too much on filling the crystal and didn't use the energy from your surroundings but your own energy," Snow said.

Mor looked at her, surprised, and asked. "How do you know?"

"I can also "feel" the energy flowing, so of course I would know it. The surrounding energy was still." Snow explained. "You need both. Gather the energy around you and guide it to the crystal. Go slow and steady until you think the crystal is filled."

"I don't want to shatter another one. You don't have an unlimited amount for me, right?" Mor said.

"Don't worry. I have enough for you to grasp the concept. Shattering a few will be no problem. The pieces are useful in making weapons, so just go ahead." Snow told him, and Mor nodded thankfully.

After breaking three more crystals, they decided to end the day and take a break on the next. Now that Mor had some free time, while Snow went and explored on her own, at her own request, mind you, he decided to talk with his friends again and went to look for them.

Mor found Orth after class in the library.

"Hey, Orth," he greeted the other boy.

"Hi, Mor." Orth nodded.

"Sorry that I ignored you the past few days." Mor apologized.

"Don't worry, I get it. It must have been shocking for you to find out the nobles were keeping secrets. I mean, it was for me that they do, but it had to be worse for you," Orth said, understanding.

"Thank you for being so understanding and my friend," Mor said, and Orth smiled.

"You're welcome. Also, I won't retract my offer because of that," Orth said.

"Before I forget, the Saphire girl came to me and seemed angry with how I treated you, and I guess I was not nice to her because of my ill temper," Mor said awkwardly, and Orth sighed.

"I can guess how it went...." Orth began, but Mor interrupted him.

"Please let me finish. I would like to apologize to Saphine for being an ass. She didn't deserve that for just being concerned about you. Could you tell me where I can find her?" Mor added.

"I don't know where she is, but I can tell her you want to talk to her again and also apologize to you," Orth told Mor.

"Where's the Ice-kin today? Aren't you responsible for her?" asked Orth further.

"She wanted to explore by herself," Mor answered.

They talked a bit about random stuff, like the last week, until they spoke of Ranbor.

"I haven't seen him for a few days," Mor said, and Orth nodded.

"He is probably angry at his punishment because his oh-so-great power is now severely limited. He will get over it and appear again, just as haughty as ever." Orth dismissed

"I hope you are right, and nothing worse will come from it," Mor said.

°*Why!? Why did you say that? Now, it will get infinitely worse. Murphy is always listening!*° The human shouted.

°*What's your problem now, and who's this Murphy?*° Mor asked.

°*Murphy is a human who said that "anything that can go wrong will go wrong"! And with you saying you hope nothing bad will happen, it will happen.*° The human said.

°*How does that work?*° Mor asked again.

°*It just does!*° The human insisted.

"It probably won't. His pride is just hurt, and he doesn't know when to stop. He has always been like this. I have known him since early childhood. He's the pampered son." Orth said.

"You knew him since then?" Mor asked, and Orth gave him an affirming nod.

"We are both high nobles. Saphine does as well." He told Mor.

"Then do you know why Ranbor has it out for me?" Mor asked.

"Honestly, it may be a multitude of factors. Firstly, you are a commoner and, therefore, beneath him. Secondly, you already beat him in a contest of wits after you aced the entrance test and, third, probably the most importantly, your mother," Orth explained.

"What about my mother?" asked Mor further.

"You don't know? Well, I think an uncle or cousin, I don't remember that clearly, acted out, and your mother put him back into place with total ease if I can remember correctly. That wouldn't be a big thing, but she later refused an open offer to marry into the Sapphire or Emerald family and gave up her status to an uncle of hers. This way, the slight against the Rubys was enhanced, as one of theirs was beaten by a commoner." Orth chuckled.

"WAIT, my mother had a marriage offer from two high noble families?" Mor was stunned by this revelation.

"Yes, how do you not know that?" Orth asked incredulously.

"I don't know that much. My mother and father are talking little about their heritage. They say their life now with me is far more important."

°*Well, it is, but at least that explains a lot. Pride is a powerful thing,*° The human said.

°*Have I told you already that I'm getting sick of this shit?*° Mor asked.

°*Yeah, you did.*° The answer came back.

Part 27

After Saphine had been left standing by Mor and further confused by the Ice-kin, she tried to get more information out of Orth, but he kept insisting everything was fine. He just has a little problem going through his mind that he might have to discuss with his family.

So, in desperation, she searched for the new girl, who started hanging around Orth and the commoner. She needed a hot second to remember the name Clare Celestyne and went to talk to her. They then met almost daily after the lessons and became fast friends.

"Why do you care so much about the commoner?" Saphine asked at one of their earliest meet ups.

Clare blushed a bit and thought of how to answer that. "I really don't know. Somehow, it feels like he is a little brother I want to support. But after seeing his body at the tournament, I sometimes want to be protected by him? I really don't understand all of this," she explained.

"What about his body? I saw it at the tournament, true he has a stronger build than most Soul-kin, but what does that matter? His magic energy is low, therefore he shouldn't be a good partner for anyone." Saphine drilled deeper.

"Well, you didn't see him up close, right? It is just strange. I understand that there can never be something between us; my parents wouldn't allow it, and honestly, I don't know if I would want it. As you say, magic energy is a big part of choosing the right partner for yourself." Clare shrugged.

"I just don't get what you and Orth see in this commoner. I understand that his mother might have been so talented that she almost married into my family. If fate had been different, he might have been my cousin or even brother, but it wasn't, and he also has none of his mother's talents, so he is just a weak commoner at the wrong school." Saphine went on.

"Really? His mother was powerful enough to marry into one of the high noble families?" Clare asked.

"Two, in fact, the Emeralds also wanted to have her in their family, but she chose differently," Saphine said.

"TWO? What happened? Why didn't she accept either one? How come she's just a commoner now?!" Clare asked, exasperated.

"I don't know, she just chose a commoner, she herself was a minor noble but chose to forfeit this title and marry into the commoner's family instead of him marrying into hers," Saphine said. "I don't understand that either."

"Does Mor maybe have a hidden talent that he keeps secret for some reason? Maybe he has really strong magic and a strong body. Do you know if his father maybe has a good physique?" Clare asked further.

"No, I never met him, and we don't have any connection to the Agatons, I just remembered the name at the entrance ceremony. But I don't think he hid something because the headmaster would have detected it by the attribute-ritual." Saphine said.

"Guess a strong parent doesn't equal a gifted child. But then why is he in this school? I think there is something going on, neither of us knows," Clare said thoughtfully.

"I can't even begin to guess. But you are right, it is strange. Being on the topic of strange, do you know what's up with Orth? He told me it is nothing, but he behaves strangely," Saphire asked, and Clare got bashful at this question.

"Well, I was with him. We waited for Mor after he got dragged into the headmaster's office by Miss Amethyne, and afterwards, he told us that the Ice-kin wanted to teach him how to gather magic from their surroundings." Clare began to explain.

"So? We also learn that, in our last year at this school," Saphine asked, confused.

"Exactly what Orth told Mor, but then we found out that Mor didn't know about something like that," Clare said.

"Why? I thought that is common knowledge?" Saphine went on.

"I thought so too, but it seems that the commoners don't get told about such a technique," Clare told Saphine, who thought for a second and then answered supprised.

"You mean, the nobles keep secrets from the commoners to keep them down?"

Clare nodded. "Seems like it. Orth told me he wanted to ask his family about that and maybe, in the future, change this inequity. He is probably thinking about how he might do this, it seems an unfathomably big ask for a single person. I told him if the time comes, he can count on my support."

"Really, why do you both care so much about commoners?" Saphine asked.

"Well, if you would try to be friends with Mor and maybe understand his way of thinking, you might begin to understand," Clare said, and Saphine laughed.

"Me? Friends with a commoner? Impossible, my status is much higher than his!" She exclaimed, almost offended.

"Well, he is friends with Orth and me. Maybe you just should try to look beyond status." Clare said, shrugging.

"I don't think so. You play nice with the commoner if it is funny to you, but I won't. The only Agaton family-member I would speak to would be his mother, the ice-empress." Saphine said.

"Your decision," Clare said, then changing the topic, "What do you think about the Ice-kin woman?"

"What question is this? She's just a barbarian," Saphine said.

"I don't know. Mor said he liked her, and I think if that's the case, there has to be more to it," Clare explained.

"You think there is more about her because the commoner said so? Sometimes, you have a strange world-view." Saphine almost chided Clare.

"Don't get snippy with me! Even you have to admit that a lot of boys are watching her, almost staring, just like a lot of girls had stared at Mor after his robes were destroyed at the tournament. And somehow, I kind of envy her, she seemed to move so fluently, and even though I don't understand why, I find myself thinking I somehow lost to her." Clare confessed, and Saphine thought for a second.

"I think I get you. She seems to move in an effortless elegance. It is unfair, that a barbarian would be somehow superior to a Soul-kin noble." Saphine agreed, getting a bit annoyed, without knowing why.

"Yeah, I guess having a good body does something to make us envious. But why? Only magic energy should affect us like that?" Clare asked.

"I don't know, but you only have the body you got. So no sense pondering why the Soul-kin women don't look like that," Saphine tried to reassure Clare and herself but failed to do so.

"But, we are all kin. So maybe there is a secret to it? Maybe you are not stuck with the body you just got?" Clare asked.

"Now you are talking crazy. You can't change a body. I already told you." Saphine said condescending.

"We could ask her." Clare offered.

"Are you mental? You want to talk to the barbarian?" Saphine asked incredulously.

"Why not? She is training Mor, a Soul-kin, so maybe she would be open to at least talk to us? If we don't speak to her, we will never know." Clare said, and Saphine sighed.

"This is stupid. What do you think this will get you?" She asked.

"I don't know, but I will try talking to her. Maybe she's nice." Clare answered.

"Really, that is your reasoning? "Maybe she's nice." You know what? I will go with you, just see how badly you fail and look out for you if she wants to hurt you," Saphine told Clare.

"Let's try to invite her sometimes! You will see, this could be fun," Clare said, excited.

Like this they both met up and just talked, sometimes while drinking tea, sometimes playing some games and waiting for a chance to invite the Ice-kin, and after a few days, their chance came. While Mor had his talk with Orth, Clare almost abducted the Ice-kin for tea and snacks while Saphine watched with scepticism.

"I still don't understand what you want to achieve with this, but well," Saphine said as they all sat down on a table filled with fruits, tea, and juice.

"Why am I here?" Snow asked and Clare smiled friendly, while Saphine averted her gaze.

"I wanted to talk to you!" Clare said and the Ice-kin looked a bit confused at this revelation.

"But why?" Snow asked again.

"Well, you seem to be friends with Mor, so I thought you might be nice." Clare offered.

"Are you friends with Mor Agaton?" Snow wanted to know.

"Yes!" Clare said, grinning. "Not really," Saphine added quietly.

"And you thought I would be nice? Because I am on good terms with Mor Agaton?." Snow asked, picking out a piece of fruit.

"Exactly! Also, we wanted to ask you something." Clare went on.

"What would that be?" Snow asked further.

"Is it possible for us to get a body like yours?" Clare blurted out.

Snow was a bit surprised and thought for a second about her answer. "Yes, maybe not exactly, but close." "I don't believe you! You can't change the body you're born with. Everyone knows that!" Saphine interjected.

"Doesn't change the truth that you can." Snow countered.

"Could you show us how?" Clare asked, interrupting Saphines next outburst.

"I could, but I won't. I have chosen Mor Agaton as the one allowed to be thaught by me. So if you want to know how, you need to ask him. I'm just surprised you didn't already." Snow told the girls.

"What do you mean?" Saphine asked.

"Mor Agaton knows this since before I showed up," Snow said, getting herself another fruit.

"Of course. The commoner knows how to change a woman's body. He's a boy! How would he know?" Saphine asked sarcastically.

"Doesn't change the truth," Snow said again.

"And why won't you tell us?" Clare asked.

"Because it is tradition," Snow said matter of factly.

After this, the conversation petered out, and soon Snow made her excuse and thanked the girls for the snacks and conversation. Leafing two confused girls behind.

"You think she's messing with us? What she says can't be true." Saphine asked.

"But what if?" Clare countered. "We should ask Mor about this." At this exclamation, Clare got a bit sad.

"What's the matter now?" Saphine questions.

"Mor wanted to have space to think about everything. And I don't want to annoy him further if I don't give him space," Clare answered dejectedly.

"True, he seemed very angry after I tried to question him about Orth. He was extremely disrespectful," Saphine added.

"Then no choice but to wait until he wants to talk to us again," Clare said.

Part 28

After this interlude, Mor asked Orth to get Saphine and, if possible, Clare to him if he found them before Mor did, and Orth agreed. That dealt with, Mor continued his training with Snow the next day.

But try as he might, he couldn't get the hang of it. After shattering another three of Clare's arrowheads, he grew frustrated.

°*I didn't think it would be that hard.*° The human commented.

°*Why won't it work?*° Mor asked, frustrated.

Snow gave looked at him strangely.

"Do it step by step. First, concentrate on the energy around you, and then get it to flow along your arms and slowly, carefully, into the crystal." She tried to explain, but Mor just sighed.

"That's what I'm trying." He whined. "But I don't get it! Also, why does this shit just shatter if I use my energy?" He went on, annoyed.

"If you use your energy, you try to fill it too fast, and then it shatters. You must do it slowly and evenly, then it can store surprisingly much." Snow explained, and Mor let himself fall backward from his sitting position to lie flat on the ground, sighing.

°*Want to try something else?*° The human asked.

°*And what?*° Mor answered dejectedly.

°*You remember how she took out Ranbor?*° The human went on.

°*Yes, of course. What of it?*° Mor asked back, his interest slowly growing.

°*I want to throw hands with her, no magic, just pure muscle power.*° The human said.

°What?! Where does this come from?° Mor asked, surprised.

°Don't know, I just wanted to try. I feel that I can remember something if I do.° The human said.

°Let's ask her, but if she says yes, I want to go first.° Mor said.

°Why that? Do you think you can do anything against her?° The human asked.

°Maybe, just let me. I did let you try with the magic thing, too.° Mor said.

°Fine, if she says yes, you can go first.° The human agreed.

Mor sat up again, and Snow looked at him, surprised. Something in the boy's look had changed.

"Snow, would you fight me? I need to get my head clear of the crystal stuff." Mor asked, and she was surprised at this declaration.

"Fight you? Why?" Snow asked, slightly interested.

"Just to see how I would fare against you. Of course, without magic or weapons." Mor answered, and Snow thought for a second.

"Sure this would help you? I will just beat you. You don't have any chance." Snow told him.

"Then let's see if that's true!" Mor said, standing up excitedly.

Snow sighed and stood up, too. "Then show me what you can do." She told him, and they both got ready.

°Round ONE, good luck!° The human said, and Mor rushed forward, using his weight and momentum to get a surprise punch past Snow's defenses.

°*Bad choice.*° The human commented, and Mor almost wanted to ask why, but Snow's reaction came faster than he could voice his confusion to the human.

Snow reacted to Mors' wild rush with a sidestep, grabbing his outstretched arm and pulling him forward. This made Mor stumble, as expected.

After she ruined his balance, Mor could feel her knee on his stomach, and she tapped him lightly on the back of the head.

"You lose," Snow told him, but was then surprised as Mor just laughed.

°*My try!*° The human exclaimed.

"That was great. Could we do another one?" Mor asked, and Snow nodded, confused.

"Sure, if you want." She told the boy, who then removed the top of his robe and put it aside.

"What are you doing that for?" She asked.

°*More freedom of movement.*° The human answered.

"I can move more freely like that, and now it's on!" Mor smiled, Snow shrugged and got ready.

After Mor let the human take over, Snow watched in surprise as something in the boy changed and knew it wouldn't be that easy now. The boy had taken a strange stance, protecting his face and body with his forearms and fists while lightly hopping in place for a few moments until he suddenly stood still and watched her every move.

Snow felt a shudder running down her spine. This boy's look made her remember the gaze of a monstrosity that had just sniffed out its prey. She felt hunted and tried to shake it off.

"There's nothing to fear. It's still just a Soul-kin boy." She thought to herself and got ready for another wild attack.

But this time, the boy didn't charge blindly at her. Instead, he closed the distance with a quick step and followed up with a fast left jab. Still, Snow reacted lightning fast and slapped away the punch, barely dodging the follow-up right fist. The boy's punches came in a neverending hail, and Snow found herself getting pushed back at the ferocity. Still, it was nothing she couldn't handle, and she began to play with him.

The boy seemingly pressured her into giving ground, but at this point, she was used to the rhythm of his punches and got ready to counterattack.

°*How are you doing that?!*° Mor asked.

°*I'm concentrating! Later!*° The human answered.

°*Soon she should... NOW.*° The human said.

Snow slapped away the left hand coming for her face and made a grab for the follow-up right, only to realize she missed her grab because no right fist was forthcoming. Instead, the boy closed, further ducking down and making a quick uppercut, touching her chin gently with his knuckles. They both disengaged from each other, and Snow looked at the boy, surprised.

"Your point." She said, slightly confused.

°*Holy shit! You won!*° Mor celebrated.

°*Yeah, I somehow remember doing something like that in my previous life. Or maybe just seeing it? It's not that clear. But also, she was going easy on me.*° The human said.

"You supprised me Mor Agaton." Snow said. "I underestimated you, but now I will take you seriously. Let's do another one."

"You're on!" Mor said.

°*Beat her again!*° Mor told the human.

°*I'll try.*° The human answered and got ready.

Snow watched the boy take on a different stance, this time a broader one. One hand stretched towards her, almost beckoning her to attack him, while the other was pulled slightly back parallel to his body.

"Try it, lady." The boy taunted her, and she happily obliged.

She closed the distance in a blur, opening up with a swipe at the boy's face, who just deflected her hand with a wiping motion, transferring smoothly into an open palm punch of his own, which she deflected.

Snow made a quick motion to get out of reach, the boy close on her heels, making a double jab, one fist aiming for her stomach and the other for her face. Snow leaned back and evaded both of them but then had to block the follow-up kick from the boy with her arms so as not to get knocked over.

Snow had no time to think about the strangeness of all of this. The boy just gave her enough time to think about her next move, and somehow, she wanted to beat this boy in earnest now. He was a fine challenger for her skills. Snow reapplied pressure on the boy with a barrage of punches, culminating in a low sweep with her leg. The boy, redirecting and blocking all of her punches, jumped backward. He made a backward arch, catching his fall with his hands and rotating his legs in a kicking motion to keep her away.

Snow had to back off, or else she might get hit by those wild kicks, and both of them took a second to evaluate their opponent. Snow was still fine, but it seemed the boy hadn't her endurance. He was breathing heavily.

°*That's really fun.*° The human said. °*To bad, we have to end it soon. We just don't have enough stamina to let it drag out further.*°

°*You still think you can win?!*° Mor asked. °*Look at her. She's still not showing any sign of slowing down!*°

°*Watch me!*° The human said, closing to Snow and opening up with a low kick of his own, which she blocked with her leg. The boy bought himself enough time, though. He rose up to standing again fluently and tried a sweeping punch to her body. Snow evaded that with a short step backward, seizing the opportunity as the momentum of the boy's punches carried him on, turning his back to her. Snow made a large chopping motion towards the neck of the boy and watched in surprise as he grabbed her arm without looking directly at her and heaved.

He turned her momentum now against herself and over his shoulder. Snow landed back first on the floor, and before she could recover, the boy had already pinned her to the floor and had her arm in a locking position where he could apply pressure to it.

"You won again." She said, and the boy let her go with a smile, his chest heaving with the breaths he needed to take.

°*You, did it!*° Mor celebrated.

°*Yeah, now be a gentleman and help her up. It was really close.*° The human said.

Mor got up first and offered his hand, which Snow took. After he calmed down a bit, he suddenly whinced.

"I think I overdid it." He said, pulling in a sharp breath. "Yes, definitely hurt something."

Snow laughed at Mor's discomfort. "You are really something!" she told him and continued teasing. "If you keep up with it and get even stronger, I might need to get my daughter to get you."

"Thank you?" Mor answered uncertainly, quickly changing the topic. But I think I'm ready to try again with the crystals."

Part 29

As Mor and Snow were just about to sit down to continue the magic training, they were both surprised by voices shouting.

"What was that?!" The first voice shouted.

"That was incredible!" The second one added.

"Are you stupid?" The third one finished.

Mor and Snow were so occupied with their little bout that they didn't notice the arrival of the intruders. Mor looked surprised at the three figures.

"Orth, Clare and Saphine?" Mor asked, surprised. "Since when are you all here?"

"Since you tried beating up the Ice-kin," Orth answered for them all.

°*Seems that we offered quite a show.*° The human said, and Mor had to agree. °*Look at the girls!*° The human teased, and Mor realized only then he was still bare-chested.

"Are you alright?" Clare asked, not looking Mor in the eyes.

"Yes, Clare, I'm fine. I wanted to test myself against Snow. I needed to get my frustration about the magic training out." Mor answered, walking over to pick up the top part of his robe, wincing as he bent down.

"You're not fine, I saw that," Clare exclaimed and rushed over to Mor. "Let me heal you!"

"You don't need to, nothing to worry about." Mor tried to calm her down after putting his clothes back on.

"Shut up and sit down. No complaining." Clare said sternly, while Snow smiled and the human giggled.

Mor let out a sigh but decided not to resist the medical attention. After he sat down, Clare put her hands on his back and let her healing magic flow into him. The warmth spread through Mor's body, slowly relieving his pain.

"Where did you learn to move like that?" Orth asked, and Snow perked up, also interested in the answer.

Mor shrugged and got a light slap from Clare on the back of his head. "Don't move." She chided him.

"Sorry, Clare," Mor said before answering Orth's question. "I just made it up. I saw how Snow moved while she beat Ranbor and just emulated it with some imaginations of my own." He lied.

Snow and Orth looked skeptical at that explanation, and Snow was the first to speak again.

"Then you are a real genius in unarmed combat." She said, still not fully trusting his explanation.

"Something is strange. Tell us the truth, commoner!" Saphine added, and Mor fixed her with an intense stare.

"I told you the truth. It was all made up in my mind," Mor said, deciding to add a piece of the truth but keeping his tone insistent that even Orth and Snow had to grudgingly accept this. For now...

Saphine looked away, and Mor could swear she was turning slightly red. He then sighed.

"Listen, Saphine." He began and was interrupted by Saphine. "I let it slide once, but you will address me properly as Lady Sapphire."

Mor raised an eyebrow at that declaration, while Orth sighed and Clare also let out a breath.

"As you wish, my lady," Mor said. "I just wanted to apologize for the last time I acted very rudely. You didn't deserve this for being concerned with Lord Obsidian." Mor could just barely hold out the sarcasm he felt.

"Good, I will be so gracious to forgive you." Saphine said, "Was this all you wanted me here for, Orth?" She asked the other boy, who nodded in surprise.

"Yes, that was it. I think." Orth said.

"Good, then I will take my leave." Saphine glanced at Mor quickly and unintelligibly before huffing and leaving.

She just turned a corner and wanted to scream. Why was she reacting like that? She almost couldn't keep a straight face looking at the commoner, but now she gets what Clare had told her. Seeing a body like this up close is nothing like seeing it from the distance of the tournament stands. Trying to get the picture out of her head, she decided to go to the library and read.

"Well, that was something," Orth said after Saphine had left.

"Yes." Mor said, "I think I made it worse."

"Don't worry, she is a nice girl but a bit stiff," Clare said. "Also, I'm done. All damage to your body is fixed."

"What?" Mor asked, surprised.

"What do you mean, "what?" I fixed whatever you did to damage your body like that. There is no damage left," Clare said.

°*Well, so much to a good, exhausting training session...*° The human complained.

°*She only ment well.*° Mor answered.

"Thanks, Clare," Mor said. "You are really talented. I felt almost nothing of your magic working.

That's very impressive."

°*WE ARE STUPID!*° The human suddenly shouted.

°*What, why?*° Mor asked.

°*Healing magic!*° The human stated as if it was obvious.

°*I don't get it?*° Mor was confused.

°*We also can use healing magic, well you can, but still!*° The human went on.

°*So?*° Mor still not getting what the human went on.

°*Clare used subtle slow magic! Like we also do while reducing pain... How can you be so dense!*° The human complained, and finally, it clicked with Mor.

Clare, Snow, and Orth flinched when Mor suddenly cried out.

"I got it! Snow a crystal, please!" Mor asked excitedly and got handed one by the woman.

And Snow handed over another crystal piece. Mor closed his eyes, imagining the crystal as not a strange stone but a magical being. Using the magic regenerating spell he learned from Amber, remembering that if someone is suffering from magic deficiency, you need to start giving them only a small amount of magic, and he slowly lets the magic flow from him.

He couldn't gather the magic around him, so he used his reservoir. This time, the crystal didn't shatter. Instead, it started to hum slightly, getting stronger with every passing moment. Snow watched in amazement as the humm got sharper and sharper until she could not hear it anymore. Instead, a glow built inside the crystal piece.

"Amazing." She said, Clare and Orth nodding in amazement.

Mor felt a resistance building in the crystal and decided to stop, opening his eyes.

"Wow, this thing took about half my energy," Mor said as he held up the crystal, looking at it from every angle. He then smiled at Snow. "I did it!"

Snow nodded, "Indeed, but you should have used the surrounding energy." She half chided the excited boy.

"Right... But now I think I have a good idea of what to do. The only thing left is to use another source," Mor said, then asked his next question, "How do I get the energy out of that crystal again?"

Snow looked at him, surprised. "You don't? Once the magic is in there, it can't be pulled out again. It's only possible to "transform" the emitting aura. Otherwise, the energy will dissipate slowly on its own. By using the crystal for attacks or by transforming the energy, it just gets empty faster. But this transformation technique is unique to the stone-kin. I don't know it." She explained, and Mor sighed.

°*Fuck! Why is this magic shit so full of limitations!*° The human cursed. °*We make a single step forward and then always end up at a dead end!*°

°*Well, at least we know how to feel the surrounding energy.*° Mor tried to calm the human.

°*True enough, and maybe this thing with the crystal comes in handy sometimes.*° The human said, calming a bit.

°*I already have an idea for this.*° Mor said. °*Crystals are also a kind of stone, right? So if we "fill" one, it gets this aura, which can penetrate the defenses of a monstrosity. This means that we are more effective than any other Soul-kin against monstrosities.*°

°You are right! And if it works against those things, it probably is very hard for other mages to defend against!° The human went on.

°Good thinking, meaning the next step, is getting the energy around to the crystal and, after that, modifying the technique to fill your reservoir faster!°

"What did you just do, Mor?" Orth asked.

"I just filled this crystal with energy," Mor answered proudly.

"And that does?" Orth went on while Clare listened interestedly.

"Well, Snow explained it gives the Crystal a magic penetrating aura, making it more lethal against monstrosities," Mor explained, and Orth let out a whistle after Snow confirmed Mors's tale with a nod.

"Might I try it?" asked Orth, and Mor looked questioning at Snow, who shrugged.

"I told you. It's your decision." She said.

"Then Orth, just slowly let your magic flow into the crystal. Like you want to heal it," Mor explained, and just as with him, Orth's first crystal instantly shattered.

"Too much energy." Mor joked, and Orth looked annoyed at the tone.

"I want to try, too!" Clare said and got herself a crystal from Snow. Then she began concentrating on "healing" the stone, and to the surprise of everyone, she succeeded on her first try.

"It's not that hard." She said, and both boys groaned at that.

Part 30

While Orth tried to get this thing with the crystal right, Clare scooted closer to Mor.

"Mor? I wanted to know something from Snow, but she said I needed to ask you yourself..." Clare began shyly.

Mor looked questioningly at Snow, who just shrugged and stayed silent. This was not her fight.

"What do you need, Clare?" he asked the bashful girl.

"I don't... How should I... You know..." she stumbled onward.

The human let out a whistle °*Lucky guy! There's a confession incoming.*°

°*A confession?*° Mor asked, confused.

°*Yes! She wants to confess her love for you!*° The human answered, and Mor was suddenly painfully aware of Clares'Clares' fidgeting and a nervous crack in her voice.

°*What should I do?!*° Mor asked, slightly panicking.

°*Well, do you want to accept it or deny it?*° The human asked.

°*I don't know!*° Mor answered.

°*Oook, so neutral to positive. Then just to the following...*° The human explained, and Mor followed their guidance.

Mor looked directly at Clare, grabbing her fidgeting hands, and said in his most soothing voice, "Calm down. Just tell me. What's the worst that could happen?"

Clare looked up, surprised. Orth stopped with his crystal attempts and instead listened in as subtly as possible. Snow just put a hand over her mouth, seemingly in shock. Finally, Clare took a deep breath and went on.

"Snow told me you know how to get a better body, and I wanted to know how!" Clare blurted out, and Orth's interest peaked.

If this was really a possibility, it was too interesting to ignore. Mor was stunned into a surprised silence, his mind processing Clare's words.

°*Ups, guess I interpreted that wrong.*° The human said.

°*What's wrong with you? Do go off saying shit like that if you are not entirely sure!*° Mor complained.

°*Yeah, yeah. Sorry, I really thought I was right.*° The human apologized.

°*Why do you always try to get me to be nice to girls?*° Mor asked further.

°*Firstly, it costs nothing to be friendly and makes you seem likable. Secondly, it's not just girls. It's just that, apart from Orth, no other boy was nice to us, so no reason to be nice to them. Third, don't you want a partner in the future? Being nice now to good girls will make it easier later.*° The human explained.

°*You know that's not possible anymore... I used my once-in-a-lifetime chance and got you for it.*° Mor said.

°*You don't know that you didn't try it again, and even IF. Maybe there is a way for me to go to the afterlife, be reborn, or whatever. When you don't need my help anymore, we can look for something like this, and maybe you can get a girl then!*° The human went on.

°*So you are just looking out for me?*° Mor asked.

°*Indeed. You never know what the future brings, so you better be prepared for anything.*° The human said.

°*Well, thank you, but please tone it down a bit.*° Mor said.

°*Got, it!*° The human agreed.

Snapping out of his stupor, Mor looked at Clare.

"You want to get a "better" body?" Mor asked, and Clare nodded excitedly.

"How do you mean that?" Mor asked further.

"Well, I'm envious of Snow, and I thought we are all kin, so I somehow could get a body like hers..." Clare explained, and Mor understood.

°*Help me explain how! You know the actual facts.*° Mor pleaded to the human.

°*Well, first ask her if she wants a "healthier" shape or more strength, with the former being easier for her to achieve,*° the human said, and Mor repeated the question to Clare.

"If you say shape is the easier one... I would like to try that, but what's the difference?" Clare asked, and Mor got another short explanation from the human.

"Shape will do not much for our overall physical strength, but honing your muscles will do that. But trust me, this muscle training thing is very painful. Because we are not using most of them and just relying on magic." Mor explained, and this time, Orth spoke up.

"What do you mean painful?" He asked.

"You know the pain if you run too much to get somewhere faster? The pain that will appear in your legs the next day or the day after?" Mor asked, and Orth nodded.

"Yes, I hate that, but at least we can easily undo this. Clare helped me after Miss Amthyne had dragged you off last time." Orth said.

"Sorry, I originally wanted to help you with that, but with the whole "nobles lie" thing, it slipped my mind. But to get to the point, you can't use magic to "undo" the damage. You can lessen the pain with magic, but your body has to "repair" itself. Only then do your muscles become stronger." Mor explained, and both Clare and Orth whinced.

"No, thank you. I will stick with magic." Orth said.

"And for only the shape?" Clare asked hopefully.

"That's easy. Watch what you eat. Expessialy as Soul-kin, we need to eat more. The Cocona-Nuts are very good, for example. Eating is not only for "not dying," but it can help your body build reserves. This means that even if you don't train hard, you get a bit stronger because your body has more fuel. Think of it like a fire. If you put in the perfect amount of material, it burns brightly. If it's not enough, it only simmers, and if you use too much, it might get smothered." Mor explained, getting a surprised look from the other students and an affirming nod from Snow. "That's it?" Clare asked. "Really? You are not lying to me?"

"That's it," Mor confirmed. "For the beginning, just eat as you are used to, and add two or three of the Cocona-Nuts. Eating too much of them will upset your stomach, and trust me, you don't want that." The boy shuddered at the suppressed memory.

"If you are used to this, you should slowly raise your overall intake of everything a bit more, and I mean slowly. We are talking about months here until you are satisfied with your looks. If you think you are too heavy, reduce the intake again or move your body, but then we are getting into the muscle training thing again.

"They are connected?" Orth asked, and Mor nodded.

"Your muscles use this "fuel," meaning they don't need magic energy for more power. No need for a body enhancement spell for simple things." Mor explained.

"That's how you can move like that while hurling other spells!" Orth exclaimed.

"Everyone thought you used two spells at once and wondered how!" Clare added.

°*Would be nice, if we could...*° The human huffed.

Mor just grinned, giving a wink to both his friends.

"Puts everything in perspective, right? I just need a bit of enhancement magic for some moves, like my high jumps, but that's just the moment when you jump upwards. After that, I can go right back to normal spells." Mor explained proudly.

"You are awesome!" Orth smiled. "Maybe I should try this, regardless of my earlier statement. Would you help me?" he asked, and Mor nodded.

"Sure! But it will be hard and painful." Mor said.

"I get that, but think about the possibilities! You and me, we could do anything. With your help, I could even become the next heir to my family, and then I can help you get better treatment for commoners!" Orth had already begun brainstorming, and Snow smiled at this youthful enthusiasm.

"You want to help the commoners?" Mor asked, and Orth nodded.

"Me and Clare both, because we are friends with one." He said, smiling.

"Thank you both," Mor said, touched, and got a grin from both of his friends in return.

After all this, Orth tried a few more times to get this crystal thing right but soon gave up in frustration.

"I just don't have any talent in healing magic." He complained, and Clare chuckled.

"That's the problem with you, high nobles. You just choose your wives according to your preferred element, and therefore, your offspring are only good in that specific magic. Well, good, might be a bit of an understatement, almost unbeatable may be the right word, but suck in everything else!" Clare laughed.

"Aren't you a noble too?" Mor teased her.

"Yeah, but not one like Orth. I'm branch family, and my magic bloodline is not as "pure" as the high born. But because of that, I have an affinity for healing and a good grasp on earth magic." Clare explained.

"Well, for everything else, you have your staff," Orth mumbled grumpily. "I don't need to be good at everything if I just can ask someone else to do it for me. Organizing and gathering talent is our main function as high nobles."

Soon, Orth and Clare waved Mor goodbye and got back to their own tasks, Orth promising to accompany Mor on his "morning runs" in the future.

°*He will hate those and probably give up pretty soon. After all, you Soul-kin are wimps.*° The human half teased.

°*Yes, probably, but I want to give him the support, he is a true friend to us,*° Mor answered.

After the rowdy bunch had all left, Snow sat opposite Mor again.

"Want to continue with your training?" She asked, and Mor nodded.

"Yes, I need to get this "energy from around me"-technique down," he said, and they began to try again.

Mor was concentrating very hard and tried to follow Snow's descriptions, and finally, after a few hours of trying, he did it. A small trickle of magic was flowing from around him into the crystal, but he couldn't make it glow anymore. Just getting it to a slight hum was very difficult.

"You did it very good," Snow congratulated him.

"But it doesn't glow anymore, like before?" Mor asked, disappointed.

"Indeed, I didn't want to say anything about it, but I saw the glowing for the first time. You probably got to the maximum capacity of the crystals. After that, I don't know what might happen." Snow explained.

°*They probably just explode, releasing all the energy at once,*° joked the human.

°*Really? How do you know?*° Mor asked, startled.

°*It was a joke! How should I know!*° The human sighed.

"So I got the technique down?" Mor asked, and Snow nodded.

"Much faster than I expected. It was worth sticking around for that. Now you just have to practice it so you can do this in a combat situation," Snow said.

"Don't you need to gather more information? You were here just over a week?" Asked Mor, and Snow shook her head.

"I had a good picture of your kin around the second day, but you were the unexpected outlier, so I had to stick with you," Snow confessed.

"So when are you leaving?" Mor asked her.

"That depends on you. Do you want to learn anything else? Do you still have questions?" she asked right back.

°*Yes. I do,*° the human said, and Mor nodded.

"Yes, Snow, I still have some things. But it's getting late today, so maybe tomorrow? Mor offered, and Snow agreed.

Part 31

The next morning, as promised, Orth accompanied Mor on his run for a while, which started many conflicting rumors, ranging from Orth just wanting to understand commoners to Mor having put an illusion on Orth to control the nobility.

Still, as Orth was just starting out, he couldn't keep up with Mor for long. Instead, wanting to lie down a bit before breakfast. Mor sent him off with a wave and a reminder to use only pain-reducing healing magic.

Orth slogged back to his room to lie down and take a nap. He was spent. This running thing was more exhausting than he believed, but he also didn't want to lose to Mor. Of course, before he could envelop himself in the soft mattress and fluffy pillow, someone got in his way.

"And what do you think you are doing?" Asked the obstacle, and Orth sighed.

"Going to bed, Saphine. I had an exhausting early morning and want to get a nap in before breakfast." Orth said coldly.

"No! You will explain yourself to me! I heard the rumors that you took up running because the commoner forced you into it, but I don't think that's what happened. I know you just feel bad for the commoner because he is not as privileged as we are, but you don't need to do this. It's just a commoner." Saphine huffed.

Orth let out a deep sigh. He was too tired for this shit. "Don't talk about him like that. He is my friend. Also, I'm doing this because I want to. Now get out of my way before I get angry with you."

Saphine flinched back as if he had struck her. "I'm your friend too! I have known you much longer than this muscleheaded commoner! And it seems you need me to protect you from your own stupidity!"

"If you are my friend, then you should support my decisions and not try to patronize me. Also, even if I explained my reasoning to you, you wouldn't understand", Orth growled.

"How could I if you don't explain?" Shouted Saphine.

"I need to be better if I want to achieve anything with my life. I can't just lay back and get handed everything like my brother... I'm the third, the spare. No one expects anything from me, but it's also frustrating because nothing I do means anything to my family. So, I only have two options if I want to change anything. Option one, become the next head of the Obsidians and dethrone my brother for it, or option two, gather enough power and influence to do it without that." Orth grumbled.

Saphine looked shocked at this declaration. She had never known such thoughts would go on in Orth's head. She slowly reached out to him to give him a friendly touch, but Orth shook her off and stomped to his room.

Leaving her feeling like an ass.

After Orth's less-than-satisfying nap and a short freshen-up, he at least felt a bit better. The brief interaction with Saphine went through his mind again, and he had to blame his exhaustion for being that mean to her, but on the other hand, it helped him express himself the first time.

"*So it's a double-edged sword.*" He thought to himself while leaving with a grumbling stomach to get breakfast.

In the mess hall, he linked up with Mor, who had just come back from freshening up himself, an already waiting Clare, and, to his big surprise, Saphine.

Clare waved both boys over. "Mor, you need to help me choose my breakfast!" she said excitedly, and Mor tilted his head questioningly.

"Why? I explained it to you yesterday," he asked.

"Indeed, you did, but I might as well get your advice if you are here already." Said Clare, with Mor just shrugging and then nodding in agreement.

"Why are you here?" Orth asked the silent Saphine, and Clare interceeded.

"I invited her. She also wanted to know the secret and just missed it yesterday." She answered Orth's question.

Saphine laid a hand on Clare's shoulder. "It's fine, Clare. I'm really here to apologize to you. I wasn't behaving like a friend earlier, and you showed me I need to do better myself. So I thought if you and Clare are friends with the com..." She let out a bashful cough. "... with Mor Agaton, I should accept that and try to at least get along with him."

Orth's slowly rising temper softened substantially. "Thank you for that. I'm also sorry for snapping at you like that. It just came out."

"Why didn't you tell me earlier?" Saphine asked.

"I don't know, maybe I just didn't want to look weak, spiteful, or thankless even with all the privileges shoved down my ass," Orth said with a light chuckle, and Saphine smiled at that.

"Well, next time, just tell me. I won't think less of you for having feelings. Were childhood friends, aren't we?" Saphine said, and Orth agreed.

°*What do you think happened?*° Mor asked the human.

°*Don't know, but it's something between them, so there's no sense in prying into it. It seems they cleared it anyway,*° said the human.

°*True enough.*° Agreed, Mor.

"I would be happy to get along with you, Lady Sapphire," Mor said honestly, getting an uncomfortable smile from the girl, extending in an awkward silence.

Luckily, with perfect timing, Orth's stomach grumbled, demanding food, and Orth's surprised expression got the other three to laugh out loud.

"I think Orth is right." Wheezed Mor. "Time for breakfast!" "Can you help me choose to?" Asked Sapphine surprisingly.

"Sure, but why?" Mor asked back.

"If Clare wants to do this, I want to do it with her. Like Orth joined up with you." Saphine said, a bit mumbling.

Mor looked at Clare, who just gave him an innocent smile.

"I told her about it, but we won't tattle any further. This is our group's little secret," she whispered, and Mor sighed.

"Please, do that." He said. "It might have dire consequences if this gets out like that. First, we must produce real results and then spread it to the other Soul-kin."

"But why do we need to be that careful?" Clare asked. "Isn't this something good?"

Orth thought for a heartbeat and answered in place of Mor.

"Yes, we need to be. Because we are disproving a known fact: "It is impossible to change your body." But we are doing exactly that. Now, think about the implications. Which rules are also false? Are the nobles really the only ones fit to rule? It could end in a war among Soul-kin, and with the world being in turmoil, with what happened to the stone kin, we can't let that happen." explained the boy.

"Yes, Orth understands. We are changing something like a natural law. This will not be a silent thing", Mor whispered, and Clare looked uncomfortable at Saphine.

"Don't worry, Clare, I will keep silent. I know when to use "politics. " Saphine calmed her friend.

With the ground rules now firmly in place, Mor helped his friends choose a more balanced and "healthy" breakfast. The one most surprised was Orth, as Mor explained what he needed for this strength and muscles to grow and, most of that, the amount he was expected to eat.

It then finally dawned on Orth that this would be something unheard of, more so as he compared his portion to the girls, who just took what they liked, and Mor adding a few "fattier" bits and bobs to their plates to make it more balanced. With the help of the human, of course.

After everyone had finished their breakfast, Orth felt somehow very satisfied. He had eaten the first time for another reason than not dying. He could almost feel the "energy" Mor had described flow into his arms and legs, which was, of course, only his imagination.

He now just wished he could take another nap as a bit of tiredness set into his mind, but he was not at all uncomfortable.

Then, after they finished the lessons for the day, Orth retreated to his room for the much-anticipated nap while the girls told Mor they were somehow fitter than most days and just went off to do whatever.

Mor went to the training room, meeting with an already waiting Snow, almost evading the incoming embrace but getting caught anyway. After this familiar greeting, they sat down again, and Snow waited for Mor to start with his questions.

°*We need two things. First, we need to know where we can get those crystals from and if she can spare us some. Second, I want you to try shooting her bow. This will probably enhance our "throw stone" spell.*° The human instructed Mor, and he went to ask Snow.

"My first question would be, where can I get those crystals you are using?" He asked Snow.

"That's easy. We call them crystals because of how they look, but they are "grown" in and on the body of the monstrosities. So just kill one, and you get more than enough for anything you have in mind. We trade those for the metals of the stone kin." She explained, and Mor groaned.

"So they are not stones?" He wanted to clarify, so Snow shook her head.

"No, they are some kind of bone?" She told him.

°*Fuck! Why is never anything easy with your stupid world!*° The human complained.

°*Maybe we can still do something with it?*° Mor put forward.

°*Yeah, no harm in having them on hand.*° The human said dejectedly.

"Then my second question would be, can you spare some more of those "crystals" for me?" Mor asked Snow, who just nodded.

"I think I can spare some, but not more than two dozen," Snow answered truthfully.

"Thank you. I appreciate each." Mor said, and Snow gathered a bunch from her sack.

She handed them over to a thankful Mor.

"And I have a last request." Mor started. "May I try out your weapons?" He asked.

"No!" Snow instantly shut him down. "The weapons of an Ice-kin are their lives. We build them, and we maintain them. They never leave our side." She almost seemed offended at the request.

°*Then, ask her if she would demonstrate how she uses them.*° The human offered, Mor forewarding the compromise and Snow nodding at that.

"Yes, this is acceptable." She said.

With this, Snow demonstrated her weapons, especially the power of her war-bow, to a very attentive Mor. The human told Mor to imagine the arrowhead as a stone. Mor then tried to replicate the speed and power of the arrowhead, with his stones mirroring every shot Snow unleashed.

He slowly grasped the power and impact this weapon could produce, and the energy requirement for his spell reflected this. It didn't push his "signature spell" entirely to group-class, but just barely.

Still, their time came to an end. The send-off was a small and somber affair. Mor, Orth, Clare, Saphine, and the headmaster were the only ones to say goodbye. But in truth, the headmaster was only there because it was required of him, and Saphine only tagged along with everyone else.

The only one truly invested in Snow's departure was Mor. To Snow's surprise, he sent her off with an Ice-kin embrace, which she happily reciprocated.

Mor was earnestly sad to see the woman go. He saw her as a kind of funny aunt, someone you could confide in, but at the same time, she would support you. Even though they only had a bit of over a week together.

In the end, Mor promised Snow he would visit after he was finished with the academy. At that she confided in him that it would be the perfect timing for her daughter's coming-of-age ceremony.

Finally, after everything was said, the Soul-kin teacher standing by to provide transport helped Snow return to her people. And just like that, like a late winter breeze, Snow was gone.

Part 32

A day after Snow left, Mor and the human held a strategy meeting about how to carry on after class.

°*Fist, we should review our strengths and weaknesses and then proceed from there. We need to figure out what to train next to become stronger overall.*° The human explained.

°*Yes. But do we even need to continue at such a fast pace? I mean, training with Snow was fun, but she's gone for now, and Ranbor isn't an issue anymore. Can't we just take it slow from here?*° Mor asked.

°*True enough, but think about this. We know that your monstrosity things are getting more active, and maybe this legendary thing has returned.*° The human began, and Mor nodded at that. °*Yes, but we are on a floating island, and the headmaster guaranteed our safety. So no need to be scared.*° Mor tried to dissuade.

°*You really want to just trust in the security of the floating city? How long do you think it will take for enough of those monstrosities to emerge until they can launch a serious attack? Call me paranoid, but I think it's better to be over-prepared than to complain about not being prepared enough.*° The human went on, and Mor had to concede the point.

°*I guess you are right...*° He said.

°*And to really get the point across, would you rather be able to help fight those things or hide like a coward?*° The human asked.

°*You can stop now. I got the point.*° Answered Mor and then asked a question of his own. °*Then what do you think we should do?*°

°*I told you. We'll first go over everything that we have in our repertoire and seek obvious weak points. Then, we'll remove them by training other techniques.*° The human said, and Mor nodded.

°Then, tell me what you think. How are we faring?° Mor proposed.

°Well, let's start out with our strengths and advantages.

First, we have a powerful and efficient attack with our "Rock-throw."

Second, we can move while concentrating or casting a spell.

Third, we have very good physical power that we can enhance with magic.

Fourth, we can use any kind of magic without pesky attribute limitations.

And finally, we have the crystals from Snow, even though we don't really know how to use them. Maybe we can even refill your reservoir with Snow's technique, but I wouldn't count on that right now.° The human listed.

°Sounds already pretty good to me. So, where do we need to get better? Except with our reservoir.° asked Mor.

°That's it. We have some glaring weaknesses, the biggest being our limited energy, but we can do nothing about that. In addition, we lost to Orth with almost the same repertoire, meaning we need something to surprise opponents like that.° The human explained.

°I get it. Even with the more potent "Rock-throw," we still would lose. And while body enhancement was a good last resort, it also has glaring weaknesses. Because we can't continuously keep it up, the energy requirement is too high, and my concentration gets broken with the feedback pain from connecting my fist. So we are just sitting at square one?° Mor mused.

°Not exactly. We now know of those weaknesses and can now work against them. For that, I have two ideas. We will leave the *glaring energy problems for now. Nothing we can do about that. Still, we should get a few minutes of use out of our trump card body enhancement. Which should be enough for most fights.*

Now for my first idea: if the feedback pain kills your concentration, we need to get rid of it. That means we must harden your skin by punching a lot, which might take too long. So, how do you feel about a weapon? We could even use the crystals we got from Snow for it?° The human asked.

°The problem would be we can't make a dagger, sword, or Snow's special arrows. So what's your second idea?° Mor inquired.

°We can't make a "metal" weapon and don't have enough crystals to waste them in arrows. But we can make a wooden club or staff.° The human explained, and Mor nodded.

°Still, what's your second idea?° He prodded.

°The second one is a long shot. You told me of elemental puppets, I know, you said a single mage can't control and upkeep those, but maybe we should just try. This would get your body out of harm's way, meaning we are not as vulnerable against area attacks.° The human offered.

°Normally, I would say, this is not how this works. BUT. We often "broke" rules, old as the Soul-kin themselves. It would be nice not to be in danger anymore. So, let's add this to the try-out list. This weapon idea is also good, so let's add this, too. You just have to describe how a "club" or "staff" has to look.° Mor agreed.

°Great, those two would give us the edge on any close-quarters fight. In addition, our "Rock-throw" also covers physical ranged attacks. Which leaves us with one more problem. What do we do against someone like Orth, who can make armor? We can't break through it, and we are at a disadvantage up close...° The human pondered, and Mor thought for a bit.

°*True, our repertoire is very earth-magic dependent because the easiest and most cost-effective pupped would also be of earth element... What to do... What to do... Well, for now, a weapon with imbued crystals would probably smash right through magic defenses. At least, if I did understand Snow correctly,*° he pondered.

°*Yes, but we can't rely solely on that. We could try to include some of those crystals in the puppet, but it might also be harmful to it. We need one more good spell we can use easily,*° the human said.

°*Well, wind magic is pretty effective against such earth spells. Maybe we need a higher level one of them?*° Mor offered, and the human agreed.

°*Yeah, it seems like it. But I'm not happy with it. It's not creative or adventurous enough. It has no surprise factor!*° The human grumbled, then got an idea.

°*Do you know a spell where you can see further?*° The human asked, and Mor thought for a second before shrugging.

°*No, but maybe we can find something like that in the library. Want to explain why you want something like that?*° Mor asked while going to the library.

°*I will. Once I know what we have to work with.*° The human answered.

On the way, Mor was surprised and then cornered by three students. He knew better than he'd like. It seems Ranbor's flunkies had waited for him and now wanted something. Interestingly, only the boys threw him scornful looks, while the girl Anna looked at Mor snotty but with a bit of hope. "Leave me alone, go play with your Lord," Mor said, and he wanted to leave, but the three exbullys blocked his way instantly.

"You will listen to me!" Anna demanded haughtily.

"No." Mor simply stated in a flat voice, stealing her thunder.

"I command you! In my function as noble, you are required to listen to me!" She tried again. This time, Mor only raised an eyebrow and sighed.

"Good! You will go to my lord's room and apologize for your insolence. And I will guarantee that you won't be harmed and forgiven for your insults!" Anna ordered.

Mor laughed at that. "I will do no such things? Why would I even?" He asked her incredulously.

And she looked at him offended. "Because I order you too! My lord hasn't left his room for the whole week! And it's all your fault because you don't accept your place in the world! Now, go apologize and beg for forgiveness. Then I'm sure my lord will rejoin us!" Anna comanded.

"Of course, as you command. My lady." Mor answered sarcastically, and as slowly a satisfied grin grew on Anna's face, Mor added.

"That's sarcasm. I won't apologize, and if Ranbor wants to be a big baby and sulk because he has to deal with the consequences of his own actions. I. Don't. Care." Mor emphasized the last words. "Listen up, peasant." Emtsor started, but Mor's stern look silenced him.

"If it's that much of a problem, get a teacher!" Mor stated, trying to walk away again and getting held up a second time.

"We tried. We didn't want to deal with you. But no one would do anything other than to go to my lord's room and ask him politely to leave. Which is, of course, fine, but it didn't help. He just answered that we should go away and leave him." Anna went on, desperation growing in her voice.

"See, not my problem. The moping crybaby will need to get over his hurt "pride" on his own. Also, if he misses enough classes, I'm sure a teacher will get him." Mor said, now pushing himself between the boys.

"They won't!" Anna tried one last time, now pleading. "You wouldn't understand, for someone as great as my lord, this academy is only a formality! He won't need to attend classes to get passing grades. It's so he can gather more social contacts for later life!"

"Oh, I'm really feeling sorry for him now..." Mor said coldly. "Still, my answer is no. He should have thought about that before bullying me! Now let me go. I have better things to do." He added and left for good.

°*How can someone sulk for that long?*° The human asked.

°*Don't know, don't care. As long as he leaves me alone, he can do what he wants.*° Mor answered. °*True enough.*° The human said and ended the discussion.

After this interruption, Mor got to the library without further problems and asked a librarian about view-enhancing spells, preferably with low energy requirements. The librarian nodded and pointed Mor to a few books that might have such spells.

Mor and the human began to read and search until finally, a few hours later, the human cried out excitedly.

°*This one! That's just what I was looking for!*° The human told Mor.

°*How will this one help? Now that I look at it, it's just a really simple wind spell.*° Mor asked, puzzled.

°*Yes.. But it uses air to form a kind of lens, and with sunlight and the right magnification, I can show you something really incredible!*° The human explained, and Mor shrugged.

°*Ok? Then add that to the try-list for tomorrow.*° Mor said, confused.

°*Nice. Then the plan for tomorrow is to get wood, try what we can do with the elemental puppet spell, and then create a sun gun!*° The human said, confusing Mor even more.

°What's *a sun gun?*° He asked, but the human wouldn't tell.

Part 33

With their plan firmly in place, Mor's training could now resume. He spent his mornings absolving his morning exercises, followed up with a run. Orth accompanied Mor every other day when his muscle pains receded, but he could not keep up the whole distance. Still, Mor encouraged his friend not to give up and promised that Orth would see improvements soon.

Clare and Sahpnie continued their diet with Mor's support but were unhappy about how slow it was going. Clare complained that no change was even visible, but Mor, with the help of the human, explained to her that overdoing it would result in overachieving and going to the opposite extreme. A balanced diet is vital, and you must give your body time to adjust.

After class, Mor would retreat to his usual training room, but as he was the only one always using it, he asked a teacher for the key. To his surprise, he got it. Probably because he chose the most distant and oldest room available.

Now returning to the first day of his training, Mor acquired some fitting wood pieces from the isles carpentry, according to the human's description. He then locked the door and prepared.

°*Great, we got our wood. Now, what would you like to start with?*° The human asked.

°*Well, after you left me hanging yesterday, I want to see your sun gun.*° Mor demanded.

°*If you like. But then we need to go outside again, we need sunlight for that.*° The human explained, and Mor sighed.

°*Why didn't you say so earlier?*° He asked, annoyed.

°I didn't think that far at the moment?° The human offered as Mor reopened the training room door and walked to a bright spot.

°So what now?° Asked Mor.

°Use that wind spell, one side to the sun, and with the other, try to hit... ah.. let's just take this stone for now.° The human said.

°Okay?° Mor said, trying to follow the humans' instructions.

The first try was a failure, as the "lens" was rotated the wrong way, dispersing the sun rays instead of focusing them. But with a quick recast, Mor got it right. He focused a needle-thin point on the stone and watched in anticipation. After a few minutes of boredom, he got impatient and asked the human.

°How long does this take? I mean, this spell is not so exhausting, but still. Shouldn't something have happened?°

°Well, try touching the stone now,° the human said smugly and giggled as Mor grabbed the stone. The human expected at least a surprised reaction.

But their expectations were subverted as Mor picked up the stone and asked *°What now?°* *°What do you mean, what now?!°* The human asked incredulously.

°Isn't the stone hot?° The human asked further, and Mor shook his head.

°Not really? Maybe a little bit? So, what did you expect to happen?° Mor asked.

°It should have heated the stone so much that you couldn't just pick it up. I know you can start a fire with this technique!° The human explained incredulously.

°I thought you didn't have magic?° Mor asked.

°*We didn't! We used a tool for that!*° The human said. °*But why won't it work?*°

°*I don't know. Maybe you made an error?*° Mor offered, and the human let out a disappointed sigh.

°*Yeah, it seems like it. Maybe the sunlight was not strong enough, or the lens was not focusing right. Shit... I need to think about this some more. So let's shelf for now and try the other stuff.*° The human sounded very disappointed at this revelation.

Mor returned to the training room, locking the door again to give them privacy.

°*Well, want to try the puppet next?*° Mor asked, but the human just groaned in a kind of agreeing way.

Mor just shrugged and started the incantation, slowly building up the pupped. Step by step, it took on a humanoid form until it stood taller than Mor and was a lot bulkier. Mor had his eyes closed in concentration to keep the puppet together.

That did the trick to pull out the human from their earlier disappointment and ask. °*Can you change how it looks?*°

°*Yes,*° Mor groaned. °*But don't talk to me, this is hard!*°

The human shut up and instead watched in amazement how the puppet looked until he saw something.

°*Huh, what's that? Maybe I can follow this...*° The human mumbled.

°*I said please be quiet.*° Mor grumbled.

°*Oh! This is awesome! Mor, look!*° The human shouted, somehow sounding far away, and Mor could hear the rumbling and grinding of moving stones.

He slowly opened his eyes and was surprised when the puppet waved at him.

°*Look, I can move....Hurgh!*° The human exclaimed, getting interrupted as Mor's concentration wavered from the shock. The human was pulled forcefully out of the puppet and back to Mors' body, groaning in pain.

°*It.*° The human finished with a pained whimper.

°*How did you do that?!*° Mor asked.

°*First, Ow. Second, I don't know. I felt a sort of connection between you and the puppet and had the feeling, I just could walk over there. Nothing ventured, nothing gained, right?*° The human answered.

°*But that should be impossible! I was only concentrating on keeping the form intact. Moving it would have been beyond me! And it should have been beyond you!*° Mor explained hastily.

°*Why though? It felt just like moving a body.*° The human said.

°*Because. To move a puppet, you have to guide the magic energy. It needs to reform the connections and make it seem like a movement. There are no muscles or such things, only magic.*° Mor went on exasperated.

°*Wait! What?!*° The human asked, surprised.

°*You must have guided the magic energy I channeled.*° Mor explained.

°*But why now? I couldn't do it earlier, which was a big problem with our first plans!*° The human wanted to know.

°*I don't know, but maybe it has something to do with the continous nature of the puppet spell. We only tried for you to use my magic on your own. But now I provided it, and you seemingly redirected it to suit your needs.° Mor theorized.

°*That means?*° The human asked further.

°*That means we can use high-concentration continuous spells! I want to try it again with a simpler, less energy-demanding spell.*° Mor said.

Mor channeled a spell for a weak whirlwind, which is normally used to sweep the dust. He kept up the energy supply.

°*Now try to move it.*° Mor told the human who did just that.

°*I don't feel the same connection... There is something, but it feels like it wouldn't hold my weight?*° The human pondered.

°*Your weight? Do you even weigh something?*° Mor asked.

°*I don't think so, but it is just a feeling I have. Maybe it only works with something of higher energy demand?* ° The human mused.

°*Seems like it, but we have to try this another time. The puppet takes too much energy to do it too often,*° Mor said, and the human agreed.

°*Then, do you want to work on the weapons? Or should we first try to adapt Snow's technique for your reservoir?*° The human asked.

°*Let's work on the weapons first. They seemed easier to finish than a completely new technique.*° Mor chose.

At this, Mor sat down with the wooden rod the human had called a baton. Mor used simple spells to embed Snow's crystals into the wooden piece. Getting the fitting right still took a lot of time because he needed to ensure the crystals would not fall out after an attack. Finally, the human was satisfied, and Mor looked at his finished weapon. The final product was just over a meter long, just thick enough to hold it comfortably in his hands, and had all twenty-four crystals embedded on the upper third of its length.

°*Nice! It looks good. Now, let's give this a few practice swings and then call it a day.*° The human complimented.

Under the humans' tutilage, Mor practiced a few different swings and attacks. He tried quick onehanded strikes, heavy two-handed swings, and some thrusts, which might stun an opponent.

Like this, Mor and the humans spent their training days practicing with their magic baton, getting used to the earth puppet, trying to adapt Snow's technique, and, to the humans' disappointment, falling back on a higher-level air spell instead of their "sun gun."

The only annoyances on those days were Ranbor's followers, who would repeatedly plead and threaten Mor to apologize to Ranbor, but Mor always refused. This got to a boiling point after they tried to pressure Orth to "order his subordinate," and Orth put them in their place with very choice words.

After three weeks of all of this, just when Mor and Orth were on their morning run and bitching about Ranbors flunkies and their constant annoyance, an explosion shook the dormitory tower.

A rumbling thundercrack echoed through the whole school. Silencing the bitching of the boys and stunning them into surprised silence and indecision. Time seemed to stand still for a heartbeat, and then the rumbling of crumbling walls and the shattering of glass windows took over.

°*WHAT THE FUCK WAS THAT?!*° The human shouted in surprise while they could see the tower crumble, lean, and finally crash to the ground.

Part 34

As the silence slowly vanished, it was replaced by the screams of panicked students, the wailing of magic alarms, and the frantic shouts of teachers trying to regain a semblance of order and evacuate their charges.

After the explosion, a single figure hobbled through an empty corridor open to the sky, leaving bloody footprints on the floor and a smoldering ruin on their robes. Ranbor stumbled along, completely lost, wondering what had happened.

He had retreated to his room after the headmaster limited his magic output, cursing the Ice-kin and the peasant with every breath. And to make matters worse, the limiter sigil on his chest itched and burned. Still, no matter how much he scratched, it would not lessen his discomfort. Soon, it was utterly chaffed.

Then his subjects would come and try to get him out of his room, but Ranbor didn't want to. If he returned to class with his punishment active, he would be a laughingstock for everyone. Even the commoner would be able to overpower him.

But after he sent them away, they would just bring a teacher, which wouldn't change Ranbor's mind. Instead, it annoyed him greatly, and his hatred would fan a wrathful flame, getting stronger with each passing day. He began to imagine all the things he would do to everyone who defied him, and then it happened.

The dormitory tower on his level exploded in a thunderous fireball, throwing him across his room, charring his robe and flesh, and leaving him in a stunned, bleeding heap.

As he continued to wander the destroyed corridors, a "whump" vibrating through the floor caught his attention. A teacher teleported next to him, reaching out and saying something Ranbor could not understand.

The thundering clap of the explosion had taken his hearing. Still, the teacher's intent was clear. He wanted to get Ranbor to safety. With a relieved smile, Ranbor reached out to grasp the teacher's hand. A secondary explosion erupted before he could touch the teacher's outstretched hand, throwing him and the teacher in different directions. Ranbor was the lucky one. He landed on the smoldering carpet. The teacher, though, had no such luck. His position relative to the new explosion had thrown him against the walls, his neck now bent at an unnatural angle, his body mangled.

If Ranbor still had his hearing, he might have heard the audible crunch of a breaking spine. Shellshocked, Ranbors mind tried to protect him with madness. He laughed, silent to his destroyed hearing but sounding unhinged to everyone who might hear him.

He slowly got up, returning to his slow, unthinking wandering, leaving a trace of bloody, smoldering footprints behind him. Ranbor only knew he needed to get out.

°*What's going on?!*° The human asked, but Mor could give no answer.

Mor stood there stunned, unable to comprehend the situation. Orth was doing the same.

°*HEY! Snap out of it!*° The human shouted!

Finally, Mor turned to Orth, looking at his shocked friend, his brain finally catching up with the situation.

"Orth! What is going on?" He asked, but only Orth blinked in confusion.

Mor shook Orth, getting him out of his stupor.

"I... don't know." The noble answered.

"The girls," he then mumbled.

"What?" Mor asked.

"This is where the noble dorms are. Saphine's room is up there, and so is mine," Orth said, still unbelieving.

°*Shit!*° The human exclaimed.

°*We need to find out what's going on. But what should we do with Orth?*° Mor asked.

°*Drag him along. We need to find a teacher or someone!*° The human ordered, and finally, Mor acted.

They pulled a stunned, mumbling Orth along, frantically searching for a teacher or someone who might know what was happening. They got closer and closer to the now-beheaded tower, finding the first victims of this atrocity. Students hurt by debris were sitting around sobbing, crying, or in stunned silence.

°*We need to help them.*° Mor said.

We can't help them all! The best thing we can do is find Adept Amber for them, but we should save our energy. We don't know for what we might need it.° The human said.

°*But, we could heal some!*° Mor countered.

°*Yes, but if the infirmary is obstructed, we need all the power we can get. It's stupid to heal some and then have to abandon everyone else because we can't get the experienced healers. We need to stay safe, and that means saving our energy.*° The human explained.

Mor nodded, feeling helpless, but forging on with Orth following him like in a trance.

The headmaster tried to regain control of the situation. He was shouting orders at the teachers, searching out stuck students, and at the same time trying to find out what had happened.

"I want to know what this was? Were we attacked by a monstrosity?" He demanded to know from a panicked teacher, who just shrugged at him.

"I don't know!" she answered, then she was sent away again to get more students to safety.

"Get everyone into the gathering hall!" The headmaster ordered. "And where are the healing adepts?" He demanded to know.

Everything was a chaotic mayhem, and nobody could tell him anything. The headmaster cursed.

"Why must it happen at this time? We don't know who was still in their rooms and who was already off to breakfast or meeting before class," he pondered to no avail.

He shook his head. Panic gripped him, but he couldn't let himself be consumed by it. He needed to stay calm and make the right decisions.

Clare was bent over Sahpines' motionless body. They were just on their way to meet up with the boys and get breakfast together when suddenly a loud crunch was followed by the groaning of stressed stone. They were lucky, as they were already on the stairs downstairs, but unlucky, as the stairs fractured and crumbled, dropping both girls and stone debris down a floor.

Clare was protected, by sheer luck, from the falling debris by Saphine, but the other girl was bruised and hurt, half buried in degree, one of her arms pointing in a strange direction.

Clare did everything she could with her healing magic to keep Saphine alive. While she concentrated, she couldn't hear the footsteps on the upper floor until it was too late.

Part 35

Mor and Orth, who finally overcame his stupor, rushed towards the infirmary. They ran past the destruction of the fallen tower and past mumbling students. While running, they noticed a teacher trying to get some shellshocked students to move to a secure area.

°*STOOOP!*° The human shouted, and Mor slithered to a halt, Orth crashing into the suddenly stopping Mor.

°*What?*° Mor asked.

°*The teacher! Ask him what's up!*° The human ordered

°*Teacher?*° Mor asked.

°*Yeah. You just ran by him!*° The human said, exasperated.

°*I didn't notice! I was just concentrating on running!*° Mor said.

°*Thought as much. You were too fixated on your task to notice your surroundings. That's why I stopped you.*° The human said, and Mor nodded.

"Why did we stop? We need to find someone who knows what's going on and get to the infirmary!" a heavy-breathing Orth asked.

"Yes! We just ran past a teacher." Mor told his friend, and they both backtracked.

The teacher was still trying to get the stunned students to move, but no matter what he said or tried, they would just stare at him uncomprehendingly.

"Come on! Stand up. You need to get to the gathering hall. It will be save there!" He tried without success. Shaking the staring student.

Mor and Orth walked up to the teacher, and as Orth was still out of breath, Mor would do the talking.

"Sir! Can you tell us what's going on?" He asked the frantic man.

"What are you two doing here? Get to the gathering hall!" the teacher shouted at them.

"No! We can help. Please tell us what is happening!" Mor said decisively.

"What's the status of the infirmary? What about the students who were in the tower?" Orth suddenly interjected, but the teacher only shook his head, tired and sad.

"We are trying to get everyone out, but many are badly hurt. I don't know about the infirmary. But something must have happened, as we couldn't get in contact with a single healing adept. Still, this is a concern for us teachers. You students should just get to safety. Leave this to the grown-ups." The teacher told them, but Mor shook his head.

"We can't do that. Orth and I will help. The most important thing for now is looking at the infirmary's status. We can do that while you can save more students," Mor said, and the teacher thought for a moment, looking at the surrounding destruction.

"Orth? The Obsidian boy?" He asked, and Orth nodded.

"Okay, I agree, but promise, get to the gathering hall if you see something you can't handle. For all we know, a monstrosity could run rampant," the teacher said, sighing.

"Then we will take a look at the infirmary," Mor said, and both boys took off again, this time with a slower pace.

"Do you think it is a monstrosity?" Orth asked as they jogged along.

"I don't know. I hope not, but what else could it be?" Mor said.

°*I have a bad feeling about this.*° Added the human.

***

The headmaster was still trying to get a complete picture, but the information was sparse. Many students and teachers were missing, and they still had no information on the infirmary.

He cursed, and his thoughts went to the two teachers he had sent earlier to inspect the infirmary. "Why were they taking so long?" he wondered.

***

The entity laughed, slowly walking after a scrambling person. It was happy to finally be free, to finally, after so much time, be able to follow its nature.

The running person stumbled, fell down, and started to cry. "Why?" The person asked, tears running down their dirty face. The entity smiled in ecstasy. It loved those faces. It slowly bent down, grabbing its victim's face between its thumb and forefinger. Their victim cried out in pain and struggled as their cheeks got burned from the heat. Then, the cry was suddenly silenced as the entity burnt its victim to a crisp. "Why?" It asked, grinning wider than anything had any right to do.

"Because it's my nature."

The entity sauntered on, looking for a new victim to burn.

***

Ranbor stumbled after his foot got caught in something. He fell, his hands crunching into something black and burnt on the ground. In shock, he slowly retracted his hands and looked at what he had just fallen into.

His look conveyed only confusion as he tried to get the dirt off his hands. The dirt from this strange lump of black something. He slowly got back up again and followed the bloody, smoldering footprints before him like in a trance, hoping they would lead him to safety.

***

Mor and Orth finally reached the infirmary and saw the destruction wrought.

°*What did happen here?!*° The human exclaimed, while Mor just stared, and Orth gasped in shock.

"The tower. It crashed through the ceiling." Mor said, looking around.

"The adepts!" Orth shouted.

Both boys ran forward, trying to take a closer look, as they suddenly heard someone call out to them and a second voice sobbing hysterically.

"Hey, you boys! I need your help!" the first voice shouted, and the boys walked over.

The picture before them was a strange one, as they were met with two teachers, one of them holding the other. The teacher being held was wailing in horrific hysteria, while the other just looked helpless.

"What's going on here!" Orth demanded to know. "Why are you just sitting here?"

"Well," the calmer teacher said. "We were sent here by the headmaster to look at the situation, but just when we decided to remove the debris. Then suddenly, Kyn here acted out. I wanted to calm her, but nothing I said could get anything out of her, so I decided to clear up this mess myself, but every time I let go of her and tried to channel my magic, she would cling and wail.

Completely destroying my concentration." She stroked the wailing woman's hair, trying fruitlessly to calm her down.

"Okay, what can we do?" Mor asked.

"You need to take her to the gathering hall. She's not fit to help anymore, and I don't know what her problem is. We need to get her to safety. Then I can get rid of all that junk." The teacher explained.

The boys looked at each other for a second, then at the wailing Kyn, and nodded in silent agreement.

"You take her. You teachers can move faster than us. We can get rid of the debris. I'm an Earth affinity mage. We can do this." Orth said, but the teacher disagreed.

"This is no job for students. Do as I say!" She ordered, trying to untangle herself from the crying mess that her colleague was.

°*I don't think she quite gets the situation. This Kyn teacher will keep clinging until she has calmed down,*° the human said.

°*Well, we could force her. She is probably a lot weaker than us.*° Mor said.

°*Yeah. Probably, but do you really want to deal with someone hysterical who can summon a fireball or something else? The best thing is to just let her.*° The human layed out, and Mor winced.

The teacher finally freed herself from Kyn's grasp. She tried to get her to go with the boys, but Kyn would just cry and shout in hysteria, conjuring up a duststorm as soon as she was let go. Orth tried to intervene and moved to calm the woman, anchoring himself to the ground, but she wouldn't listen.

With a desperate shove, Mor pushed the other women to the crying Kyn, under loud protest, mind you, but that did the trick. As

Kyn could hold on to the other teacher, the dust storm receded, and calmness settled in.

°*Good thinking.*° The human praised.

°*It was a gamble.*° Mor answered.

"You take her. We will look into what's going on with the infirmary," Mor ordered, and finally, the teacher nodded, defeated.

"Be safe, boys. I will be back as soon as possible or send help." She said, dragging the wailing woman away from the destruction to a more intact space. With a silent "pop," she was gone.

"Let's get to work. We need to free the entrance!" Mor said, and they got to work, shifting away debris and, in Orth's case, crushing bricks to powder. Mor was still saving as much energy as possible, only using some when shifting a wooden beam.

***

Amber was cursing her luck. She and the other adepts were fine, but the door wouldn't open, and the rumbling had cracked the masonry. In addition, they could not leave by teleport, as the supporting runic circles were "cracked." It might still be possible, but she deemed it too dangerous to try it. Still, if no one came soon, they might have to take the risk.

"Why is no one coming?" She asked, and another Adept shrugged, trying not to panic.

"Amber! We need to teleport right now! There could be hurt students outside!" Another added.

"I told you no! Your safety is also important. If you get hurt by this, you can't help anyone!" She chided.

"I don't care! I want out of here!" The other said, and before Amber could stop the idiot youth, he finished his incantation and was gone with a sickening crunch instead of the usual "pop" or even the less controlled "whump."

"Do you think he did it?" The other Adept asked Amber, who looked concerned.

"I honestly don't know. I hope so." Amber sighed.

***

Just as Mor shifted another beam, a crunching sound occurred, and the human called out in alarm.

°*Doge!*° The human ordered, and Mor threw himself aside just in time to evade a bloody ball of crunched something.

"What is that?" Mor asked, and Orth looked in shock.

"I don't know?" He answered.

°*You also don't want to.*° The human stated, just as it dawned on the boys.

Mor grew pale and retreated to a corner, emptying his stomach at the realization. Orth didn't get that far. He just turned around, trying to hold back the bile with his hand and ending up puking through the gaps of his fingers.

After a few moments of calming themselves and trying to ignore the bloody clump, they returned to work. They worked more frantic, unable to concentrate on any spells but doing anything to prevent their attention from returning to the crushed body. Finally, they could see the door, blocked by the debris. They made only a small gap in all the rubble, just enough to let someone climb over and out, but they were now standing in front of another problem.

"How do we open this up?" Mor asked, shaken.

"I don't know. It opens outward." Orth answered likewise.

"Can't you just destroy it with your earth magic?" Mor answered, but Orth shook his head.

"Can't concentrate right now. Every time I close my eyes, I..." Orth answered, forcing down another raising of bile.

°*How about you?*° The human asked.

°*Same as Orth, the second I concentrate, the pictures flood my brain, and my concentration is gone.*° Mor answered, getting slightly greenfaced.

°*Then no choice! Let's kick it with your strength!*° The human ordered.

°*How can you stay so calm?!*° Mor shouted.

°*Don't know? But remember, I'm probably also dead, so something like this doesn't seem to shake me,*° The human said.

°*I can't.*° Mor whimpered.

°*It's fine. I will do it,*° The human said, and using Mors's body, they kicked with everything that lean body had to offer.

Amber looked up as loud bangs came from the door and walked over quickly.

"Who's there?!" She shouted.

"Amber?" Came the response of a familiar voice.

"Mor?" She asked back.

"We can't remove all the rubble. Can you somehow destroy the door?" The boy shouted back.

Amber almost scolded herself because she hadn't thought of that.

"Yes, get away!" She ordered, and the boys scrambled away.

Amber concentrated on her magic and let the door fall out of its frame. She only had to remove the holdings from the wall. Amber could make out the dirty and scraped-up forms of two pale and shaken boys as the door fell inwards. Still, she was delighted to see them.

Part 36

"Headmaster! We have new information." A panting teacher shouted and continued to make his report.

"Miss Pyrith and Miss Kunzy returned from the infirmary."

"Very good. What do they have to report?" The headmaster asks.

"Well, Miss Kunzy is hysterical and completely out of it. We are not sure what happened to her. Miss Pyrith told us it just happened suddenly. In addition, she reports that the entrance to the infirmary is blocked." The teacher went on.

"Why didn't they do something about it?!" The headmaster interrupted. "Bring me to them!" The reporting teacher nodded and led the headmaster to a secluded corner. There, he saw both women, one stroking the hair of the other, who seemed to be sleeping. He could see some streaks on her face, seemingly from crying, and her eyes looked puffed.

"WHAT!" The headmaster started to shout but got shushed by the awake Pyrith.

"Quiet, she finally fell asleep." She whispered.

"What are you doing here?! I sent you to get the status from the infirmary!" The headmaster continued in a stern whisper.

"Yes, and I told it already. The infirmary is blocked by debris. I don't know why the Adepts can't teleport out or if something worse happened. But just as I wanted to clear it, Kunzy here went hysterical and ruined my concentration." Miss Pyrith explained. "Then why didn't you return immediately?" The headmaster chided.

"Because I thought I could still do something, and at first, it looked like it, as two boys made their way to me. I immediately instructed them to get Kunzy to safety, but this was a bad idea. So, those two decided to get a better look at the infirmary. And if that idiot next to you had only a bit of intelligence, he would already have sent help for those boys! Like I asked him to." She went on.

The other teacher started defending himself, but the headmaster silenced him.

"We will discuss that later! Now get going!" He ordered, and the teacher rushed away, only to be stopped by an elderly voice.

***

Mor scrambled into the infirmary, followed by Orth, and both broke down in mostly relieved tears, but those also entailed a bit of something akin to horror. Amber instantly reacted, got them some blankets, and looked at their hands.

In shock, she recognized their dirty, scraped, and wound-covered hands.

"Did you dig with your hands?" She asked, trying to keep a calm voice.

Mor looked at her and nodded.

"At first, Orth got rid of the stones, and I used my magic to remove everything else, but then... and because of... we had to remove the rest with our hands. We needed to get you." Mor tried to explain in a shaky voice.

Amber quickly glimpsed at the other boy, who got even more pale and pressed his lips together.

"What happened?" She asked carefully.

"It... He.... She... It was so much blood...." Mor stuttered, and Orth tried his best to get the recurring pictures out of his head.

Amber nodded towards another adept, and with a few head jerks, she got the adept to look at what had the boys so shaken. The other adept crawled out of the hole the boys had dug and noticed the crumpled remains of someone on the ground. She had to hold back a horrified scream and quickly crawled back.

The adept leaned down to Amber, who was still tending to the boys, and whispered.

"It seems like there was a failed teleport attempt, and with how shaken those two are, it wasn't long ago. Meaning it's probably Adept Amborin." She said, and Amber nodded.

"It's fine boys. You saw something bad happen, and naturally, you reacted like this. You just saw someone die with a failed teleport. This is also why you must be careful with spells like that." Amber explained to Orth and Mor.

°*Listen to her. It's not your fault. It was just bad luck, but remember, you must get out of this. You need to be able to protect your friends, right? Wouldn't all that hard work be for naught if you just give in to horror and panic right now?*° The human asked, calm and soothing, and Mor took a deep breath, trying to steel himself.

°*Good man, after all this is over, you can cry and panic all you like. But until this crisis is over, we need to be able to act.*° The human added.

°*You're right, still... I don't know if I can.*° Mor answered.

°*I know you can. I believe in you. You are stronger than that.*° The human reinforced, and finally, Mor nodded.

"Thank you, Amber. It was just horrifying how it almost dropped on me." Mor said, still shaky but doing everything to fight down the horror. "Dropped on you?!" She asked, shocked.

"Yes, I could just get out of the way before it would have hit me." Mor nodded, and Orth took a sharp breath at the memory, trying not to puke again.

Amber ruffled Mor's head.

"And you two still continued on? Now I understand how your hands ended up like this. Come on, let's fix that up first." Amber said.

"Yes, we needed to get you. Many students are hurt, and you are the best healers." Orth mumbled and got a ruffle of his own.

"I'm proud of you. You two did very well. You are real heroes!" Amber told them, and both seemed to latch on to this, regaining a bit of confidence.

"But now you need to be brave again. We can't teleport out of here, so we need to get out and see if the sigils outside are fine." Amber explained, and again, both boys turned a shade paler, but to their credit, both nodded.

"The teleport things should be fine. Another teacher already left earlier." Mor said.

"We were told to gather in the gathering hall. It seems the teachers are getting all the students there." Orth added.

"Very good. You are very helpful. Now, let's fix up your hands and then get moving." Amber said, but the boys shook their heads.

"We can do this later. It's more important to get you to the most badly hurt." Orth said.

"If you say so. But then I will take care of your wounds. And I will allow no protest then!" Amber said, but Mor still opened his mouth in protest.

"I can..." He began, but Amber shushed him softly.

"No, I need to thank you two. I will take care of you." She said, and Mor nodded.

°*Let her do this. You need to accept the thanks. It will help you.*° The human said.

After the first adept clambered out of the infirmary, taking a blanket with him. The boys followed soon after, and luckily, the adept had enough foresight to cover the awful on the floor. Therefore, their reaction was less extreme than the first time.

The human put one of Mor's hands on Orth's shoulder the whole time, and both boys gathered strength from that touch. While Amber nodded at that proudly. Those two would come out fine after this was over.

Finally, the adepts invoked the teleport, and with a bunch of "pops," the group appeared in the gathering hall, just to hear the headmaster order the next teacher to go find them.

"No need, headmaster. Those two freed us, and we are ready to help." Amber said, ushering Mor and Orth to a safe spot next to Pyrith, who nodded a thankful greeting.

"You did it. Great work, boys." She said.

Amber and her adepts quickly got to work, healing the students with the worst wounds until she finally got back to the two boys and took care of their hands. To no one's surprise, both had fallen asleep from exhaustion, covered in their blankets. Then, at Amber's touch, Orth awoke and asked.

"Where's Saphine and Clare?"

Part 37

After Orth had spoken his question, Amber ruffled his hair and said.

"I go ask. You need to rest up. Healers orders."

But now sleep was something that would not come to Orth anymore. He had first nodded off because of the exhaustion, and therefore, it was pleasantly dreamless, but now his memory showed him pictures of that bloody, crunched body again.

At Orth's fidgeting, Mor also awoke, looking around a bit confused.

"Did we fall asleep?" He asked, and Orth nodded.

°*Yes. Exhaustion and shock got the better of you.*° The human added.

"Amber is going to ask about the girls," Orth said, and Mor sat up a bit straighter.

"Aren't they here?" He asked, looking around.

"I don't know. I hope they are safe." Orth answered.

While the boys were getting more nervous by the second, Amber walked right to the headmaster and demanded to know where the two students were. The headmaster almost wanted to shout at her, but he thought better of it. Instead, he sent her to the teacher, who was keeping track and trying to regain a semblance of order in the huddle of students.

"Miss Amber, what can I do for you? I'm very busy right now, getting a sense of who's where." He greeted her.

"I need the status of two students, one Saphine and one Clare," she said calmly but sternly.

The teacher sighed.

"Just a moment, I need to look over my lists. Do you have the family names and years of those students?" He asked, and Amber shook her head.

"I don't. But they are probably first-year girls." She answered.

"That, at least, limits it a bit." He mumbled, looking through his lists.

"Let's see. We still have twenty-five first years missing, so let's look there first," he continued. While the teacher was looking, the headmaster came closer, wanting to ask Amber about the hurt students.

"Miss Amber, how are we on injuries?" He asked her.

"Everyone here is through the worst. We only healed the most serious wounds for now to save our energy for emergencies. We will still get to every student, but it will take a while. Two of my adepts are seeing to that right now. They are in a rotation of healing and regaining energy." She reported, and the headmaster nodded.

"So, no losses here?" He wanted to confirm.

"Yes. We could get to everyone in time. Now it's only nonfatal injuries." Amber confirmed.

"Found them!" The teacher said suddenly.

"Miss Saphine Sapphire and Clare Celestyne! They are... still missing..." He added and flinched as the headmaster rounded on him.

"HOW ARE THEY STILL MISSING? HOW MANY ARE?" The headmaster shouted.

"Were they missing twenty-five? Of the first years, a hundred overall?" the teacher mumbled, cowed.

"But. We already have three teachers on that, who are tasked with getting the students out of the collapsed tower," he added defensively.

"How long are those gone?" The headmaster asked, skeptical.

"Just about half an hour now! They are a bit late, but if the teleport runes are destroyed, it might take longer than expected." The teacher explained, and the headmaster took a deep breath, trying to calm himself down.

"Who did you send?" He asked in a forced calm.

"We sent... Ah here!... Miss Amenist, Mister Pietersiten, and Mister Kunzy. All of them solid mages." The teacher answered, and Amber nodded.

"I know Pietersiten. He has a good talent for healing magic. Good choice." She agreed, but the headmaster looked over where the two boys sat when the last name was mentioned.

He didn't look at them but at the two figures next to them and cursed.

"How are you such a pencil pusher?! You know we have a hysterical Miss Kunzy sitting over there, and you never! Not even once! Thought that this might have something to do with her soulpartner?" The headmaster really wanted to scream and punch this administrative idiot.

The teacher looked confused and said, "I don't understand," but Amber caught up much faster. "Hysterical, and her soul-partner is overdue?" She asked.

"Seems like it?" the teacher answered, and instantly, the headmaster and Amber were rounding on him.

"HOW DID YOU NOT CONNECT THIS?!" They shouted at the teacher, who only wanted to escape this situation.

The headmaster let out a pained sigh, draining his aggression away.

"We need to assume that all three teachers are dead. Whatever destroyed the tower may still be up there threatening the cut-off students. Get our most combat-capable teachers together. We need to get up there!" the headmaster ordered, and finally, the administrative teacher reacted. Quickly, a team of mages was assembled, including the headmaster himself and an adept of Amber's retinue.

"We have some missing students, and some may be alive. In addition, whatever is responsible for this atrocity may still be in that tower. We will go up there and get everyone out, but remember, we probably can't teleport back out. Keep alert. We don't know what destroyed the tower. It might be a monstrosity. That means we will go in as four teams with two members each." The headmaster ordered.

"Now for team composition, Miss Amtis will go with me. Miss Prehn and Miss Spinel, you are a team. Miss Sugilty and Mister Malachy, you will build the next. And finally, you are the final team, Mister Magnesitor and Miss Hematon. Priority is getting everyone out! Destroying whatever is rampaging is secondary. And stay safe!" He continued to a gaggle of nodding teachers. With a bunch of "pops," the eight of them were gone, reappearing with a "whump" back on the top of the destroyed tower.

"Fan out, find everyone you can." The headmaster ordered, and all of them scattered.

***

Clare was breathing heavily, her energy was almost drained, and the headaches were brutal. Still, she couldn't give up now! Saphine depended on her healing power. Clare's desperate attempts were suddenly interrupted by a voice calling out.

"I found some! Are you alright?" It called.

Clare looked up, tears in her eyes, finally noticing the woman looking over the broken edge of the staircase. Clare wanted to stay calm and answer, but her emotions got the better of her, and a crying voice answered.

"Saphine... I'm not powerful enough." Clare howled.

Miss Sugilty recognized the precarious situation.

"Mal, get over here and help me!" She called back.

She dropped down to the two girls, and the other teacher was close on her heels.

"We need to get the stones away," Malachy said, and without waiting, he turned them all to dust. "Couldn't you wait with that?! What if this destabilized the staircase?" Sugilty chided the other teacher, who just shrugged.

"It couldn't. I controlled first. I'm not stupid," he countered, and Sugilty let out an exasperated sigh. "And you didn't tell us?" She started but then waved it off, instead concentrating on Saphines injuries.

"We need to get her stable and then out of here. This is something only the adepts can cure." She said, letting her magic flow to at least stabilize the most grievous injuries. Malachy kneeled next to Clare and laid his arm around her.

"Good job. You saved her." He said soothingly, but Clare just threw herself against his body, crying. "I got her!" Sugilty shouted. But we need to be quick now! I don't know how long my treatment will last."

Malachy nodded, got up, carefully picked up the hurt Saphine, and with a gigantic leap, he was gone.

"I really wish he would communicate a bit more." Sugilty sighed but embraced the stunned Clare and flew after her colleague.

***

There was a commotion in the gathering hall as all available healing adepts rushed to the entrance, and Mor and Orth got up to take a look. They finally reached the building entrance and the cluster of nosy students. There, they found a sidelined Clare.

"Clare!" both boys shouted, and she raised her head, tearing up and charging them. Orth got hit by her almost tackle, being the one further forward and, therefore, the first target. The force of Clare's impact threw them down to the floor. Mor just got on his knees to get down to them. After a few short moments, Mor got a hug himself.

"Clare! What's happened? Where's Saphine?" Orth asked, and Clare started to sob again. "The adepts... I tried... But I couldn't." She sobbed, and both boys looked in concern at the wall of bodies.

"Calm down. Now that she's with the adepts, she will make it. Saphine is more tenacious than you think." Orth tried to calm Clare while she continued to cling to him.

"I go ask!" Mor decided and tried to force his way through the mass but couldn't make headway. °*Calm down. She will be fine. Remember, she isn't that malnourished girl anymore, even if they don't see that. Her body has now reserves,*° the human said calmingly.

°*But I need to know!*° Mor complained.

°*She's alive, or the adepts would have already stopped treatment. And that would be pretty obvious. Let them work, and calm down. Saphine will need support from all three of you.*° The human chided, and finally, Mor nodded and returned to his friends in defeat.

Part 38

Soon after Saphine and Clare were brought to the gathering hall, the teachers brought in more students. The healing adepts did what they could, and in a feat of monumental magic power, all the students brought were also saved. What was not communicated to the students was that not every missing student had been found, and a lot were still missing without hope of being found alive. After Saphine was released from the healer's attention, her unconscious form was brought to Orth, Clare, and Mor. The three friends used the boys' loaned blankets to make Saphine more comfortable. They marveled at their luck, that everyone in their little group was still alive.

***

The headmaster was gathering his little group for a last pass in the hope of finding a few students they had missed when they heard the silent splat splat of footsteps and a voice.

"Hello, hello. Amethyne~" The entity smiled broadly. "Just the one I was looking for." It giggled.

The headmaster turned around. "Mister Ruby, why?" he asked.

"Hhheadmaster... help... please." The now Ranbor thing croaked.

"Shhh... Stay quiet. The adults are talking." The entity shushed.

The headmaster stared in disgust at this creature, and with a simple nod, he telepathically conveyed his plan to his strike team.

"We need to capture it! We might be able to reverse whatever Ranbor has done to himself." He conveyed

"I'm against this. We need to put it down." Magnesitor disagreed.

"I'm with the headmaster," Amtis said.

"I can hear you ~" The entity interrupted their telepathic communication.

It started to laugh eerily.

"It's very naughty to exclude someone you are speaking to." It continued.

"What are you?" The headmaster asked, giving an almost unnoticeable nod to Malachy, who was already shuffling over.

Malachy acted fast, catching the entity in a stony grasp and leaving only its head free, just as Amethyne created a sphere of vacuum around this stony prison.

The entity laughed silently, stopping after a second and saying something. Then it got annoyed that no one could hear it, its stolen body slowly running out of air.

The headmaster smiled, giving a grateful nod to Malachy.

"Good job, it was easier than expected. Now we just need to keep this up until it passes out."

Malachy nodded and answered. "No problem."

But just as they let their attention slip for a heartbeat, the eyes of the entity lit up, and Malachy burst into flames, letting out a silent scream of pain and agony until, a moment later, his charred ruin of a body crumpled to the floor. The shocked silence was deafening as the entity continued to laugh silently in its prison.

The shock broke the headmaster's concentration, and air rushed back to the entity.

"That was not nice." It said.

"Though I need to applaud you, depriving me of air was a good idea. Well, it would have been if I needed air at all." It cackled.

It looked at the others of the strike team and smiled. Amtis flinched at the piercing gaze while the others tried to stay calm.

"Now, who's next? ~" The entity asked sweetly.

The headmaster again moved first, now supported by the remaining six. Everyone unleashed a stream of water magic, cutting, drowning, and battering the stationary creature. This barrage of attacks generated an obscuring wall of steam, and while four of them kept up the pressure, the headmaster and Sugilty combined their power, creating a lance of ice and hurling it into the fray. The strike team was rewarded with a pained scream of pure fury, followed by an exploding wave of steam and heat, tumbling them around. The entity walked out of the carnage, grimacing, with the melting lance of ice lodged in its body.

"You are DEAD!" It raged.

"I wanted to save you for last, Amethyne! I wanted to be polite and show my thanks because, without your limiter, I might have never amassed enough power to completely take over! But that's over now! You hurt me!" it continued to wail.

As the teachers tried to get back on their feet after being thrown down, the entity fixed Amtis with its fiery gaze. She just had enough time to throw up a defense of water, but because no one was able to support her, it got broken a heartbeat later. With this, the second member of the strike team was incinerated and turned into ash.

Any trace of amusement was wiped from the entity's face, replaced with a hateful expression. It walked slowly to where the headmaster had fallen, flames generating in its hands, forming long whips of licking heat. It cracked its flaming whips across Sugilty's face as she tried to buy her colleagues time to get back in the fight. Inflicting a gnarling burn scar across Sugilty's formerly unmarred face and dropping her in a cry of pain.

Amethyne scrambled back to his feet, reengaging with a barrage of vacuum slices, but this would be no more than a distraction, and that was all it was meant to be. He just wanted to give the remaining teachers enough time to disengage and get away. This thing was too much for their power. They would need more mages.

The remaining teachers got up, Hematon limping over to Sugilty, trying to help her. The others were getting ready to rejoin the battle. The headmaster recognized this error and shouted a warning.

"Get away! Get help!" he ordered, stunning the teachers into indecision, which would cost them dearly. Hematon was first to react, trying to get Sugilty to safety. This, in turn, drew the entity's attention to the fleeing woman. With a double lash, both fire whips caught around both of their necks, and with an audible snap, the entity pulled back, snapping both their necks in the process. This, in turn, enraged the remaining combatants, and they redoubled their efforts. However, with the entity's countering barrage, they didn't find enough time to use their most effective ice attack anymore. So they just did what they could. The teachers tried everything, and a few of their attacks had an effect. They wounded "Ranbor's" body, weakening the entity, but as one after another ran out of energy and, in turn, was burned to a crisp, the victor was set.

The headmaster, the last alive of his entourage, fell to his knees into the dust that was once his colleagues, looking up at the Ranbor thing in defiance. It, in turn, cocked its head, the broad smile returning to its face.

"Seems I was too much for you. Funny how this all fell together. You burned out before me!~" It said.

"Now, my dear friend, tell me. Where are the others?" It asked, the headmaster silently shaking his head in defiance.

"Oh! I know. Every time I have to ask, I will hurt you," the entity said like it had the best idea ever. The headmaster's eyes opened in panic as the hand of the entity was placed on his chest, burning a hand-shaped wound through his robes and onto his skin. He screamed in pain, still not telling anything. But the entity now had time and patience. It would get the information, and if the headmaster croaked before that, it would just have to go look. Right now, it wanted to enjoy inflicting pain.

***

Sometime after the last student was dropped off, a wounded student brought in a badly burnt figure. The adepts instantly wanted to help, but something in the student's gaze held them back. Maybe it was the eyes burning like wildfire or the smile broader than what should have been possible.

"Look what I found~" The student was saying.

"Now, now, where is my good friend? Saphine!~" Ranbor continued.

"We have something to settle before I fulfill my heart's desires!"

Part 39

The Ranbor-thing smiled into the stunned silence until, finally, some teachers encroached on the creature.

"Ah, ah, ah!" it cautioned, lifting its victim a bit and forcing the attention to the body it held. "Stay back. Your precious headmaster is still alive, but if you intervene, he won't be for long," the entity said.

"Now! If you would be kind, I must discuss something with little Miss Sapphire." It continued. The teachers stopped in indecision, trying to find a way out of this situation without risking anyone's life. Amber tried hard to read the headmaster's body. Trying to verify if this Ranbor thing was lying, and to her relief and horror, she had to recognize that the headmaster was indeed alive, if barely. She whispered her discovery to a nearby teacher, who nodded in turn.

"We must treat the headmaster fast, or he will die." She urged.

All the while, Mor, Orth, and Clare tried to make sense of the building situation.

"Is that Ranbor?" Mor asked.

"I don't know? Looks like it?" Clare added.

"What did that idiot get himself into now?" Orth asked.

°*This looks bad. He wants Saphine.*° The human interrupted.

°*Yes, but she's still out. Also, I won't hand her over. That asshole is entirely unhinged. We can't even begin to guess what he would do to her.*° Mor answered.

The burning eyes of the Ranbor-thing snapped to Mor, and the smile grew unnaturally wider. *"There you are!~ Little Miss Saphine is unconscious? Too bad. But this makes it easier for me~* "It whispered into Mor's mind.

°*Did it hear us?*° The human asked.

°*Impossible. No one can hear you. You are in my mind!*° Mor said.

"*Don't be such a bore. Of course, I can hear you. You are the same as little poor Ranbor here. Though I must wonder... Why do you let yourself be imprisoned?*" The entity asked, and Mor took a surprised breath.

°*Fuck off.*° The human growled.

"*Now, now. Don't be that abrasive.*" It answered.

"Mor, is everything all right?" Orth answered, at Mors surprised breath.

"This thing is dangerous. It isn't Ranbor anymore." Mor whispered.

"How do you know that?" Orth asked.

"Trust me. Not even Ranbor is that stupid and powerful." Mor continued, and Orth nodded.

The Ranbor-thing stood there, putting a finger on its chin and then snapping it as if it had a brilliant idea.

"I know!" It shouted happily. "If you give me the Peasant and my dear friend Saphine, I will give you what's left of your precious headmaster, AND you all get to live."

A scared murmuring went through the gathered students, but the teachers took a more aggressive stance.

"We won't negotiate with something like you. You can't have either!" one of them shouted, gathering his energy for a massive spell. The entity's gaze snapped to the teacher, its eyes brightening creepyly. And like the others before him, the offending teacher instantly combusted into a pillar of flame, dropping dead a heartbeat later.

"Seems I needed to make an example of one of you. Now, let's all be cordial, or I will end your precious headmaster for real." It chuckled.

A gasp went through the gathering hall as the horror of this sunk in. Some of the teachers clenched their fists in helpless despair, while some students tried to get as far away as possible. Mor ground his teeth, slowly standing up, while Orth tried to hold him down.

"He wants me," Mor growled.

"No! Stay here. He will kill you!" Orth tried to reason.

"I can't endanger everyone. It's not my style. I just need to beat that thing down into the ground." Mor tried to encourage himself and calm Orth.

"Then I will help you!" said Orth, also getting up, but Mor shook his head.

"You need to keep Saphine safe." He disagreed.

°*He's right, though. This one will kill us,*° *the* human said, and again, the Ranbor thing gave Mor an evil smile and nodded.

°*Yes, probably. But what else can we do except fight? If we run, it will kill Saphine and rampage through the whole school until it gets us, same if we want to hide. I don't want to die, but if taking the slim chance at victory will stop further atrocities, I will take it. I won't cower while others die in front of me.*° Mor said, trying to sound confident.

°*Welp, no choice then. I'm in!*° the human said, and a nervous smile crept over Mors' face. The Ranbor-thing grinned and gave a mocking bow as Mor walked forward. Mor passed scared students and teachers who tried to dissuade him but could not stop him.

"Look at that. The peasant is no coward. Well, I wanted to keep you for last because my generous donor really wanted you to die last after you pissed yourself in fear." It tapped its chin again in thought. "But I guess you wouldn't allow me to finish off Saphine first, right?"

Mort shook his head, "Forget it. True, she always looked down on me, but at least she tried to be a friend. And I won't just hand over friends to their death, more so if she can't protect herself." The entity laughed at this.

"Look at him, everyone! While the nobles cower in fear, and the teachers shake in their boots, the peasant stands against me!" It shouted.

"Then let's play~~." It purred.

Mor took out his baton, took a deep breath, and concentrated on the crystals, one after another. He looked at the Ranbor thing and pointed at the crisp body, still in its grasp. "Hand over the headmaster first." He demanded, and the entity chuckled.

"So chivalrous. A true hero." It mocked while chucking the unconscious headmaster into the onlooking crowd.

"Now come!" It chuckled. "Show me how a poor, magicless peasant dies."

°*It's on, motherfucker!*° The human shouted, and with a burst of enhanced speed, they bridged the short distance to the entity, slamming their magically charged baton into the side of its head. Mor had moved faster than anyone else could react, and now he was damming the teachers to stand by in fear of hitting this stupid student.

At first, the Ranbor-thing laughed at their bravado, but then the baton connected. With a pained yelp, the entity was thrown to the ground, its face distorted with bone-crunching damage and pain, while flames started flickering to life around it.

"I'll kill you!!!" It raged.

Part 40

With the sound of the first hit another sound was drowned out. With a bunch of four "pops," some new people joined the gathering at the end of the hall, noticing the tense atmosphere and trying to make sense of it.

One of them wanted to instantly charge into the fray but with a finger snip of another. She was locked in place, the third shaking his head.

"I want to see how this will go." The second said, with a voice full of authority.

The fourth was looking around in surprise and confusion, not understanding what was going on.

***

Amber rushed to the prone form of the headmaster, trying to save his life, and was just in the process of berating Mor for his idocity as the first hit smashed into the entity`s head. She decided, at this moment, to have faith in the boy.

***

°*How did you like that?*° The human asked in contempt.

Mor wound up for a following attack, not wanting to give this thing any chance at retaliation, but he was to slow.

With an enraged roar, the Ranbor-thing unleashed a torrent of flame engulfing the boy, burning, consuming, a distraught cry echoing through the hall. Then there was a "swhoosh" parting the fire prison, and an unharmed Mor charged out of it, his wooden baton smoldering but still holding strong.

°*Fuck. This thing won't hold forever, we need to keep up the pressure.*° The human commented, contorting Mor's body into another strike.

Mor supplied this movement with magic enhancement, but they were to slow. The entity had already gotten up in a burst of flaming energy, evading the incoming strike. Mor followed up with a quick thrust, launching his baton right into the stomach of the entity, forcing it into a pained gasp.

The entity roared again, creating a flaming saber and countering Mor's quick attacks, with a fainting strike, it slashed across the hemp of Mor's robe, setting it ablaze.

Mor jumped back at this, firing three quick rocks to buy himself some time. The rocks impacted the body of the entity, smashing rips and tearing skin, but seemingly to no noticeable effect. Still, Mor had bought himself enough time to remove his burning robe, revealing his upper body completely. This time, though, no reaction was forthcoming because everyone watching was captured by the duel.

The entity growled, and with the sound of a roaring wildfire, it unleashed a flaming breath to overwhelm the weaker boy. And again, Mor slashed through the inferno before he could take damage, unleashing another barrage of fast stones and following up with a charge.

The entity dodged the stones, melting one into slag in the process, but then couldn't evade the downward swing of Mor's baton. The attack smashed through its shoulder bone, disabling the fire sword-wielding right arm, and was instantly followed up with a wide sweep against the entity's left side.

The entity slid out of the follow-up, regaining ground and screaming like a wounded beast, just as the first crystal fell out of

Mors smoldering baton with a silent clink, shaken loose by the impacts and the slow burning of the wood.

In the breathless moment of the battle, this silent noice sounded almost deafening to Mor, distracting him for a heartbeat. That distraction almost cost Mor his life, as the entity changed its tactic, dismissing the sword in favour of a burning whip, lashing out and capturing Mor around the neck.

Mor had expected a sword strike and had raised his baton in defense; that way, he was not completely helpless. With a strained groan, Mor used his strength to press his baton against the fiery bond and then escape. He again got himself some distance, on hand going to the now burned streak across the back of his neck, coughing, his eyes tearing up from the pain.

°*Fight, through it! Don't let yourself be distracted!*° The human shouted, and Mor took a deep breath, trying to ignore the pain.

Mor refocused as the flaming whip lashed towards him, sidestepping it. He closed the distance, swinging his baton in a two handed baseball swing, his thundering strike folding up the entity, losing another crystal in the attack. Mor continued his attack with a kick that he instantly regretted. The touch of the entity's skin, left a burn mark through Mor's pants and on his skin.

With a pained howl, Mor hopped back, holding his pained leg. The entity, in turn, burst into flames, every cut and open wound of Ranbors body adding to the inferno.

"You unworthy bastard!" The entity roared. "I'll kill you!"

With a bunch of unhealthy crunches, the entity fixed its broken arm, burning brighter every second. The heat was almost unbearable. Still, Mor held his ground, rubbing his burnt leg and casting a quick healing spell to heal it up a bit.

The entity unleashed a tidal wave of fire, trying to overwhelm the boy and still getting denied by the power of Mor's baton. Mor, back in the fight, rushed forward again, kicking one of the crystals on the floor towards the entity, forcing it to dodge and following up with another two-handed swing, aiming right for the entity's legs.

The heat of the entity gave Mor an instant sunburn on his exposed skin. Still, Mor clenched his teeth, finishing his magically powered swing with every bit of force he could muster, breaking both of the entity's legs in the process. But instead of falling to the ground, it started to hover, not relying on its legs anymore.

°*That's bullshit!*° The human complained.

The entity unleashed another firestorm, forcing Mor back.

***

Saphine awoke, dizzy, recognizing shocked gasps from nearby students and Clare's despairing sobs. In confusion she looked around, seeing Orth standing there, his knuckles white, his jaw clenched, shaking in helpless rage.

"What's going on?" Saphine asked in a quiet, pained voice, surprising Orth and Clare.

"Saphine! You're awake!" Clare cried, hugging the confused girl and, after that, returning to uncontrolled sobbing.

"Mor... he's..." Clare tried to explain, her words failing her.

"Ranbor did something. But I can't even fathom what, and it created that thing." Orth said, nodding to the heated carnage.

Saphine looked to where Mor brawled with the entity, recognizing the beat-up form of Ranbor, but had to agree with Orth. Whatever that thing was, it was not Ranbor.

"Why is Agaton fighting it?" Saphine asked. "Why aren't the teachers doing anything?"

"He fights it because it wanted you and him. I can only guess that a bit of Ranbor is still within it, giving its rage direction." Orth answered, holding back a deep fury.

"Me?" Saphine asked, and Orth nodded.

"It said if we give you and the "peasant" to it, it will spare everyone else." He answered.

"But why aren't the teachers doing anything?" She continued to ask.

"Because they can't. It killed one of them with a single gaze. It even defeated the headmaster." Orth explained.

Saphine looked over in shock, where she could see a few teachers averting their gaze in humiliation.

"Why didn't he run?!" Saphine demanded to know. "He's good at that! He could have just left!" But Orth shook his head again.

"He couldn't. Else, he would have danmed you and everyone here to death. Additionally, whatever Mor learned from Snow is seemingly the only effective technique against that thing." Orth said.

"And all I can do is watch... How can I call myself a noble, but my legs aren't moving." He mumbled in despair.

"Why would he protect me?!" Saphine asked again.

"Because he sees you as a friend," Orth stated simply.

***

°*How are we on energy?*° The human asked, but Mor only grunted.

He could feel the headaches slowly growing; they would need to end this soon. With this in heart, Mor continued his attack, choosing a flood of wild swings against the entity. It blocked and evaded almost every one of those uncontrolled swings, damaging the wooden baton more and more, but Mor hadn't planned to end it with those wild attacks. He wanted to corner the thing, limiting its movements, and finally, he put all his might and magic into his final attack; he forced his double-handed swing through the firey defenses, cracking and shattering the baton on the entity's head. The remaining crystals were cluttering to the ground, with the body of the entity. Mor let out a shout in victory, the whole gathering hall erupting in cheers with him.

Orth, Clare, and Saphine rushed towards him, just as the teachers did. His friends embraced the exhausted boy while the teachers took a look at the entity. The teachers quickly noticed that the thing was still alive, and combining their might, they formed a lance of pure magic energy with the intent to utterly destroy its soul.

Part 41

The visitor almost wanted to dispel his magic, releasing his overeager retainer, but something bothered him. He had the feeling that it wasn't over yet. His second retainer started walking towards the finished fight and got held up himself.

"My lord?" The retainer asked, and the other one shook his head.

"Not yet." He simply stated.

And he would be right. As the lance of energy touched the entity's body, it opened its eyes and began laughing.

"Thank you ~" It cackled. "You idiots!"

The entity took a deep breath, consuming the gathered energy and releasing it in a firey explosion, throwing everyone back. Only Mor could keep his balance and stay on his feet. Everyone else tumbled to the ground and away, sustaining a variable degree of burns.

°*Stay fucking dead!*° The human growled as the entity rose back from the ground, its energy replenished.

It focused Mor with its fiery gaze, and in an instinctive motion, the boy dodged, evading the erupting flame by the nearest margins. Mor cursed, firing off a barrage of stones, but without the magic-interrupting properties of the crystals, the attacks had no effect.

Just as the entity's smile returned to its face, a blast of water doused its form. But as before, the entity's heat evaporated it into steam. Saphine stood up, putting her hands on her hips.

"Cool down! You idiot!" She shouted, and the entity returned to cackling.

"Little Ranbor is gone. I'm all that's left. Only fire and I will consume everything!" It celebrated. "And now, little water mage... burn!" It ordered.

Time slowed to a crawl, and Mors' mind began to race. He could see the fire forming, rushing forward, and his body moved on its own.

°*Don't...!*° The human started, but Mor put himself between the incoming fire and Saphine, crossing his arms in defense.

°*Puppet!*° The human shouted in alarm, and luckily, Mor understood.

Mor unleashed his power with a monumental effort, the stone puppet forming disturbingly slow in the span between heartbeats. Still, it had been enough. The pupped blocked the devastating attack but got damaged beyond repair in the process.

Saphine looked in sheer panic as the fire rolled towards her, closing her eyes against the heat, but the pain didn't come. She slowly opened her eyes again, seeing Mor standing protective before her, his half-assed stone puppet defending against the worst. Her fast-beating heart and Mor's muscular form stopping her thoughts.

The teachers knew they had been premature at this display of power from the entity. They got up hurt, burnt, and groaning, giving Mor space again and concentrating on protecting the bystanders. The commoner boy was their greatest hope to get out of this. Clare scrambled back to safety, vulnerable with her drained energy, and Orth moved up to protect Saphine.

°*Again!*° The human ordered, and Mor obliged, rebuilding the puppet.

The stony humanoid charged forward, following the humans' control, rushing in an erratic pattern over the ground until finally launching a punch at the entity.

°*I won this gamble!*° The human shouted smugly, plastering a confused look on the entity's face. *"You're bluffing,"* it countered with absolute certainty. Then, the fist of the stone puppet crashed into the entity's face.

With a loud crack, the punch launched the entity into the next wall, drowning the gathering hall in shocked silence. The crumbled wall exploded, throwing debris everywhere.

"HOW!?" The entity roared.

The puppet took on a fighting stance, beckoning the entity with one hand. There, set into the earth and stone, the glittering of familiar crystals could be seen.

°*Show me your moves!*° The human taunted.

The entity charged forward on a pillar of flame, forming a greatsword of condensed fire. It slashed at the puppet, catching another punch in the face as the puppet evaded and countered. °*The boulder is disappointed.*° The human said, never letting their concentration waver for a second.

The entity roared again, attacking in wild grand swings, which the pupped dodged with smooth movements. The entity disregarded its defense in favor of wilder and more furious swings. "Die!" It shouted.

°*The boulder will use the weakness!*° The human said, delivering another thundering punch, throwing the entity back into the wall.

Mor groaned. His energy was reaching his limit, but he had to keep going. He couldn't afford to lose. The human, recognizing the magic supply flickering and slowly getting weaker, redoubled their efforts.

They rushed after the entity, hammering the thing flat with earthshattering blows.

The whole hall rumbled and shook with the unleashed power, the human hammering down on the thing like a jackhammer. With another roar of fury, the entity freed itself from the barrage, getting some distance. Then its gaze fell onto the concentrating Mor, an evil smile growing on its face. "You know. You might be problematic for me. But, you depend too much on the energy of your host." The entity told the human, unleashing another attack against the now defenseless Mor. Luckily, Saphine reacted fast enough, protecting them both with a water shield. The entity grinned and split its fire. While it obscured the puppet's vision with one hand, it increased its power against Saphine's shield with the other. Only Orth's supporting earthwall saved them from being burned, but it was not enough.

Mor cried out in alarm as the brutal firepower overwhelmed their defenses. Their situation became desperate in an instant. Then again, they were saved as the puppet threw itself between the young mages and the wall of destructive force. The human had sacrificed their arms to escape the concentrated fire and now used the rest of the puppet's body to protect Mor and his friends. °*Fuck off! I won't let you!*° The human shouted in defiance as the puppet was engulfed in heat and fire, melting to slag, and as Mor's energy supply finally gave out, he felt something missing.

°*Are you ok?!*° He asked, concerned, but the human wouldn't answer.

"I got it!" The entity cackled. "I killed your little pet.~"

Mor looked up in shock, his mind racing. *"The human gone? But that's impossible!"*

"Oh, it is possible. I just had to burn its soul from the puppet." It laughed, and with this, Mors's mind broke, the shock and horror of the day returning in force and overwhelming his young mind. His partner was gone, the one who had always been on his side, protecting, guiding, and supporting him. Mor dropped to his knees, gathering a confused look from Orth and Saphine.

"What?" Orth began, just as Mor let out a desperate scream of pure despair.

Mor couldn't believe it, he didn't want to! He would murder this creature, but he was out of energy! All the held-back emotion vented in his despair, and something inside him cracked. A blockade he didn't know he had, just shattered in his madness.

Mor pulled on his surroundings, drinking in the magic around him, not caring where it came from. He pulled on the energy of entity and on the reservoirs of his friends. His whole body began to feel nauseous, but he continued to draw on the power.

"I need more! More! MORE!" His mind reeled.

Orth looked in shock as a burning whirlwind formed around Mor. Lazy discharges of energy playing between his friend's fingers, water dripping down in a drizzle of rain. Orth could feel the ground rumbling and sensed something just outside his field of view, all while Mors' wounds closed rapidly. Orth wanted to run, his every instinct urging him to get away, but something rooted him to the ground, pressing down on him. He tried to scream, but this display of cataclysmic power denied him even this.

While Mor screamed and screamed without needing to breathe, two figures closed in. One with the shout of a wailing banshee, the other in thundering footsteps.

The entity pulled its captured gaze from this dangerous development. It could feel its energy getting drained by this boy. The entity tried to get some distance, to get away. It wouldn't let itself be consumed. Then, a hail of icy thorns pierced it on its whole body.

"Hands of my boy!" the banshee woman screamed, freezing the lower half of the entity to the spot. Meanwhile, the other, a man in black stone armor, fought his way step by step through the unleashing magic of Mor, putting a hand on the boy's shoulder.

"Calm down, son," Morokhan said calmly.

Mor's outburst devolved into pained sobs at his father's firm touch. Morokhan dispelled his black armor and gathered his son in a hug. "I'm proud of you," he simply said.

The third figure approached the carnage, looking undisturbed at the unleashed magic of the woman.

"I', impresse,d Morokhan. Your boy is indeed as talented as you claimed," the third figure, crown prince of the soul-ki,n said, and Mors' father nodded.

"I knew he was," Morokhan stated.

"Still, we need to discuss a few things he did today. Some of those shouldn't be possible," the prince said.

"As you whish my liege." Morokhan answered.

"Also, could you please reign in your wife?" the prince asked, and this time, Morokhan shook his head.

"Impossible, even if I could. I wouldn't want to. I only held back because of your orders. Otherwise, I would have crushed it myself." He stated matter of factly.

The entity struggled against the icy prison, trying to escape it, but it just wouldn't melt. The entity cursed the boy, who stole so much of its energy, and the mage before him, who could conjure ice all on her own.

Sophie Agaton unleashed everything her reservoir would give, creating a localized ice age around the entity. Piercing the entity repeatedly with lances of never-melting ice, she shredded its form and froze its soul. The woman was a force of nature. Finally, she smashed the frozen body of the entity with a giant frozen hammer, shattering it into a thousand pieces. Still, she wouldn't stop there until no discernable piece of the entity was left, its existence wholly eradicated in the unrelenting cold. As the last pieces were shattered and her emotions were brought into check, she turned around, tackling her sobbing baby boy in a mother's embrace. Morokhan knew when to retreat and released Mor from his arms. Instead, he stood up and brushed himself off.

"Is it destroyed?" The prince asked, and Morokhan nodded.

"Yes, my lord. Sophie used about three-quarters of our energy. Nothing would survive this." He informed the prince.

Sophie held her boy, stroking through his hair, whispering calming words while sometimes throwing a stinkeye towards her husband and the prince. Slowly, Mors' sobbing subsided, replaced by a depressed calm. He looked at his mother, but his brain couldn't comprehend her presence.

Mor opened his mouth to speak but then closed it again, falling deeper into despair.

°*Please come back.*° He begged, already missing the humans irritating remarks and bad jokes. But he only got silence in return for his pleas. He didn't want it to be true. How could his pillar to lean on just be gone? Mor just stared blankly as Orth came closer, exhausted but smiling and didn't recognize Saphine's look of new-found approval. His ears heard that they were talking to him, but still, his mind would not process it.

Mor would take a look at his hands and his body, unable to find even the trace of burns or cuts. Nothing but pristine skin, and it creeped him out. He wanted to be hurt, to feel the pain, to know that he fought with all he had. But it was denied to him, denied by something he didn't understand. Orth looked at him, his smile slowly turning to a confused frown, and babbled something again. His look of excitement turned sour and concerned. Orth called out to someone, and in a rush of concern, Amber entered Mor's view. She instantly took stock of his well-being, barking questions and getting no satisfactory answers. Then she reached a decision, and Mor was ferried off, trudging along, his parents helping him walk.

He was brought to a secluded room, far away from the mayhem and the attention of the other students. His mother stuck with him, while his father accompanied the prince to make sense of the chaos. Clare, Orth, and Saphine gave additional company.

But nothing they did would rouse Mor from his stupor. As the evening dawned, his friends went to find a place to sleep, only his mother staying by his side. He fell deeper into the dark hole the humans' death had burnt into his soul.

Mor just sat there, not eating for days, nothing able to get him out of his despair. The prince got more agitated because he wanted to know what was up with this boy, but Mor's parents always got in between this.

Until, to Mor's surprise, Saphine visited him in a lonely moment when his mother was not smothering him. She looked annoyed at him and took a deep breath.

"Snap out of it! I won't stand for this. You decided to fight and protect me and everyone else, and I won't allow someone I'm indebted to sit around commiserating his lot." She scolded the reactionless Mor.

She stomped in annoyance, and then inspiration struck, literally in Mors' case, as Saphine slapped him across the cheek.

"Stop whining! You're better than that!" She shouted, and Mor blinked in confusion, feeling the pain radiating from his cheek.

"It would have said the same." He mumbled, offering his first reaction in days.

Saphine sat down before him, forcing Mor to look at her.

"Who would? Orth and I both heard what the Ranbor-thing had said before you lost? Control? What did it kill?" She asked, and Mor's eyes watered in the prelude of tears.

"My friend." He answered in a whisper.

"Your friend? What friend?" She carefully pressed further.

"The human," Mor said simply, not noticing her confusion and not caring about this secret anymore.

"And this human, was this important to you?" She continued, in a calm voice, trying to lure Mor out of his despair.

"You wouldn't understand. It was my first friend, the one who helped me get stronger and stand up for myself. Without the human's help, I'm nothing", Mor stated, his body racked by sobs.

Saphine pulled Mor close, embracing him in a tight hug.

"Let it out. But remember, you have Orth, Clare, and me. You're not alone anymore. We are not an adequate replacement for your friend, but you are not alone. Grief all you need. We will be there for you." She whispered softly, and Mor broke out in tears, crying, letting his emotions run free.

"Bad timing?" A voice asked from the door.

Saphine looked around in surprise as the prince shuffled into the room.

"I had to wait for a good opportunity and sneak in. His parents are very protective of him." He continued while Saphine turned bright red at the awkwardness of the situation.

But she couldn't escape as the much stronger Mor clung to her, crying.

"This is not how it looks!" She started, and the prince chuckled. "I just wanted to help a friend!" She tried again, but the prince just raised an eyebrow in disbelief.

"I'll leave you two alone. I think if I just let you go on. I might get the answers I'm seeking." He grinned and silently closed the door again, leaving the exasperating Saphine and the crying Mor behind.

Saphine now really wanted to hide herself in embarrassment, but at least she could help her friend.

The misunderstanding could be cleared up some other time.

Part 42

Mors' crying slowly ebbed off, and he stopped clinging to Saphine, leaving a wet spot on her robe from his tears.

"You slapped me." He said, and Saphine nodded apologeticly.

"You wouldn't react to anything, and even Orth didn't know what to do. Still, I'm sorry." She apologized, but Mor shook his head.

"No. I have to thank you. I needed this." Mor answered.

"Great, then we're quit," she said haughtily, but she couldn't keep it up and began chuckling. Her giggling was contagious, and soon, Mor couldn't help but start to giggle, too. His mother chose to return at this moment, looking surprised at her son and the girl. After a closer look at her boy, she looked furious at Saphine.

"Why has my boy the imprint of a hand on his cheek?! Did you do this?!" Sophie demanded, cowing Saphine to an embarrassed nod.

Sophia took a deep, outraged breath, getting ready to scold this stupid girl, but was stopped as Mor started to laugh.

"Mother, stop it. You should be thankful to her. She did the right thing." He said, and just as fast as Sophia's anger had risen, it vanished. She rushed into the room, throwing herself against her son.

"My boy! I was so worried!" She shouted.

Saphine looked awkward and slowly got up.

"Well, I think I have to go," she said, but Mor freed himself from his mother's smothering and said.

"No. I have much to explain, and you, Orth, Clare, and my parents have to hear it.

"I would like to hear this, too." The prince said, opening the door and revealing Morokhan and Orth.

Mor nodded, then stopped in confusion for a moment.

"Mother, Father, why is the prince here with you?" He finally asked.

Morokhan looked at his boy and sighed.

"He is not here with us. We are here with him," he said simply. "We all need to explain a lot of things.

"I will go and get Clare. You want her to hear your story, too, right?" Orth said, and Mor nodded thankfully.

With this, Orth left while everyone else sat down on the floor, even the prince.

"What did I miss?" Mor asked while they waited for Orth and Clare.

"The headmaster survived, thanks to you." Saphine begun. "Amber wanted us to thank you for this, even if your action was stupid." She continued with a smile.

Mor nodded and also smiled, *"That's good news."* He thought.

"Well, the headmaster decided that the school year was over, and everyone would return home. There was just too much damage done and too many people wounded or killed." Saphine almost whispered the last word, but still, it plastered a grim expression on Mors' face.

"Yes. It's a bit simplified, but it's still right." The prince said.

"Ok, but why are you here? Your Highness." Mor asked.

"Lucky accident." The prince said.

"Your mother." Morokhan sighed.

"Well, Mor hadn't answered to my letter!" Sophie protested.

"Ah..." Mor said, remembering the moment.

The prince started to laugh at this strange situation.

"It's fine, Moro. I did want to come here and take a look at this school. We're just a bit ahead of schedule," he said. "Also, now I know that my sister will be in good hands." "I don't understand?" Mor asked, confused.

"Well, you were chosen to be the guard for Her Royal Highness when she joins the school next year. Of course, I would have tested your ability on your break, but I was sure it would be fine. But then your mother thought something was wrong and pressured the prince to take her here," Morokhan said.

"And I was right!" Sophie said triumphantly, pulling Mor close to her again.

"I still don't understand?" Mor asked again, even more confused.

"It's rather simple. The Agatons are the royal families' guards, going back since the founding of the Soul-kindom," the prince revealed, and Mor looked at him in disbelief.

"Of course, no one is allowed to know this. This means the Agatons aren't given any titles and live as commoners. This serves another function as the connection between the common people and my family. It's a rather handy practice and has stopped a riot on more than one occasion." The prince continued.

"Wait, wait. Meaning, my parents aren't simple guards?!" Mor asked, and even Saphine looked surprised.

"Yes. Did you never wonder how you were allowed to come to this school?" The prince asked.

"Because of my mother's talent?" Mor asked back.

"Only a guise. It was also a test of how you would do. I wouldn't have revealed all this to you if you had failed. Being an Agaton is an honor, and the position is only given to the most promising mages." The prince said.

"He is right. Neither your mother nor I was born an Agaton. I was adopted into the family, and your mother followed me. To hide this secret, my records were removed from my original family," Morokhan explained.

Sophie just shrugged, "I was in love. Of course, I would follow you." "Was?" Morokhan asked, teasing.

"Still am." Sophie agreed, getting a cringeworthy sigh from the prince before he let out a cough and resumed.

"The only problem is your small energy reservoir, but well, you are probably just a late bloomer like your father. And even if that's false, you proved your ability today. More than enough," the prince added.

Mor looked in confusion at his father, who looked away in shame.

"Father had low energy reserves at my age?" Mor asked, unbelieving.

"Yes, he did!" The prince laughed. "He went to school with me. But even with his strong earth affinity, he was as weak as anything."

"You didn't have to dredge this up, your Highness," Morokhan said, but the prince laughed only louder.

Mor looked in confusion but then also had to laugh at this.

"Is it a problem that I heard all of this?" Saphine asked, and the prince looked at her like he had just noticed her.

"True... It would be a problem if you talked. What to do?" He asked himself, and Morokhan sighed while his wife wanted to erupt in protest, but before she could get up to speed, she was interrupted by a stern gaze from the prince.

"I know!" The prince said, all smiles again.

"You two just need to bond and become the next generation Agaton!" he said as if it were the most normal thing in the world.

"What?!" Saphine and Mor shouted.

"Don't worry." The prince said with a wink.

"I should have cleared that misunderstanding right away!" Saphine thought, lamenting. "Impossible." Mor simply stated, earning a happy look from his mother and confusion from everyone else. Saphine even bristled at that.

"And why not! Am I not good enough?" She asked, insulted, her pride speaking faster than her brain could follow.

"That's not what I mean," Mor stated. "But for this tale, I want Orth and Clare here." They waited a few more minutes for both to return, Saphine in embarrassed silence as her thoughts had caught up with her mouth, the rest in interested confusion. Finally, Orth and Clare entered and took their places.

"Good to see you up again, Mor." Clare greeted him warmly, and Mor nodded with a smile.

He took a deep breath, trying to order his thoughts, and finally let it out with a long sigh. "As I joined this school, I had big problems with Ranbor and his flunkies. They tormented me at every chance they got." He began his tale, his mother holding him closer again.

"I didn't want to be used anymore, and neither lives in constant fear, but I didn't know how to do this. Then, I made the worst mistake in my life and took my greatest chance. I tried to replicate a soul-bonding ritual, like in the children's stories, and well, it succeeded." He said with an earnest look.

A surprising gasp was going through the room, the prince staying silent and attentive.

"But at the same time, it failed. I wanted to bind an earth elemental, but I got something called a human instead. It had no magic, so my failure was undetected by the headmaster, and I can guess what you are all thinking: why am I telling this? Simply put, the human helped me become more confident. Protected me against illusions. And while we had our differences. In addition, it always questioned our Soul-kin traditions and helped me shatter many of them." Mor continued.

"And now, you think you can't bond anymore because you already did?" The prince asked, erupting in laughter, and Mor confirmed it with a nod.

"This is too funny. What you young ones don't know is that there are two rituals, and it seems you did the second by accident. One is the traditional, binding two Soul-kin together. The second is a forbidden one because it would bind your soul to a bodyless being, and history tells of Soul-kin going out of control because they would be taken over by this being. The question, therefore, is, why didn't it happen to you?" The prince explained.

"Because the human just wanted to be my friend and have fun?" Mor offered while the prince shrugged.

"Your guess is as good as mine." He simply stated.

"Is what happened to Ranbor the same?" Orth asked, and the prince nodded.

"Seemed like it, and that's why it is forbidden. Don't try to do this!" The prince said sternly. *"Still, I need to find out where this Ranbor got the technique from. From the boy's reaction, he's clear. No sense giving your secret to your enemy."* He continued in his thoughts.

"What about me?" Mor asked.

"Well, it's done now, if I understand it correctly. Therefore, I will just overlook this. Just don't try to repeat it. What you did was very stupid," the prince stated, and Mor nodded, ashamed.

"So all your body training and strange movements were because of this human?" Orth asked, and Mor nodded.

"Yes. I'm sorry I have hidden this from all of you. The human was also the one who beat Snow," Mor confessed.

"It could move your body?!" Clare asked, surprised, and Mor nodded again.

"Not only mine but also one of my elemental puppets." He explained, and the prince nodded, finally understanding how some of the "impossible" things were possible.

"Very interesting," he said simply. I almost want to talk to this human. It sounds very different and interesting."

Mor smiled at the memory. "It told me that it comes from a planet called Earth, and there, no one has magic."

"No, magic at all?" Orth asked.

"Yes," Mor confirmed

"Then I have a question. What did you do at the end of your fight with the thing?" the prince asked, and Mor looked confused.

"I didn't do anything. Mother killed it, and father came to protect us kids." He stated.

"You don't remember?!" Orth asked, and Mor just looked even more confused.

"Remember what?" He asked back.

"You lost control over your magic and just absorbed it from around you. But it felt like nothing we Soul-kin know." Morokhan explained.

"I don't know. I can't remember. There was only despair and ..." Mor said, trailing into his failing memory.

There was a sullen silence for a moment, but then the prince broke it with his next question.

"What did you do to enhance your body this way? You look more like an Ice-kin than a Soul-kin." Mor snapped back, getting a rueful smile. "The human told me how. It didn't allow any kind of objection and said that our knowledge of our bodies reeked of laziness. And well, it was right. You only have to push through the pain."

"Pain?!" His mother interjected. "My poor boy."

Mor shook his head and answered, "No. I'm very grateful. Yes, sometimes I hated humans for their stubbornness, but the results speak for themselves. Also, moving my body is even fun right now." "True enough, I feel the same way." Orth agreed, and the girls nodded.

"You're all in on this?" The prince asked, and the young mages all confirmed.

"But we're keeping it in our little circle because we don't know what this could cause to the Soul-kin," Mor said, and the prince let out a calm breath.

"Yes, please keep it that way. This information is not allowed to leave this room, just as everything else we discussed." He looked at Saphine at this, and the girl looked away, embarrassed. Orth and Clare just looked in confusion at this reaction.

°*Oh, I like this one.*° Mor twitched like he was stung.

°*Human?*° He asked, thinking he might have imagined it.

°*Who else? What did I miss?*° The human asked.

°*I thought you were killed!*° Mor shouted, both in his mind and aloud, surprising everyone else.

"Mor?" Clare asked carefully.

"Give me a moment, I need to rip that ass a new one!" Mor said, confusing everyone else even more.

Orth leaned over to Saphine and asked in a whisper. "Think, he snapped again?" But Saphine was not so sure.

°*Well, it was close. But why would I die? Also, why are you so angry?*° The human asked.

°*I thought you died! The Ranbor thing said it killed you!*° Mor scolded.

°*And you believed that?*° He human chided right back.

°*You didn't answer me!*° Mor growled.

°*Yeah! Because I was busy not dying! It's pretty hard to get back if your "bridge" is gone!*° The human argued back.

°*And why are you only talking to me now?!*° Mor wanted to know.

°*I just woke up! Because it was hella exhausting! I just passed out once I got back!*° The human growled.

°*I was worried!*° Mor said.

The human paused for a second and then offered a truce in a calmer voice. °*Sorry, I didn't want to worry you. But well, I'm back?*°

°*Yes, sorry for snapping at you. I'm glad you're back.*° Mor accepted.

The others watched the silent argument, Mor gesturing wild, sometimes in a typical Soul-kin way and sometimes in an altogether alien way.

"I guess this is not over. It seems I do have to talk with you again," the prince said sternly.

Part 43

The prince thought for a second before speaking again.

"I just wanted to wave your offense because your bonded creature had died. Therefore, it wouldn't be a problem anymore, but now that's impossible. Meaning you will have to answer to me," the prince said sternly, shushing Mors` parents' attempted protest.

Mor gulped at this, now getting really nervous.

"I want to speak with young Agaton alone. I have to decide, without any influence from you all, what I will do." The prince continued, and no one dared to protest. Everyone filed out of the room, leaving Mor and the prince alone.

"Now, Mor. If I interpreted everything right, this human can hear and understand us, right?" He began, and Mor nodded nervously.

"Good, then relay its answer to my question. How? Where did it learn our language?" The prince asked.

°*Wait? I never thought about that. Isn't it because your magic mumbo jumbo is weird?*° The human asked, and Mor relayed the answer.

"That's not how this works. But I guess both of you wouldn't know that. Listen to me. I will explain exactly how this ritual came to be and how it works. BUT you will swear never to share this secret."

"Do you understand?" The prince said.

"I understand and swear." Mor accepted, still cautious about a possible punishment.

°*Yeah, me too!*° The human agreed unheard.

"Good. This specific ritual, which you somehow did without knowing how, was created by our ancestors at the end of the second cataclysm. Against common belief, we didn't create the floating islands to survive but developed another technique. It was called elemental possession and is the basis for creating the first affinities: Earth, Water, Fire, and Wind.

Our ancestors would use this technique to bond with the magical powers of the elements and strengthen themselves to survive, but it had a catch. The first technique was crude, meaning the longer this had to be done, the more our pre-Soul-kin mind would influence the elements, giving them a will of their own," the prince explained.

°*I can guess where this is going.*° The human said.

°*Yes, me too.*° Mor agreed.

"The elements used their will to free themselves," Mor simply stated, and the prince nodded in agreement.

"Indeed, because of this, the pre-Soul-kin were almost eradicated. The ancient leaders then decided that this technique was to be forbidden, but the threat of the monstrosities would not allow our most powerful weapon to be left aside. In grim determination, the "Sacrificial" were created. The most adept mages would use the elemental possession and launch themselves in suicide attacks against the monstrosities, killing as many as they could before either dying or getting overtaken and then killed." The prince continued on.

Mor sat there trying to imagine the dread, fear, and desperate situations, shuddering at them. "The pre-Soul-kin could hold back the monstrosities, but barely. Still, they were trying to survive, and on the basis of the elemental possession, they created the first ritual for soul-binding. Instead of an elemental, Soul-kin would bind to one another and create stronger mages that way. This was also when our ancestors found the floating islands, perfect places to defend and refine this new technique. After establishing their settlements and completing their defenses, they enhanced this new technique, forbidding the old one completely and trying to bury it in obscurity and legend." The prince finished.

"Then how did Ranbor find out about this?" Mor asked.

"I don't know, but I will find out. And may mercy grace the one who broke the ancient law because I will crush them." The prince answered in an icy voice.

"But now that you know human, how are you talking our tongue?" The prince repeated his first question.

°*I think this question might go further. Mind if I try speaking for myself?*° The human asked, and Mor thought for a second until reluctantly agreeing.

"Ah... Eh... Ih... Oh... Uh... Ok, this is fucking weird. Btuhtat isttlrlanwgoerk..." The Mor-human said, biting its tongue.

°*Outch!*° Both exclaimed.

°*Ok, we need to go one after another. Just tell me here if you want to add something.*° The human proposed.

°*Yes. Still, this is strange.*° Mor said.

°*Yeah, it feels wrong talking in your voice. This will probably be the only time we will do this.*° The human agreed.

At this strange uttering, the prince got defensive.

"If you take over the boy, I will murder you right here and now, creature!" He threatened. **"Keep cool. I'm just doing this so I can talk to you directly. Also, if you want to hurt my buddy, I'll break every single bone in your body."** The human confronted the prince.

This gave the prince pause.

"I will accept this for now. IF you answer my questions truthfully. Now again, where did you learn our language?" He asked.

"I don't know. But if this is no strange magic mumbo jumbo, then we're all speaking a human language." The human said, shrugging Mors' shoulders.

"Interesting, that means this human language is the same as our kin-speak." The prince mused.

"Strange."

"Yeah, very." The human and Mor agreed.

"Well, then, what else do you want to know? This situation is strange, and I want to get it over with," the human said, leaning back.

"Why aren't you taking over the boy completely and instead playing along?" The prince asked directly.

The human laughed at this.

"I like this directness, and you just expect me to tell the truth. You're bold and funny! But I will stay true to my promise. It's pretty simple. Because I'm human, we're known to pack bond with anything, objects, animals, whatever if we think it's cute or friendly." The human explained, giggling.

"I don't understand? Also, animals?" The prince asked.

"Animals are the "monstrosities" of my world, but not as dangerous without your stupid magic rules. But to explain, in human evolution, we worked together with other creatures, hunting and living together. Those later became our pets, and we now treat them like family. But if a human is lonely, they

might bond to anything to escape that loneliness, even something like a ball." The human explained further.

"So your species has a very ingrained social need?" The prince asked.

"Ya got it." The human said. **"And I see little Mor here as my packmate. Meaning I will personally kick everyone's butt who wants to hurt him."** "Even without a body?" The prince teased, slowly relaxing.

"I will fucking find a way." The human confirmed, grinning. **"Anything else?"**

"No. I will give you the benefit of the doubt. Mor seems to trust you, so I will defer to his judgment," the prince said, receiving a surprised/interested look.

"Why? Shouldn't you be more distrusting as a "prince"?" The human asked, and the prince grinned.

"Simple, as the next ruler, you must delegate and trust your subjects. Also, I see Mor more like a nephew because Moro and I are close friends, even if he addresses me like my status demands since I became crown prince. Meaning, if you want, Mor, you're allowed to call me Uncle Dino." He answered.

The human laughed out loud for a split second, retreating and giving Mor his body back. Mor instantly stuttered something, then tried again.

"Why are you so casual?!" He finally shouted.

"Easy, it makes me more relatable to the common folk, but if you want, I can be regal with you." The prince said, taking on a more imposing position.

"As crown prince of the Soul-kin and your ancient appointed ruler, I, Dinothom Diamond, demand of you, Mor Agaton, to address me as your uncle." He stated in an apparently practiced voice but then devolved into chuckling again.

"I get it. So, no punishment?" Mor asked slyly, making Dino laugh even harder.

"As long as you don't do anything to destroy the Soul-kin, I will trust you." He said between laughing fits.

"Also, tell me, what's between you and the Sapphire girl?" He continued to ask, interested, Mor slightly turning red in embarrassment.

"Can you even understand how strange this is for me right now?" he asked. Also, she's my friend.

We're not romantically involved!"

"Yes, yes. But Moro didn't want to introduce me to you, and now I'm catching up to that." Dino said with a wink.

Mor let out an exasperated sigh while the human laughed in his mind.

"Now, back to the girl. Doesn't knowing you could bond with her change your view?" Dino teased further.

°*Yeah, Mor. Tell him how much you're lovey-dovey with Saphine.*° The human joined in. "Shut up! Both of you! She's a friend!" Mor shouted, the other two starting to laugh at his embarrassment.

The prince wiped away his tears from laughing too hard and put a hand on Mors' shoulder. "I mean it. If you have any trouble, I'm here to help. And with the Obsidian boy and the Sapphire girl, your influence is pretty significant. Don't underestimate this if you have a revolutionary idea or need help." Dino said, smiling.

Mor nodded, a bit embarrassed at this. "Thank you, uncle." He whispered.

"Very good. Now, I just need you to get along with my little sister." Dino said.

"Right! I completely forgot about this!" Mor shouted. "How should I interact with her? Father said I'm supposed to be her guard!"

"Simple, take care that she doesn't hurt herself," Dino said, producing a sealed letter. "And if she makes trouble and doesn't want to listen to you, show her this." "What's this?" Mor asked, taking the letter.

"Your letter of enlistment." Dino simply stated.

"My what?!" Mor asked.

°*Ok, this sounds serious. Read it!*° The human said, and Mor did so after breaking the seal.

***

I, Dinothom Diamanond, crown prince of the Soul-kin, slayer of monstrosities, forger of treaties, shadow hunter, and conqueror of tundra, hereby name Mor Agaton as fit to fulfill his role as guardian of the royal family. With this letter, the mentioned Soul-kin may only be ordered by His Royal Highness, the King, Her Majesty the Queen, and myself. While exerting his duty, he will be allowed to order anyone else, be it royal, noble, or commoner, with the same authority as myself. Furthermore, Mor Agaton is only to use this authority if he deems it indisputably necessary and not to use it for personal or political gain. He is ordered hereby to conceal his influence until the rulers mentioned above deem it necessary to reveal it or necessity demands it. Should he decide to misuse this trust, he will be outlawed and sentenced to life-long imprisonment or death.

***

"Death?!" Mor asked in supprise.

"Yes." Dino nodded gravely. "If you accept this position, these will be the consequences of your standing. But as long as you don't misuse it for your own gain, then you're safe. Your parents were given the same contract." "I can refuse?" Mor asked.

"Of course. But then, you must stay silent and live as a common guard at the palace. We can't let this information get out. The Agatons are our secret final weapon." Dino said.

"Even if Orth wants me as a retainer?" Mor continued.

"I would probably make an exception for that, but you will not be able to live as you please," Dino said.

°*He knew we wouldn't just agree and told us all this shit to capture us. Now I see his "princely" side.*° The human grumbled.

°*Well, true. But I don't think this is that bad of a contract. True, the consequences are harsh, but our rights are also impressive. We could even order the high nobles around if the situation demands it. Also, if your hunch is correct and the "First" is back, we need every scrap of power we can get. I'll accept this.*° Mor said.

°*Your decision, but I will support you.*° The human relented.

"I agree." Mor simply said, and Dino smiled.

"Good to have you at my back, but don't tell your friends that this is official. I will just play this with the Sapphire girl off as a joke and inform your parents of your decision in private. For now, can you try to look a bit meek? Like I gave you a bad scolding?" He said, and Mor nodded.

As they opened the door and rejoined everyone else, Mor looked to the ground, not making eye contact with anyone, his shoulders shuddering, while Dinothom had a stern look plastered on his face.

°*You suck at acting!*° The human said.

°*Shut it, I'm doing my best!*° Mor defended himself.

He looked to the ground and evaded eye contact, not because he was crying but because he was trying to suppress laughter.

"I'm finished with this one. His punishment is dealt with. Also, Miss Sapphire, I have to apologize for my tasteless joke. Please forget about it," Dinothom said in his most authoritative voice.

Orth and Clare gave Saphine a clueless look, but she just bowed in gracious acceptance.

"Very tasteless, my liege." She grumbled.

Part 44

While Mor was talked to by the prince, the others were waiting in the adjacent hallway, and now, as the imitating presence of the Royal Highness was gone, Orth gathered his courage and spoke up. "Mister Agaton, Sir black knight." He opened up and then got nervous as Morokhan fixated him with his gaze.

"What do you need?" He asked, trying to sound relaxed and friendly, but his concern for his son was glued to his face.

"I'm a big fan of yours, but now I have some questions." Orth continued on, and Morokhan made an inviting nod.

"Why are you accompanying the prince?" Orth asked.

"Sophie and I went to school with the prince. That's how we know him. In addition, she's the reason why we are accompanying the prince. She was worried about Mor, and I learned early on not to stay in the way if she sets her mind to something." Morokhan chuckled at some bitter-sweet memories.

"I thought this school was only for nobles?" Orth continued his questioning.

"I probably can't fault you for not knowing. This school isn't only for nobles. If you have the right aptitude and a letter of recommendation, even a commoner can join. Just like my son did, it's just a tad harder than the "commoners" schools," Morokhan explained.

"The teachers also said this school is only for nobles." Clare interrupted, Saphine uncharacteristically silent.

"Yes, they would say that. There is a rift between nobles and us commoners, a rift the prince wants to close, and he is working hard towards this goal. But in fact, the teachers are wrong. It's not never, it's just seldom." Morokhan said, grateful for the distraction.

Sophie shushed them all, trying to listen to the discussion between the prince and her boy, but she couldn't understand anything.

"Sophie, could you please calm down? You're making me nervous," Morokhan said with a deep sigh.

"Be quiet. I can't understand anything. What if Dino sentences my boy to be killed?" She hissed. "He won't. Mor will probably just get a slap on the wrist and a deserved one. Depending on how his "human" conducts itself." Morokhan said, hoping he was right.

"Well," Orth said, changing the topic. "Could I ask you a favor, Sir Agaton?"

"You may. Also, just call me Morokhan. You're a friend of my boy, so this much familiarity should be expected." Morokhan continued his discussion with the boy.

"Could you train me, please?!" Orth asked straight out. "I don't need to return to my family over the

break. Nobody will even be home, and I wanted to learn your black knight spell." Morokhan was taken aback at this request and gave it some serious thought.

"If you're fine, living like a commoner for that time, it's okay with me." He answered, looking at his wife for a second, contemplating asking her too, but then abandoning the question. Right now, she wouldn't pay attention.

"Also, it might be good for Mor to have a friend and training partner close. I don't think he is completely over everything that has happened. He's just suppressing it very well." He continued. "Now

I'm jealous," Clare said, pouting. "I have to return home, my parents want to see me... But I also would rather stay with the two of you."

"Right," Saphine added, "Your parents aren't living on Diamond-isle." "Yes..." Clare said grumpily.

"I don't like that. I wanted to continue to spend time with you over the break," Saphine said, a bit sad.

"You two will see each other next school year. Don't be too sad," Orth said, and Morokhan whinced at that sentence. *"The folly of youth."* He thought and would be right.

Saphine and Clare rounded on Orth, who suddenly found himself on the back foot.

"You're just lucky! How would you like to be separated from all of us for the whole break!" Saphine scolded him.

"You are mean!" Clare added.

Orth looked to Morokhan, pleading for help, but the man just gave him an apologetic smile and chose to stay out of this.

"I didn't mean it that way!" Orth tried to fix his predicament, but he might as well try to order the sun to stop shining.

"How did you mean it then?" Saphine asked.

"I..." Orth began, and Morokhan knew the boy was only digging his grave deeper. "I just wanted to say it's not so dramatic. We're able to meet again after the break."

"So you say it's okay for us to be separated like this!?" Clare asked unbelivingly. I thought we were friends!"

"You're tactless, Orth!" Saphine chided him, but then it was Sophie who came to Orth's rescue as the heated argument pulled her ire.

"I told you to stay quiet!" She hissed, ending the argument in an instant.

Sophie then returned to try listening back in on the princes and Mors' discussion without success. "Don't you also want to learn from the "Ice empress?" Orth tried to change the subject.

This again drew Sophie's attention.

"I will not allow it. I won't be the "reason," she articulated mockingly, "for you to spend time with my boy. No matter what Dino says, I won't agree to a possible bonding between you two!" Saphine turned red in embarrassment at this, and Orth and Clare looked surprised.

"You and Mor?" Clare asked. "Since when?" Orth added.

"I didn't agree to that!" Saphine tried to defend herself. "I just now accepted Mor as a friend. I don't see him that way. No chance ever I would bond with him!"

Morokhan smiled at that vehement refusal, remembering himself after Sophie declared her intentions the first time. *"Funny how those things could turn out," he thought.*

He watched the kids argue for a while, Orth and Clare drilling Saphine for more information, and decided he liked this little band of friends. Then the door opened, and a cowed Mor and a stern Dinothom walked out.

After this last bit of excitement, the rest of their time at the school went uneventful. Mor was asked to visit the headmaster and then thanked for saving the school, while Amber berated him for his stupidity at every opportunity. True to the headmaster's words, the school year was over, and all parents had been informed, some of them not taking the news well.

Slowly, the remaining students were carried away by the wind-magic-powered flyers. The last one to leave the ruined school carried the prince, Orth, Clare, and the Agatons.

With that, Mor was swept away from this chaotic first school year, and while he napped in peaceful silence, his dreams let him wander through everything that had happened: the good, the bad, the awesome, and the crazy. A wild ride with lots of hardship but also lots of opportunity.

Sophie and Morokhan watched their son's sleeping face, filled with pride that he had accepted the prince's offer. Both knew he would go far, as they always had believed.

***

Just how far no one could begin to guess, but that's a story for next time...

I'm closing this book, for the next part deserves one of its own.

Excerpt from "The Hero's Journey Vol.1," researched and put to pen by Nalomel Amazonik.

www.ingramcontent.com/pod-product-compliance
Lightning Source LLC
Chambersburg PA
CBHW050904050425
24616CB00045B/1755